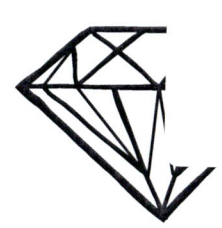

Elizabeth, Peter & Me
THE STORY OF A GEMS HEIST, GRAVE ROBBING AND BINGO!

BY MARK BAXTER

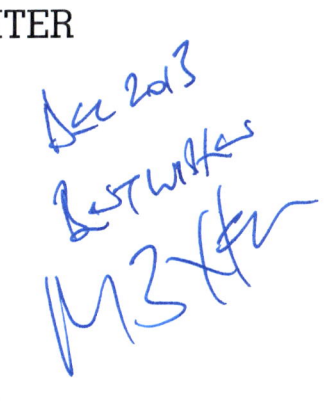

MONO MEDIA
PUBLISHING

Copyright © Mark John Baxter – 2013

All rights reserved

The moral rights of the author has been asserted

First published in Great Britain in 2013 by
Mono Media Books (London)
163A Elmington Road
London
SE5 7QZ

ISBN – 978-0-9555573-1-6

No part of this book may be reproduced or transmitted in any form or by any means without written permission from the publisher, except a reviewer who wishes to quote brief passages in connection with a written review for insertion in a magazine, newspaper or broadcast.

A catalogue record for this book is available from The British Library

Dedicated to my mum Jeannie Baxter for her unconditional love and for making me attend Camberwell Green Library and read during the ages of eleven and twelve!

Based on an idea by Mark Baxter and Paolo Hewitt

Acknowledgements

To my Lou for the love, support and proof reading.

To Sharon Purcell for dotting those 'i's' and crossing those 't's'.

To Phil Dias and Rafael Rizzolo at Karma Creative, for the fantastic design work.

Thanks to Eugene Manzi for looking the part.

To Iain Munn for de-coding the barcode.

To Jean Servais and Jules Dassin.

To my agent Rebecca Winfield for the support and advice.

To Lee 'Coggers' Cogswell for the film work.

And finally. To all who bought The Mumper. I've always admired your taste.

Bax
South East London, Autumn/Winter 2013

Eyes down for a full house....

1.	Thank You Elizabeth Taylor	1
2.	God's Waiting Room	31
3.	Wimpy And Chips	52
4.	That Takes The Flaming Biscuit That Does…	84
5.	Back In The Naughty Square Mile	104
6.	The Michael Aspel Fan Club	131
7.	Dig For Victory!	163
8.	Round And Round The Garden	195
9.	The Shopping Trolley Hard Men	213
10.	Goodnight, God Bless	229
11.	Like Putty In My Hands	246
12.	Call My Bluff	266
	Glossary Of Terms	285

1

Thank You Elizabeth Taylor

'Diamonds stolen from Star Actress' screams the headline on an Evening News placard on a windy, rubbish strewn south London street.

Funny.

It came out of nowhere. I could see that headline as clear as day. One minute I was sitting there watching the FA Cup final between Chelsea and Liverpool on the telly in the early May of 2012 and then, wallop, I'm in a trance daydreaming....

It's the 23rd of September 1962, just after five o'clock in the afternoon and I'm all suited up. Well, all the chaps were back then. Midnight blue mohair whistle from Albie Jenkins down The Cut; fresh, crisp, brilliant white shirt with starched collar with wrap around cufflinks complete with a green emerald (paste) diamond in the middle. Navy and cream striped Slim Jim knitted tie, black Oxford lace up's polished to an inch of their life. Barnet, short and neat, with a parting that had been burnt into my scalp by an over enthusiastic Italian barber.

A nice kettle finishes off the look; I always did like a nice watch.

I'd bought a copy of the first edition and ducked down a little non-descript alley as I looked round and read the headline and the story.

'Police Suspect Cat Burglar Break-In At Top London Hotel Room of Actress Elizabeth Taylor During Her Recent Stay in London - Hundreds of thousands of pounds worth of her jewellery feared stolen.'

As I read on it turned out the silly mare had thrown her prized tomfoolery all over her bed, whilst she was deciding what piece to wear at that evening's celebrity studded function.

After selecting her favourite bauble, bangle and beads she left the rest where they lay.

Well, I thought as I looked up and scouted the faces walking by, that was simply asking for trouble.

I finished the article, then folded the paper in four, longways, and placed it in my left hand jacket pocket.

I looked round, again. And then again.

I was about to set off to see a man about a dog, some geezer called Samuels. Maurice 'Maury' Samuels to give him his full title. He was situated over in the East End of London, which was a bit of a schlep from my side of the water, but needs must.

I hopped on a number 35 bus and headed for Spitalfields. As was my routine, I sat up on the top deck and sparked up a fag.

The area that we reached after travelling through the Borough, over London Bridge and past the bowler hatted army ants of the city gents was very run down round there then.

Not like now of course, with it being all super trendy and Hoxton'd up.

Back then it was a right khazi. Most of the houses had ten families in them, sharing one bog, with boarded up windows and methers having a punch-up in the streets outside, fuelled by drinking a local delicacy of 'Jack' - a heady mixture of milk and methylated spirits.

Samuel's told me he lived in a first floor flat on a little side turning, off Folgate Street. Flat 2, number 14, Duke Road.

All the walls on the buildings I now walked past were covered in graffiti written in white chalk and I began to read them as I walked along.

I already knew 'Kilroy Woz Ere', but it was news to me that 'Alan Iz a Ponce'.

Most of the streetlights weren't working, so I found it hard to read the door numbers in the early evening gloom, well, those that had numbers in the first place.

Finally I found number 14 and walked through the left open main front door into the building and climbed the two short flights of creaky wooden stairs, carefully ducking under the washing hanging on an old bit of fraying rope, which was tied to the bannister rail directly above my head.

All the wallpaper on the walls was torn, chipped and yellowing.

I knocked on the door to flat two.

'Who's that?'

I heard a woman's frail old sounding voice. Which surprised me.

I then heard another one straight after.

'It's alright ma, it's for me.'

I recognised that one as sounding like the Samuels fella I spoke on the dog to earlier that morning.

The door opened slightly, and a well-fed face peered round it, it's two jet black eyes looking straight into mine.

'Yes. Hello. Can I help you?'

'Er, I'm Vinny, I believe we spoke earlier, I...'

'Schtum, schtum ...I beg of you.'

I noticed his voice had fell into a more cockney tone.

He looked over my shoulder down the stairs behind me.

'Been expecting. On your Pat Malone are ya?'

'Yeah, yeah, course. Samuels, is it?'

He nodded to confirm his name.

'Yeah, on my own mush, no one I noticed anyway.'

This chubby unshaven-faced little fella had the baldest head I have ever seen. I reckon I had more hair in my comb than he had on his nut.

I noticed his clobber weren't too badly made though. The style was an old one, so I guessed he'd had the suit a few years. But it was of a decent make from quality cloth, which sadly had been ruined by the fag ash and food stains splattered all over it.

Samuels opened the door a little further, which was just enough for me to squeeze into the room.

This gaff looked in a right state on the first glance round.

Samuels caught me weighing up the sight in front of me.

'My old mums place. Myra, that's her there.'

He nodded to an old lady sitting in an armchair by a three bar electric fire.

'We like it this way. Keeps prying eyes off any scent.'

And what a scent it was by the way, boiled veg and blocked drains, if memory serves.

'No one will bother us here. Understand? Peaceful like.'

It was also as dark and gloomy in here as it was out in the street. The room was barely lit by different sized church candles all poking out of old empty milk bottles. Pages of old newspapers were all over the floor, with pots and pans covered in food scrapings sitting on the draining board or hanging out of a discoloured old enamel butler sink.

I guessed Mum was only too glad of the company when her Maurice was there and it obviously suited his purposes, so he put up with state of the place.

'Cup of rosy Vinny?'

I looked to my right at the rows of brown stained, chipped and battered tea cups hanging from rusty metal hooks above the utensil covered draining board and thought better of it.

'No...no, ta though. I'm alright, just put one out on the corner café as it 'appens.'

Narrow escape that I thought to myself.

I looked at his old Mum and nodded as if to say 'ok to crack on?'

The old girl had her long greying hair scraped back hard on her head, held in place with loads of kirby grips. She had a pink, green and red floral wrap-a-round pinny on as well as a pair of brown tartan slippers that would have been new when the old King come to the throne, but which by now had seen better days, signified by her big toes peeping out of each of 'em.

Maury thankfully had got my drift and nodded back.

'She's alright. Aint ya Ma? Blind as a bat as it 'appens.'

'Handy that' I said smiling.

His old mum just nodded and grinned a gummy smile.

'He's a good boy my Maurice.'

I could sense her son was very keen to crack on, don't think he wanted me dwelling the box too long here. I could tell his bottle was twitching.

'What' ya got then?'

His old pump was now going twenty to the dozen. We call it the thrill of the chase in this game.

I had called him earlier from the trombone in 'The King Louis The First' a boozer I used from time to time over in Camberwell and I had lined up my visit East, but kept the details of what I was holding to myself just in case some cheeky bleeder was earwigging all my moves.

So Maurice here didn't know what to expect. It could be rubbish or top drawer and that was why his heart was now beating a fast rhythm against his collar-less whitish shirt.

I reached into my inside breast pocket and pulled out a black velvet bag on which was the name, stitched in golden thread, 'Elizabeth'. I loosened the ties and I un-rolled it onto the table in the middle of the room. The sparkles that came tumbling out of that bag caught the glare of the candles and lit up the ceiling.

'Oi vey....' said Samuels smiling 'Pretty, very pretty.'

'Tasty eh?' Said I, already seeing that Samuels, with his expert minces, had clocked the name on the bag and now the goods, and suspected he knew he was looking at the real thing and where they had come from.

'You've been a busy boy and you done well my son, very well.'

I could hear the cogs going round in his swede.

'If I'm not mistaken, I heard the paper sellers earlier talking about these, well I guess these are them, from yesterday?'

He looked at me for confirmation and I slowly nodded.

Samuels wasn't as soppy as he looked. He immediately knew what was in front of him and that they were a trifle 'warm' to say the least. He also presumed I would be very keen to shift them on at a very good price. He presumed correctly.

He picked up his loupe and gave the tom the once over. He was almost drooling.

'Tasty, very tasty. The best I've personally seen and, indeed held.

A real pleasure to be this close up to such fine work.'

'So kosher then?' I asked.

'Sure, double kosher. Yer actress friend knows 'er onions.'

'What you got bubelah? Eh? What you got Maurice?'

Old mum was now very curious. Her minces weren't good enough to see what was in front of her, but she still wanted to know.

'It's the best Mummy, the best…' Maury was purring.

'Good boy, my Maurice, good boy he is.'

Mum was happy if Maurice was happy.

'What price though?' Said Samuels 'and it'd be such a shame to break such fine work down to sell on.'

'Hold tight Samuels, slow those horses' I said 'As it 'appens, I was wondering if there was any chance you could hang on to them for a day or two?

Samuels stroked his bristly chin and looked at me puzzled. I explained.

'I want the heat to die down a touch first and then we make our movements. Obviously, I'll look after you and Mum for baby sitting them.'

Samuels still looked perplexed.

'I presumed you would be looking to off-load as quick as possible.'

'Well presumption is the mother of all fuck ups innit.' I snapped back at him.

In truth, I was getting fed up with his challenging tone and it showed in my somewhat aggressive tone of voice.

'Look, whoever will be in the market for these, and we're talking all the top boys here, will guess I am looking for a lively sell and offer short money.

And as we both know, that is once in a lifetime stuff you've got in your paws there Maurice. I don't want to break them down, hear me.

I've got to make a real decent drink out of this, so want to take my time and not nause it.'

Samuels nodded; He knew he too was in the big league here and if he played it right, could make a nice tidy profit.

Looking at him, looking at the tom, I don't think he could

have actually brought himself to break the gems down to sell them on anyway, which would have been how he earnt his corn normally.

'There has to be a collector out there who would buy without asking too many questions and the grapevine has told me that if anyone knew the name of those collectors, it would be you son.

Which explains why I'm here.'

'Ummm...' he said, his ego suitably stroked 'I might know someone?'

'Thought you might.' I said smiling.

We both knew the plod will be sniffing round us both in a couple of hours with our track records, so had to box clever and tread carefully.

I looked my new Jewish friend straight in the eyes.

"Ok, I don't know you and nor you me, but we understand each other, and we both know where we are with this. Am I right?

Samuels nodded.

'I'm trusting you to store them for me, and nothing silly happens here, now let's have it right?'

He looked straight at me square in the face.

'On my old mums eyesight.' he said.

We both smiled and then laughed gently, as we both saw the funny side of that particular statement. I held out my right hand and Samuels shook it, which is as good as any paper contract in our world.

In truth, I had little choice but to leave them there. My local factory knew me well for jobs similar to this, though not on this scale to be fair, but it wouldn't be long before I had a visit from them, spinning my gaff over in the event I had pulled a stroke.

And that was odds-on if they drew a blank elsewhere.

Simply a process of elimination.

I looked at my wristwatch. It was fast approaching seven. I'd been here long enough. Time to go.

'I've gotta shoot Maurice.'

'Yeah make you right. Best that way.' he said assertively.

Maurice was as keen as I was to get me off the premises.

We shook hands again and I was off and out of the traps.

As I walked back down the threadbare-carpeted stairs and out of that stinking flat, my mind was running over the question of whether I had done the right thing in leaving them there?

I mean, I didn't know this geezer Samuels from a hole in the ground, though he had come highly recommended by top people in my field. One thing was for sure though, if he played silly beggars with this and tucked me up, it would be the last silly thing he'd do.

I slowly drifted back to the present day and noticed it was now 2-1 to Chelsea and the cup looked to be theirs. It was now nearly seven o'clock, cos of the late kick off and the thought crossed my mind that back in the days of that robbery, I'd just be getting ready now for a night on the town.

Funny how I'd gone from that world to this one.

Because now, aged seventy-one, I was living in a sheltered housing complex, surrounded by mostly old women. Got to fucking chuckle when you think about it.

And to think I once had myself down as a twenty year old Jack the bleedin' lad...

I had married my childhood sweetheart Brenda three months before that little caper with Miss Taylor and we had a son, Matthew two month after that. You can do the maths. It was like that back then. If you got a girl up the stick you did the decent thing and anyway, I loved her, so there was no dramas.

She was a year younger than me, just nineteen but everyone we knew of our age was getting married and then having kids, we were just a bit out with our timings.

I loved being a father though, and Matthew was a little cracker. I just loved seeing his smiling chubby chops each day. I decided once he was born, that the life of crime was over for me. I would settle down and get a proper job and all that went with it.

So, on the surface, we looked a lovely little family, but there was trouble brewing. It turned out, I wasn't the settling down type really and soon got bored with the sitting in each and every night with the telly, which was now supposed to be the highlight of the evening.

Brenda on the other hand was really content. Being married with a nipper was all she really wanted growing up. With me, well, it wasn't enough.

She knew me well enough when we were courting, to know I had been a bad boy for years, but believed me when I said I'd settle down and leave all that behind.

To make her realise I was serious, I got a job in a food warehouse, and though I hated the clocking in and out, somehow stuck it for a month.

Then the poxy foreman accused me of having a bit stock away. I mean, I had been tempted and nicked the odd tin of soup and that, but so did every other fucker in there.

It was seen as a bit of bunce, perk of the job, but it appeared that word had got out about my previous and reputation, so I was an easy touch to get rid off.

So, I was out of work.

Back then I could have got another job the next day; there was work all over. But I knew in my heart of hearts, it wasn't for me. Within a day, I was getting offered plenty of jobs in all types of skullduggery and within hours of leaving that warehouse, I was back at 'it'.

To keep Bren off the scent, I told her I had found a number as a petrol pump attendant, working the late shift over in the West End and she bought that.

For the first week I went home and told her we had that Des O'Connor or Alma Cogan getting petrol last night and she loved all that.

In reality I had drifted back into my old occupation. I had a couple of tickles going, which gave me a bit of gelt to pay Bren her housekeeping. The poor cow was none the wiser.

I was biding my time, waiting for that one tip off, that one big job which would give me a bit of breathing space.

Which is where you came in....

It was just before 6pm the day after I had seen Maurice when I popped in 'The King Louis' on my way over to the West End to have a mooch about and to meet a pal.

As I entered, the landlord Neville shouted from behind the highly polished jump that he had a message for me.

'Can't make head of tail of it meself, but I writ it down, hang on....' and with that he fumbled about in his trouser pockets trying to find the bit of scrap paper with the message written on it.

After a few seconds, we had a half finished packet of Polos, a losing betting slip and a bit of used tissue on the bar. He then he pulled out a bit of lined notepaper.

'Ere ya go.' he said triumphantly.

He handed it over to me. On it, was scribbled...

'Myra's son has found a punter. Call him urgently'

I scrunched the bit of paper tight as I made a fist and popped it into my right hand jacket pocket.

Flaming hell, didn't see that coming so soon. I had given Maury the pubs number at our meeting. Thought it would be a couple of days before anyone popped up. I felt a couple of beads of sweat form on my head, one of which started to trickle down the left side of my head.

I dabbed at it with my white breast pocket hankie.

'Not bad news I hope cocker?' said Neville, clocking all this, his jowly chins wobbling as he polished a dimpled pint pot with an old dishcloth.

'What? Nah, no Nev...sounds like a mate as found a buyer for an old wardrobe me and Bren are getting rid of.'

I smiled as I tried to style it out.

I carefully placed the folded again hankie back into the breast pocket of my jacket, smoothing it out carefully before ordering up a top shelf Malt, straight as it comes, which I downed it in one.

God that almost felt as good as the news from Maurice Samuels, as it hit the back of my throat giving a warming feeling.

I made my way over to the pub telephone, put in a couple of coppers and belled Maury. His number at the other end just rang and rang and rang.

Odd.

I decided to give it another five minutes. He must have popped out for a bite to eat I told myself. I ordered and downed another scotch and then had another go on the trombone.

Again, it rang its head off, but no one answered it.

Ummm...What's occurring here?

The time had come for me to make a move for my meet in Soho at 7.15, so I paid Nev for the drinks and bade him farewell.

On the top deck of the number 12 bus over to Piccadilly I was mulling over the possible reasons why Maurice wouldn't answer his telephone. I tried to dismiss the obvious one that he had been pinched, cos it was giving me the horrors.

Nah, he's probably popped out for that grub or taken the old lady for a drink in their local. Yeah, that'll be it...

I got off the bus at the second stop on Regent Street and headed for Brewer Street. Once in the Naughty Square Mile itself I noticed the red of a telephone box, caught in the glare of the colourful neon advertising signs all around it.

As I pulled open the heavy metal door, I hoped to find the phone working. The box may have stunk of piss but at least it had a dialling tone.

I tried Maury again.

No joy.

I was running late now, so I walked up quickly into Dean Street as I made my way to meet my pal Eric in 'The French'.

I ordered up a Scotch and we crammed ourselves into a corner of the crowded bar.

Eric was rabbiting away twenty to the dozen, about some bird he'd pulled, about a club he was planning to go to and… something else, but it was no good, I couldn't concentrate.

Eric soon sussed this.

'You alright mate? Don't think you've heard a word I've just said.'

I smiled at him and nodded.

'Sorry mate, not with it tonight.' I sunk the remaining liquid of my drink and put the glass on the bar top.

'Got got to shoot and sort some business out, but all being well, I'll meet you and that mort later in that club you've just mentioned. See, I was listening.'

We both smiled as he watched me head for the door and out into the Soho evening.

I found myself heading back to that phone box on Brewer Street.

I tired Maury's number again. Nothing. Nish. No answer.

I was now panicking. Only slightly, but it was definitely panic.

One thought was going around and around my head. Maurice...where... the... fuck... have...you... gone?

I also heard myself muttering under my breath 'I swear I'll do for him if he's had it on his toes. I'll swing for him.'

This was useless. No other way round it now, I had to get to his flat, find out the SP.

I looked at my watch and it was a quarter to eight.

I headed up through Soho Square and jumped on a number 8 bus on New Oxford Street. I felt the sweat trickling down my face again as I headed up the stairs. I loosened my tie as I sat down, I felt so restricted.

Added to all this, I was trying to pick out faces in case Maurice had been captured and had talked, dropping me in the cart.

I can't deny it. At that particular moment; the paranoia was rife and alive.

I clocked all the punters in the seats around me, but no one stuck out and all seemed ok.

Relax Vinny boy, relax son.

No one it would appear was on me tail.

I then began to wonder if the OB might have gone round home tonight. Poor old Bren would be in a right state, bleeding plod would have woken Matthew up and...and...

Hang on Vinny boy, you're losing your bottle son. Never a pretty sight that. I had to get a grip on myself, sharpish.

'Phew.' I exclaimed as I puffed out my cheeks, making the old lady now sitting next to me on the bus jump a little.

'S'alright lady.' I said as I smiled at her 'just doing my breathing exercises.'

The old dear smiled politely and went back to her crossword.

I looked out of the window as the bus approached

Liverpool Street Station.

I began to straighten my tie and took a couple of deep breaths.

I pressed the bell at the top of the stairs and prepared to get off at the next stop.

Once again, I checked all clear behind me as I walked to Samuels' gaff, making sure no one was onto me.

I was up those stairs of his building as quickly as I could and knocked on his front door. I could hear voices the other side, but not one of which I recognised. I knocked again.

An Indian looking bloke, who was now staring blankly at me, finally opened the door.

To say I was startled would be an understatement.

'Alright mate. Er, Maurice in?'

The fella rattled off a stream of chat in his own lingo, his head weaving from side to side. My heart slowly sank as the fella rabbited on and on.

I thought that's easy for you to say mate, but where's old Maurice?

'Maurice?' I repeated. 'You got Maurice in there. How about Myra? Eh?'

This Indian fella standing in front of me in an ill-fitting suit was just staring at me blankly.

Obviously, this was useless. Nothing else for it. I pushed him to one side and walked into the flat.

It looked exactly in the same state I had last left it twenty-four hours or so earlier, but was now occupied by what looked like this geezer's family.

A woman I took for his missus then starts waving her arms at me and wailing at the top of her vocal range.

I suddenly felt very hot and sweaty and the room began to spin round quite fast. I loosened my tie once again and made for the door to get out of there.

I felt like I was on the verge of passing out, but somehow I managed to get my bearings back, just as I was about to topple over.

Fuck! I've been tucked up! Maurice and his mum have gone...

The room was spinning faster and faster now and I was now sweating profusely. I felt physically sick.

I had to get out, I had to get out.

I stumbled out of the room and down the first flight, almost going over twice.

I began muttering to myself.

'I'll kill that Samuels I will, if it's the last thing I'll ...'

"Lookin' for Maury, dearie?'

The voice asking me this stopped me dead in my tracks on the middle of the stairs.

I looked down from where the voice had come.

It belonged to a middle-aged sort, who was tarted up like the dinner of a dog. On first glance, she looked like a two 'nicker Brass.

That's because she was and she wasn't over charging. She had peroxide blonde hair with a road map of black roots amongst it.

She was stood at the bottom of the stairs and I was plunging straight towards her.

She looked straight at me.

'You don't look well love, very peaky. Had a shock have we? Want to pop in here, for a, er, lie down...?'

She motioned her head towards her front door of her ground floor flat opposite.

'Eh? Nah, I'm alright.' I lied as I steadied myself. 'You seen him then? Maury?'

I was now right up close to her and I made my move as I grabbed her by the shoulders of her lime green polyester cardigan.

'Eh? Seen HIM? EH? HAVE YA?'

I was losing my rag very quickly here.

'Alright, ALRIGHT!' She said as she struggled to free herself of my clutches. 'Ferfucksake…Keep yer syrup on…. Jesus!'

She tugged her arm from my hand and I let her go. In truth, she was too strong for me to hang on. She was as tough as a Glasgow landlady with hands as rough as a monkey's foot.

'Bit strong all that weren't it?' She said 'No need for that was there. Not sure I want to help ya now.'

I didn't need to hear that. I'd had just about enough of this nonsense. Poxy East End, all wrong 'uns over here.

On top of Mr. and Mrs. Commonwealth upstairs, I now had this bird driving me garrity, and all of that on top of Maurice and his disappearing Mum.

I just didn't want any more of it. I could feel the anger rising up in me.

'Talk, you slag…TALK! You hear me!' I shouted.

'Blimey, bit stressed aintcha? You'll have a seizure if you carry on mate… ' The saucy old mort had plenty of chat.

'One-Way to stop all this aint there? TALK you brass.'

'Alright, All right. No need to get personal.

Look, Myra died last night didn't she and he's been at the funeral today up at that Northside cemetery they use. Them Jews don't piss about do they; they bury them whilst they are still warm. Funny like that they are…'

I was in no mood for laughing, and thankfully this trollop had tumbled that and carried on.

'Apart from his own missus and their boy, he didn't have

any other family he was worried about waiting any time for, so bish, bash bosh up there today, first available slot. In, done and all over in minutes'.

Well fuck me I thought, I wasn't expecting that bulletin.

Funny thing was though, as I stood there letting that information sink in slowly, I felt better hearing that news.

Not that fact that his old mum had crossed over only a couple of hours after I left them, no don't get me wrong, not that, but the news that Samuels was still on the manor was comforting, I've got to be honest.

'What about the flat upstairs though? What's all that about then? Quick turn around that weren't it.'

I said this as nonchalantly as I could manage.

'Well. See, I saw Maury at the paper shop earlier today, when I was getting my fags and a pint of milk and he told me he had seen the landlord first thing and gave him the keys back.

He wouldn't be coming back to the flat he said, too many memories and all that, so the fella rented it out to that mob upstairs.

Fucking waiting list a mile long for gaffs like these...They were pulling up outside within an hour and moving in.'

She looked me up and down and licked her red painted lips.

'You sure you don't want a drink and...a..bit...of...er, Sponge Finger.'

I smiled at the saucy cow. I looked over towards the door to her flat and noticed a pungent smell of cheap perfume drifting over from it. I declined her kind offer of hospitality and made to leave.

'It'd be better than a poke in the ear with a pencil wouldn't it? I could make you lose a bit of that stress you are carrying around with you.'

For a split second I must admit I was tempted. At the end of a long day, what harm could it do?

I looked at her again, closer this time, and reckoned underneath all that war paint she had slapped over her boat, she was probably as old as my old mum.

Suddenly that temptation began to fall away.

'Some other time perhaps' I said lying.

'Really? Well, if you're sure. Don't forget Mimi's door is always open.'

Nice of it to keep your legs company I thought.

'Oh, one last thing.' I asked as I made to walk out of the main door.

'Do you know where can I find Maurice?'

She looked at me with a look of complete pity, a women scorned if ever I saw one.

'Don't know his home address' she said sharply 'but he takes a pint in The Griffin, when the Rabbi aint looking. It's round the corner, left as you leave here. See ya sailor.'

And with that parting shot, she stuck her nose in the air and went back into her drum.

Quite an exit.

I turned left as I left her building and began the search for The Griffin.

Looking for a pub was perfect after that little lot, as I could now do with a livener myself.

I walked no more than a hundred yards and found myself walking over a wooden delivery hatch outside the public bar doors of the aforementioned battle cruiser. It was covered in heavy brown glazed tiles on the outside, with the name The Griffin picked out in gold lettering high above the main door. All the etched frosted glass windows had small mauve velvet curtains held up on brass rings covering half of them, so I couldn't see what I walking into.

I pulled myself together before I made to enter.

I pushed back the double doors, only to be met by heavy curtain's made from the same mauve velvet I had seen earlier.

I parted these with my hands and walked in.

I was met with everyone in there turning round to have a good look at me, the 'Connaught', who had just entered their patch. There must have been fifteen men in there, most of them still dressed in their working cloths - boiler suits and heavy boots. Factory workers probably.

I met a few steely gazes with my eyes through the heavy smog of fag smoke, which I hoped showed I wasn't one to be intimidated and then nodded a fond hello to the young, pretty peroxide blonde sort behind the ramp. She smiled back a weak smile, which I was happy to accept, guessing that this the best I could expect from this visit.

She looked like Diana Dors' younger sister, complete with two handfuls up her tight sweater. Her bottom half wasn't on view as of yet. I found myself looking forward to a glimpse of that.

I ordered a couple of bottles of light ale.

As I waited for the bar maid to hand them over I noticed the top of the bar counter was covered in foreign coins of all shapes and sizes, from all over the World – India, Africa, the US and Europe and I guessed they were given to the landlords by those who had returned from various trips over the years.

Above the bar was a long thin glass 'yard of ale' supported by a wooden bracket. An old cribbage board and domino set sat next to a large ornate brass till. A couple of old wooden crates full of small glass bottles of tonic mixers were placed nearby in readiness to be stacked on the shelves. Packets of KP peanuts hung in rows above the till and a cardboard box with a hole in the front held bags of Golden Wonder plain crisps captive.

I paid young 'Diana', picked up the two bottles in one

hand, and my tall thin pint glass in the other and made my way to a nearby empty table covered in water ring marks left behind from a hundred previous drinks. I poured the liquid from the light brown bottles in to the glass, tilting it slightly to one side as I did so. I watched as it foamed up at the top and congratulated myself on pouring a decent pint. I supped the drop and it tasted good. Very good. I placed the glass back on the beer mat in front of me, upon which the words 'Watneys Cream Label Stout' were printed and settled back in to the high backed wooden chair, rested my right foot on the little shelf half way up the metal legs of my table and waited.

And waited.

I looked the pub over as I did so and it was much like any other old back street boozer I had spent time in. A battered old dartboard was up in one corner, with its scoreboard still covered in badly written chalk numbers from a previous game. A couple of mangy looking plant pots sat on top of an old upright piano. And along a back wall was a shelf full of brass figures in the shape of dray horses, carts and working people. A metal sign caught my eye advertising 'Klondyke Cigarettes' and I then settled on a more familiar one telling me it was a 'Lovely Day For A Guinness'.

Occasionally I could feel the gaze of someone on me. I would turn round slowly and nod at the accusing stare and it melted away.

I also found myself thinking about Maurice's old mum.

Poor cow, gone just like that. One minute you're ignoring the washing up and the next....Gone!

I raised my pint glass to her, toasted her memory and sunk a bit more of it.

Still the waiting went on.

I had a further three pints and was about to order up the fifth when I noticed Maurice finally walk in. It was now just short of 10pm.

He made straight for the corner barstool like a homing pigeon, so it was obviously his usual perch.

I watched as he was spotted by the young bar maid who had served me earlier.

'Ello Maury' she said 'sorry to hear 'bout yer mum love.'

'Aah ta Daisy' Maury sighed 'bit of a shock as it happens. A terrible experience.'

'Usual?' Daisy asked.

'Yes please girl, treble mind...'

'I'll get that.' I said, as I made my way to his chair.

Samuels spun round, startled by the sound of my voice.

I looked at him, trying to reassure him I knew the situation without saying a word. He seemed to get the picture quick.

'Heard about old mum, come to pay my respects like, sorry I missed the burial.'

Maury looked sad for a second or two.

'Ta. All a bit sudden like. One minute she was fine and then bang, dropped down dead. Heart turned it in.'

'Come and join me over here.' I said as I ushered him towards where I was sitting. He was a little resistant at first, a wary look in his eyes, but gradually he made his way over.

We settled in, placing our drinks sitting in front of us.

'How'd ya find me?' Maury asked, his voice just above a whisper.

'Mimi.' I said.

'Oh, her.' he said as a smile played on his lips.

'Got some 'lunch' aint she?' I said ' She'd never drown.'

Maury just smiled. After the day he'd had, I knew all he wanted to do was get pissed and I wasn't going to stand in his way. But first, I needed some answers and quick.

'First off Maury, really sorry to hear the news, truly I am. But mate, I nearly joined your mum in a box of my own when

I turned up at the flat earlier, fuck me I thought you had tucked me right up son.'

He looked down at his drink and then took a slow belt of it. He cradled the glass and the rest of the drink in his hand.

'Buried my old mum today, so not really in the mood for this Vin, and you know what? I especially resent that remark. Not my style to tuck anyone up, hear me.'

The last few words were hissed at me.

I felt a little ashamed to tell the truth. Greed does terrible things to your morals, and I was so greedy to see my gems again.

'Sorry, I was out of order there. Really, sorry. But, you know... put yourself in my place for fucks sake.'

But Maury wasn't finished just yet. He was coming back at me off the ropes, his voice slowly getting a little louder.

'Bloody stroll on. Look, you... you, tripe hound. How was I tucking you up eh? I belled you cos I had lined up a buyer.

Geezer I know, he guessed I might know the coup on where the gems were, and he was talking telephone numbers to have a slice of it all.

So, I called you, you flaming second division chancer. I mean that's hardly doing a runner is it? Eh?

I've had to put up with all sorts in the last twenty-four hours.

I've had the filth round my own house already. Thankfully I weren't there, but they put the wind up my missus something rotten and I'm getting cauliflowered ears from the verbal's she's giving me.

She said they kept saying my reputation went before me, they knew I would be approached eventually. Master of my game they called me.'

He took another belt of his treble and somehow looked quietly proud to be considered a top fence by Her Majesty's finest, the soppy sod.

'Pleased for you mate' I said as I grinned his way 'surprised the commissioner aint pinned a medal on ya already. Fuck me. I might be second division mate, but lets have it right, I've hit the jackpot here. We both know that don't we?'

We sat in awkward silence for a minute, supping our drinks and sulking really, suddenly realising neither us really knew the other that well.

'Look' I finally said as I drained the last drop of my light ale 'all I need to hear is that you still got the wassnames.'

I looked round as I spoke.

'I had to move fast' said Maury 'things were going wonky. First, my old mum turns her toes up and then Lily Law appear on my doorstep. So I had to act quickly.'

I sympathised. I had already told him that. But I noticed he wasn't answering the question.

'Yeah I know all that. You've just told me. What you aint told me is what I need to hear Maury.'

Any of the faces I could feel now looking at me and Maury could have been a grass or plain clothes, so I didn't want to dwell too long in this company, what with him being so well known locally for his particular trade, and especially as he was slowly getting three parts and gawd knows what he was going to say next.

'Sorry to labour the point Maurice, I am. Truly. But I noticed you haven't answered my question. Have you still got the bleedin' tom?'

He slowly tipped up the remainder of his treble scotch into his mouth and then began to smile.

'Well, there's a funny story there.' he started to say before I cut him stone dead.

'What is it with you mob over this side of the water, eh? You all want to make everything a funny story. First that brass and now you. Fucking bunch of stand up comedians the lot of ya.

Tell you what, in this instance, let's not make it too funny eh?'

The light ale I had been sinking for the past couple of hours was beginning to make me a little aggressive. I edged my chair to move nearer to him.

Samuels flinched a touch, sensing I was getting very impatient.

'Alright, slow down, slow down. As soon as the news crept out, my ma's friends started calling at the flat, so many people turned up, people all over the place suddenly. What with them and the Rabbi, well, the flat was soon full up and it became obvious I couldn't leave your ill gotten there, right? My own drum was under starters orders from the local plod, so...'

Yeah, I was sitting there thinking, so yeah, so what?'

Maurice's bald head was suddenly covered in small droplets of sweat. Noticing the coal fire wasn't actually alight in the pub, I began to sense bad news.

He continued. 'So, I er, (gulp) er, I had to move fast didn't I? So I er...put them in er, mums coffin...'

With that he nodded to young Daisy behind the ramp, indicating he wanted the same again drink wise.

I sat there dumb struck. Did he just say he put them in the coffin?

Fuck me. His old mum was now sharing her last resting place with Liz Taylor's trinkets.

Seriously, there and then, I didn't know whether to believe him or not, but the story of his old mum pegging out seemed to be kosher and had been backed up by everyone I had met in the last couple of hours. In the circumstances he had described earlier, I suppose a desperate man would do desperate things.

Silence enveloped us for five minutes, as I debated what to do next. Maurice had already knocked back the second treble scotch he had just ordered and before too long he slowly began to slip down his chair and looked boss-eyed drunk. He shut his eyes as he landed on the fag burnt carpet, and seemed out for the count within seconds.

Fuck me, what a cock up this was turning into.

I looked at Maurice laying there and by now the entire pub was looking our way. I knew I'd be well and truly on offer if I stayed here much longer. Nothing else for it, I had to make a move.

On my brisk walk to the bus stop, a million permutations went round my head.

What if had already sold the jewels? What if his old mum wasn't really dead? What if, what if, what if!

No matter how I looked at it, I felt like I had been tucked up, my arse well and truly felt.

On the bus home back to the South, I was in a state of shock. One minute I had bundles of wedge coming and then pop!

Nothing to show for it.

I hardly slept a second that night and I was in a right daze at the beginning of the next day.

I just had no idea what my next move was going to have to be, but one place I had to visit was that cemetery that Mimi had mentioned.

When I got to Northside Cemetry, I wandered around for a while til I found an area full of flowers from funerals that had taken place a day or so before. I nonchantly looked around here and found a couple of cards pinned to bouquets addressed to a Myra.

I asked a nearby gardener if there was a grave to visit for

her, and was told there was, but it had no stone to mark it as of yet, too soon after the event, so to speak.

So, it was kosher.

His mum had gone.

And according to Maury, she took a bit of my shopping with her.

On the tube back home, the thought occurred to me about some mad half-baked scheme in which I dig up the grave to see if Miss Taylor's gems were really in the coffin.

As I said earlier, desperate men, will do desperate things.

Obviously I couldn't tell a soul what had occurred, but instead of that sunshine holiday I had planned to surprise Brenda with out of the earnings, I know knew I had to get grafting again.

We'd already knocked the rent man twice and Brenda was beginning to fret.

A few nights later, me and a couple of mates, hit a goods wagon parked up over in a west London depot.

I planned to knock out the load of hooky radiograms I had walked away with, but the OB raided our flat early one morning and they were found in my shed.

The local factory then piled on a couple of other trumped up numbers on me, including bashing a night watchman, which was absolute bollocks and I ended getting a double handful, a ten stretch, for GBH as well as the thieving.

My Brenda and my Mum had a severe case of dock asthma when the sentence was read out and I didn't feel too clever either I can assure you.

Here I was, a young man of just twenty-one, with a wife and young son and I was looking at years away.

I knew my wife wouldn't be up to any of this; it really wasn't her world.

Sure, she came to see me a few times in there in the first

few months, but you could see she hated those visits and she never once brought Matthew 'No place for kids.' She'd say and I couldn't argue with her.

The trip to Brixton nick was full of the horrors for me. I was in a van with a couple of other faces, who kept smiling at me, having guessed it was my first time inside.

As the van pulled through the metal gates and onto the concrete courtyard, I felt a dread in my heart.

I looked up at the thousands and thousands of red bricks making up the prison and thought my life was over. I just couldn't see any way forward from this very spot.

I was put in a cell with a couple of other new blokes and we quickly marked out our territories by putting what little personal effects we had by our beds.

I would get to know those white washed walls of my cell well, very well. I sat and looked at them for hours and hours.

At first, I kept my head down and didn't get too involved with those around me. But gradually I soon learnt that a bit of stir can make you go mental, potty, as you try to cope with the endless hours banged up.

For those first few months, I was being eaten up with thought of the lost opportunity I had just experienced, with an absolute hatred for Maury, convincing myself he had done me up and a real rage against the world in general.

This wasn't how it was supposed to be. Not this, not prison.

Thankfully, I slowly began to lose that anger and somehow began to get accustomed to my situation. Thank God I did, otherwise I would topped myself I think.

Frequently in that first year I was inside, I would think of getting my hands on Liz Taylors assets (in more ways than one as it happens) but gradually I put those gems to the back of my mind, basically for my own sanity.

I just couldn't afford to think of them too much. It just

wasn't healthy.

So, once I accepted I was here for the foreseeable, I began to mix more with the fellow inmates, and see what they had to offer.

And where better to learn more of the darks arts of thievery in all of its forms than in the shovel?

I had a right touch of the 'fuck it's' by the end of the first six months, and thought well why not, lets learn what I can and get back on it when I get out.

Only I wasn't getting out any time soon was I?

And as time went on, as one month followed another and one year came round as slowly as the last one, I was basically rejecting a life of crime and swearing I would never set foot back in here ever again.

And you know what, I never lost that resolve and when I got out I went straight. As an arrow. Never deviated.

Of course, by this time I had lost complete touch with Brenda and my boy Matthew. I hadn't had any news from those two in years.

So, I threw myself into the job I found myself in. I was driving artic's all over to Europe. Never turned down any job I was offered. My thoughts were if I kept moving, I would never get tempted by my old stealing ways.

As the years rolled by and time went on and I got older, I forgot about my old life.

And I was like that until I retired.

I got used to the long overnight trips, greasy food in transport cafes and kipping in any bed I could find, or even in the cab in some remote lay-by if needs be.

Finally though, that life-style began to take its toll. No job for an old man.

I finally retired aged sixty-seven in 2008, proud that I had stayed out of trouble for all those years.

The company I worked for, thanked me for the years of service by buying me a watch. They knew I liked a nice kettle.

Pity they didn't know where to buy one though. The one they presented me with was terrible. So bad in fact, that I would have left it behind if I had found it in my robbing days.

You know I said I forgot about my old life?

Well I did, mostly.

But occasionally, just now and then, I found myself remembering 1962 and Elizabeth Taylor and today was one of those days.

2

God's Waiting Room

I first arrived here on a cold, winters day in February 2012.

Here, being The Benhill Care Home, in Camberwell. I knew the manor well as I was born not more than one hundred yards away from this very site.

After all my travels around the globe I was now back in SE5.

Christ, I felt like a bleedin' boomerang.

My GP had got me in here. He's a good 'un him. I had received a letter from the council, who had found out I was recently retired and was living in a two bedroom flat round the back of Blackfriars, which they now wanted to give to a young family.

They were trying to transfer me to the middle of an estate in Peckham, but I felt too old to start all over again on a sprawling council estate and told them to shove it.

So, I mentioned it to my GP Dr. Knowles when I was up there when my chest was all wheezy and he said 'Let's face it Mr. Hawkins, you're getting no younger, have you considered the option of sheltered housing?

At first the mention of a place like that left me cold, I thought sod that for a game of dominos.

I mean, for a kick off I'm no doddery pensioner; I still dodge about as much as I ever did, if, only a little bit slower.

But the more I thought about it and began facing up to the fact that I wasn't getting any younger as Dr. Knowles rightly pointed out, I decided to visit it and have a nose round.

On arriving outside, I had to admit it looked OK. The complex was made up of various boxed shaped buildings, constructed in red brick. There was a nice garden area in the middle of it, which I particularly liked as I kept my garden looking great at my old flat. There was a security door system, which gave it a feeling of safety.

I pressed a button for the reception and I was buzzed in after telling the voice at the other end my name.

As I walked in, I noticed the general décor of the place was fine, if a little dated, and the carpet and that, looked alright if a bit shabby in places. I had seen worse. But that was in prison.

I was met by and shook hands with a big old lump of a bird called Maureen Wiloch. This was the name on my paperwork, which explained she was my point of contact there. She turned out to be from South Africa, and introduced herself in a heavy accent.

She was well over weight and was dressed in combat trousers and a padded puffa jacket. Dainty was not a word that sprung to mind.

She seemed ok though, if a little abrupt and rude at times as she showed me round. As it happens, I've noticed that the few South Africans I have met over the years have had that about them.

Germans with suntans my old my mate Denny on the trucks called 'em.

Maureen wore these big-lensed glasses, which had the effect of making her eyes look enormous. She showed into a lounge area and that was where I saw some other residents for the first time. A few old people among them, I mean older than me. I'd guess in their nineties some of them.

'Welcome to God's waiting room.' she said with a smirk on her face.

She caught me off guard there. Nice to see all that money spent at the charm school wasn't wasted I thought.

As she continued to walk me round she sold the idea of staying there to me as 'independent living', but also reminded me that if I found I needed a bit of extra help, she was there as a warden with a couple of staff on tap to take care of my needs.

I had to be honest with myself; it looked ok in there. I asked her the rent, and found out that my pension would nicely cover that, so I told Maureen I'd think about it, and I would.

One real thing in its favour was that Benhill was close to what was my pub of choice for many years, namely 'The King Louis'.

I decided to set up a base camp there for an hour or so and have a good think about it over a couple of pints.

'Oi oi. Look at you done up like Selfridges window. Where you been, court?'

Neville Junior had clocked me as I walked in the pub.

He had taken over the pub from his late father Neville Senior in the late 1990s.

'Flaming cheek. Aint telling ya anyhow, you'll only laugh.' I replied.

'No straight. I won't, go on tell us' it was obvious young Neville wouldn't be letting go

'Well, er... I 've just been looking at sheltered housing. I might be going in.' I then waited for the laughter to start.

'Great idea that Vin. My old Nan was in one. Put years on her life that did. Well comfortable and looked after she was. She had real peace of mind in there. When you going in?'

Young Neville has surprised me there. I thought he'd rip

the piss out of me something terrible. I then realised it was my own prejudices about the idea that was getting in the way. And to top it all off, everything he said, had made perfect sense. Maybe it was time to face facts?

By the end of the second pint, I had decided to do it. I quite liked the idea of being looked after if I'm honest.

No time like the present, so I supped up and went home to let the council and Maureen know what I wanted to do.

Within a week, the council had sent round a removal team and sorted all that for me which was another weight off me mind.

They were well happy to get my two bedrooms. The waiting list round here is at least a ten stretch.

At Benhill, I was given a ground floor flat, a one bedroom. Small kitchen, but that did me as I intended to mainly eat out at 'The Louis'. It was decently decorated, and painted a mainly beige colour.

I had a decent sized bedroom, but I often don't get into bed. That's the result of all those years of getting my head down in the cab of my lorry. I usually kipped in the armchair and that did me. Besides I'm a terrible sleeper. S'pose my spell inside was the kick off for that.

Don't spread it about, but I've even been known to wear a sleep mask.

If I get a glimpse of light, then bang, I'm wide-awake, no matter how early it is. I also have to spin round all the clocks in my place to face the wall before I turn in at night. That's because, say I get up for a gypsy's in the middle of the night and I see the time is only say two in the morning, as soon as I settle down again, I just sit there thinking I've got hours to kill before another day begins.

Which also explains why I'm always an early riser.

One thing I was delighted to find at the back of the flat

was a nice bit of garden outside of the back door. My own little patch of earth. Not too big, but enough room to grow a few toms, runner beans and spuds. I got into the green finger habit when I was inside and it's one that continued when I got out.

We had an allotment in the shovel and I volunteered to keep it tidy, well no one else was bothered. I knew next to nothing about gardening, but I liked being out in the open as much as possible.

After being banged up all day in the peter, it was nice to get some fresh air in my lungs. Subsequently I developed a liking for it, gardening. So nice to be able to grow a bit of produce here.

On my first visit, Maureen had informed me that is was mainly women living here. Turned out there were only fifteen of us blokes among the eighty residents in the various sheltered housing blocks. The chaps round here rarely out-live their wives.

Not surprising really, when you think most of the fellas my age would have grafted since they left school at fourteen, so many were worn out and brown bread by the time they hit sixty-five/seventy.

Loads of widows in Benhill. Sad but true.

I soon had my few things about me and all sorted in the flat, though I didn't really have a lot of furniture. Most of it was provided anyway if you wanted it and though a bit bashed about, a lot of the stuff already in the flat did me.

Never really been one for too many possessions. A decent telly and DVD player and a photo of my Matthew on the wall was all I really needed. The rest of the furniture I brought with me, was years old, but it did for me. I got it from the Heart Foundation shop on the Old Kent Road.

As for venturing out of the flat, well I bottled it really and I decided to keep myself to myself at first.

Believe it or not, I was a little nervous. I was so used to my own company, very much a loner, but never really lonely, that I was unused to making new friends. In here, because we all lived under one roof, I knew that was part of the set up.

I didn't know anyone there and well, I had got used to my own company, what with the break down of my marriage, the life of a lonely long distance lorry driver and my time at Her Majesty's pleasure.

Before all that, I was the life and soul of any party. Always first up the bar and last to leave.

Thinking back to my time in nick, that was when I became a different person. When released from the shovel I knew there wouldn't be a brass band waiting for me at the prison gates in 1971. But I wasn't expecting to see no one. Not a soul. That was when I knew I was on my own.

By then, I had lost touch with Brenda good and proper.

She came those few times to see me and then suddenly stopped.

The signs were there though, that this wasn't what she wanted; it was no life for her, being a prisoner's wife. It was written all over her face.

She wrote me a letter that I was given after nine months of stir or so, explaining that she felt she had to move on and bang, she asked for a divorce.

It had a drawing in it from little Matthew, who I hadn't seen since I was nicked at home. The poor little sod screamed the place down when the old bill turned up that morning and booted our front door down.

At the time I wasn't too worried as I was sure I would only get a "bed and breakfast" sentence, but I was betting without copping the dodgy charges that were lumped on top.

I was very bitter about all that at the time, but Bert, the old lag I was sharing my first cell with, soon put me straight.

He told me if you put yourself in this line of work, there was always the chance of a stitch up from plod. He told me to stop whining and just do the porridge.

At first I fought what he said, it felt too much like accepting it all, even though that all wrong and those first nights in there were terrible.

I kept up a front and gave it the 'Jack the Lad' performance, giving it the big 'un about the daring jewel raid I had done and what was waiting for me when I got out. But truthfully, my insides were churning over every time a door slammed or a set of keys rattled in a lock.

I used to stare at the white washed brick walls and get the horrors as I thought about the life I was had compared to what I was living now. Living? This wasn't living, this was surviving.

I wrote back to Brenda three times, but they were handed back to me by one of the screws, with 'NOT KNOWN AT THIS ADDRESS' written across them in red biro. I knew she hadn't moved, she was too close to her mum who lived nearby. On top of that, the poor cow didn't have a pot to piss in and barely a window to throw it out of, so this was obviously her way of saying no more, it was all over.

Can't really blame Bren when you look at it in the cold light of day. She was a young bird, who hated my life of crime and told me so often.

I simply hadn't done right by her, no; I was Jack the Biscuit weren't I? Cocky bollocks.

Well, here I was now banged up for the foreseeable.

Not so clever now are you boy?

I must have read her letter at least a hundred times. And time and time again as I read the words I could also hear her voice saying those words.

'Got to think of the boy, he needs a good father, and that

can't be you can it? it's only fair.'

Fair? Yeah can't argue with that. Whatever I was, I wasn't fair.

Of course it hurt not to think that I would not hear from her again, but I sort of got used to it. My solicitor came and visited me three years into the stretch and informed me I was now divorced.

Terrific I thought, and good morning to you too sir.

In reality, I hadn't put up any resistance to the idea. I couldn't could I? It was over. I wasn't happy with the plan, but I had no one to blame but myself?

By that third year, I was well and truly conditioned by the place. The words that Bill had told me had well and truly sunk in.

I even found myself occasionally forgetting about the little family I once had. Had to really, you just do it in there to keep sane; it will drive you stark staring potty otherwise

Despite all the silence and non-visits from Brenda, for some reason, I secretly hoped my Matthew would be waiting for me when I came out. I had decided to write and tell him the release date once I was given it.

He would have been only nine then, but I was hoping someone would have brought him down to Sussex where I finished my sentence in the open nick.

As I walked towards the lump of a warder unlocking the big metal front doors, I crossed my fingers as I emerged.

But, as I said no one was there.

No kid, no family and none of the mates I once had. Sure, for the first year I was in there, I had one or two turn up on visiting day's to say hello, but they had soon stopped coming.

In all the nine years I was inside, I'd only had two visitors after that first year. My mum being one, bless her heart. Sadly she died four years into my sentence. Thankfully I was given permission to attend her funeral; I think it would have killed me to have missed that.

As for my old man, well he had scarpered years ago when I was a baby. So I knew he wouldn't show up, unless he turned up to share a peter in the nick with me...

Oddly enough, the other visitor was one Maurice Samuels.

Yes him, that Maury. He had the strange habit of popping up once a year, near the anniversary of the Liz Taylor blag, as regular as clockwork.

When I first saw him in the room with all the relatives of the other prisoners, I've got to be honest, I feared the worst.

I was two years into it and I was sure he was only here to tell me bad news that somehow the gems had gone.

We exchanged pleasantries, the weather and all that, but I just wanted him to spit it out - go on you berk, tell me.

Instead, he assured me he had been 'keeping the grave clean and tidy in my absence'. He just wanted to let me know he visited his mum's plot every week and everything was as well as it could be expected. I didn't know whether to laugh or cry back in my dingly dell later. Knowing they were still there was worse somehow than knowing they had been sold on. I just kept thinking about them for days after his visits, imagining them, just lying there!

Him popping in to tell me all this, was certainly doing me no good.

I finally got out a year early in 1971, when I had just turned thirty. It took me days to adjust to the outside I can tell you. I somehow felt like an alien in my own city.

Those were days of the Troubles in Northern Ireland, Enoch Powell and his rivers of blood and even worse than that, Arsenal doing the league and cup double. That bit of news in particular didn't make me feel any better I can tell you.

There had been massive changes in those nine years and I had done my best to keep up with it all from inside from reading the papers and listening to the radio, but it was still a shock to the system when you were actually walking around in it. Everything was so loud and busy. Took me a long time to get my bearings.

As I had nowhere to stay, my probation officer got me temporary accommodation locally, which turned out to be an old Seaman's Mission in Deptford.

That place was as bad if not worse, than prison. I wasn't sure I could stand too much of it to be honest. Old, dirty geezers, coughing and farting all through the night, and the grub made the prison look like The Talk of Town.

One morning after getting out of the mission as early as I could I escaped the stench of the place and decided to go round to my old house.

I knew I wouldn't get the warmest of welcomes from Brenda. I expected the worst, but I hoped she'd let me see young Matthew at the very least.

I stopped at florist's barrow on the way and weighed up the idea of buying Brenda some flowers, but bottled that at the last moment. It began to feel awkward so I left it.

I had a tidal wave of nerves roll up on me as I walked through the iron front gate and up the glazed tiled path towards the black painted front door of our old house in Walworth.

I now remembered a time before having the same feeling in the pit of my stomach as the one I was experiencing at this very second.

It was when I was led from my cell into the dock on judgment day back in 1962.

Yeah, that bad.

I rung the brass doorbell and then took a step back as I

heard a dog bark. Dog eh? Woman alone in a house with no man about, well none that I knew of, made sense.

The door creaked slowly opened.

'Yeah? What d'ya want?'

I looked down to where the voice was coming from and was startled to be challenged by a young girl on a pair of metal roller skates, their red leather straps keeping them on her shoes, looking at me.

'Oh, alright?' I said, trying to not look too puzzled. 'Does Mrs. Hawkins live here?' I looked again at the rusted door number as I said 'I got the right house? '

Without saying a word to me, the kid spun round on her wheels and shouted 'Auntie Bren, there's some bloke here for you.'

I heard my ex-wife's voice shout, 'alright Trace, be out in a minute.' and then saw a handsome little face peek round the door and which was now looking very intently at me.

I knew straight away it was my Matthew. He had long shaggy blonde hair and piercing blue eyes. He also had the same shaped nose as my mum and me, and he looked, well, big.

He was nine now, coming up to ten, not far away from his teenage years. He looked a cracking young fella.

I somehow knew it was him.

'Alright, Matthew... it's me...dad.'

He looked down at the floor and then up again.

'What d'ya want?' he asked kindly.

I smiled. The thought struck me that I hadn't seen him since he was baby. Grew up to be nice kid. A good boy, I could tell.

'Just passing like, thought I'd say hel...'

With that the front door was pulled further open sharpish

and Brenda was standing there, her right hand holding a dog's lead attached to the collar of her dog, who was pulling very hard towards me.

'Thought I recognised that voice.' she said 'What d'ya want Vin?'

Her tone was harsher than Matthew's. Much harsher.

I smiled as I looked at her; she hadn't changed a bit really. Maybe a little fuller in figure, but still well dressed and her brown hair nicely cut.

'Hello Bren.' I said 'how are you? I was just saying to er... Matthew here. I was passing and I thou...'

'Look Vin, been a long time innit? Let sleeping dogs lie and all that. We've all moved on. Best you do too mate'

I looked straight at her, getting a little humpy if truth were told, in that she had gone straight on the attack.

'I know Bren, I know. Believe me I have moved on. But he's my kid as well as yours and I just wanted to say hello is all. Let him know I'm out and, well, just wanted to say hello. I've changed in there Bren. Just wanted...'

'Matthew knew you were coming out Vin. Passed on your letter as you asked and he read it. He's a good reader, doing well at school. Told him if he wanted to meet you out of the nick, I wouldn't get in the way, but he decided to leave it. How it is now. We've all moved on.'

I could also see, no, I could feel, she was expecting me to turn up. Her body was shaking ever so slightly. She had been waiting years for his moment, knew it was coming. Probably practiced this moment in her head, maybe even out loud when no one was about, a hundred, no, a thousand times.

I could see I was going to get nowhere here today.

'Who's the girl?' I asked out of nowhere, throwing her off kilter.

'Girl? What girl?' Brenda suddenly looked lost.

'Kid who answered the door, the mystery?'

Brenda nodded as she grasped my train of thought. 'Tracey.' she said brightly 'that's young Tracey.'

'My girlfriend' said Matthew cutting his mother off in her flow.

I smiled. 'Girlfriend eh? Marriage plans are there mate?' and Matt smiled sheepishly. 'Me and your mum weren't much older than you two when we first met, were we Bren?'

But Brenda was closing the door.

'Gotta go Vin. Good to see you ok, yeah, but got to go.'

'Wait Bren, please, can't I come in for a cuppa or something? Bren. Brenda!'

But it was no good, she just shut the door, pulling the dog in as hard as she could. At that precise moment I wanted to kick it down and the Mr. Angry inside me was brewing up, ready to do it, it would let her know how strong about I felt and…and…

But I suddenly saw sense. This was crazy thinking. I mean I've only been out a couple of days and already I'm thinking of smashing up my old family home.

Brenda would have a field day and say 'See, he aint changed.' and everyone would nod and agree. Once a bad boy, always a bad boy. Well, they didn't know me anymore.

Time to get going here. Time to leave it. It will happen; I will see the boy for a bit longer. Just not today.

I went in to see my probation officer on my way back to Deptford, and well, I'm not ashamed to say I cried. I sat down, and I cried at his desk.

Cried for not seeing my kid for nigh on ten years and I cried for the loss of those ten years of my life. Yeah, hands up, I was a naughty boy and I had got punished. But I had done my time and it was now time to get some life back.

The probation officer made me a cup of tea and over that

told me the good news, that the council had allocated me a flat in Blackfriars, fairly new build's. The estate it was on was built just after the Second World War, so low rise unlike some of these horrible social housing schemes going up around then.

This news brought a small smile to my boat, at least I could now get out of that flea-ridden flop I was currently stewing in.

In the coming weeks, I also managed to secure the job I mentioned earlier. Got it through someone I met in 'The Louis'. The fella wasn't too choosy who he employed, so my prison record wasn't a problem.

So, I began the job I would be doing to my retirement day. I ended up travelling between London and Europe for the next thirty-five years or so. Solid job, nothing special, driving containers about.

Importantly, it kept my mind occupied and me out of nick.

Those days were over, well and truly over.

Funnily enough I found I never thought much about Samuels and his mum and her grave. I couldn't afford to dwell on it at this point in my life. If it popped into my head occasionally, I quickly dismissed, I wasn't getting back into that. Done and dusted.

With the nomadic life like I was now leading, I tended to have a few birds tucked away here and there. Never serious enough to want to settle down with any of them though and that suited both parties. There was Rosie in Amsterdam, Birgit in Denmark, Davinia in Paris…you get the picture. If anyone ever got too clingy, possessive like, I spanished 'em. I was determined to not go down that road again.

Once bitten… and it fucking hurt!

Thankfully over the next twenty years, I managed to build my relationship with my Matthew. As soon as he got to sixteen, I started taking him football on a Saturday, down the Old Den, if I was in town. He loved it, a couple of cheeky pints for me and him on the way to the ground and same again and a chip supper on the way home.

It was slow going at first, but then he gradually opened up. He once told me I had hurt his mum bad, and that she'd never forgive me. Hard to hear that from your own son, but he took after me in that respect, him being a straight talker.

Actually, it meant the world that did in a way, as I took it as a sign that I was gaining his trust. Hard going at first as I say, but we got there.

We now get on like a house on fire and I feel blessed to know him and have him in my life.

After that first hesitant week in Benhill, I started to open up a bit I suppose. Started saying hello to a few other residents, who seemed a decent bunch on the whole.

One thing I did begin to notice however, as I walked about a bit more, was the real condition the place was actually in. Threadbare stair carpets, filthy windows, rubbish not being collected, security doors not closing properly and generally an air of neglect about the place.

Now the majority of people in here, myself included, were paying a service charge in with their rent, which should have taken care of all that I have just mentioned.

We had an on-site cleaner, but as far as I could make out she was always hiding somewhere, reading the paper and dunking her custard creams in her tea.

It also soon became obvious to me that Maureen runs this place with a rule of fear and intimidation. This approach was not what I had expected at all.

Her accent had maybe softened after her years in London, but the occasional word would get out and remind you of where she came from. As it happened, I wasn't too sure of her from our first meeting and that 'Gods waiting room' crack and before long I knew I was a good judge of character, because she revealed herself to be an eighteen carrot wrong 'un.

I knew screws like her in the shovel, bitter and twisted bastards they were.

Even from my first couple of days of circulating, I couldn't believe how she was going about things in here. I noticed that her and the staff took full advantage of the ill health of some of the residents.

For example, I noticed if anybody wanted a packet of fags or a newspaper from the nearby newsagent and they were incapable of getting there themselves, they had to use one of the staff to go and get the stuff for them, for which they'd be charged a fiver or a tenner to do so.

The lovely Maureen would then take a cut of that personally.

With eighty people people staying here, and two thirds of them incapable of standing up, let alone going shopping there was a tidy few bob to be made. I really didn't like what I was seeing, but I had just got here, and didn't want to get too busy just yet, but believe me I was watching.

Apart from all that, I settled in quite well I suppose. Never one for sleeping much, I tended to watch old war films or a decent Cowboy one with John Wayne in to the early hours, with the sound down to a minimum.

However, during my second week, around midnight I kept hearing loud pitched screams and shouts of 'GET OUT, GET OUT!" coming from the flat above mine, number twelve. At first, I thought it was row going on or a loud telly or something and was loathed to put my head out and take a look. But by the third night of this, I'd had enough. I left my flat and walked up a flight of stairs and into the flat the noise was coming from, its front door wide open.

Upon entering, I found Maureen with one of her assistants Daniella, holding down old Nelly who lived there and from who all the shouting and hollering was coming from

' Maureen.' I said as calm as I could. 'What the flaming 'ell is going on?'

She was startled to see me. Really startled.

'Got nothing to do with you Mr. Hawkins – get back to you flat immediately.'

It was obvious I wasn't going to get any sense out of her, so I decided to ask Nelly, only she looked like she was drugged up or something.

'Nell, NELLY! Can you hear me mate'

'Is that one of them Maureen, is it, eh? Nelly seemed in a really confused state.

'Yeah that's one Nelly, told you we'd flush them out.' Maureen said.

' Flush one out?' I said. 'Will someone tell me what is going on?' I was now getting the needle.

'That's it Nelly, you lay your head down' Wiloch was now letting go of my neighbour and laying her down on her own settee. Old Nell looked exhausted.

I tried to stand in the way as Maureen got up to leave and without a word she just brushed past me.

'My office, ten in the morning!' she barked in my general direction and she was then gone with her lap dog Daniella by her side, she also giving me a filthy look as she went by.

Fuck knows what was happening here, but I was determined to find out. Poor old Nelly was now soundo, snoring her bleeding head off and I was left standing there like a right lemon.

I shut her flat door behind me and returned to mine. A couple of heads were quickly pulled back to behind curtains as I walked down the corridor, so obviously others had heard the commotion, but they had decided not to get involved.

I sat up all night, going over in my head trying to suss out what was occurring here…What the flaming hell was all that about?

Early next morning, before Maureen reached the office, I went round to see Nelly.

She was up early and looked in good cheer. A tiny woman, with a boy's haircut, she was well into her eighties.

'Hello Mr. Hawkins' she said as she opened the door ' What can I do for you?'

I was surprised to hear that question really; I thought she would know I would want to get some answers.

"Its about last night Nell' I said.

'Last night? She looked puzzled 'whatever do you mean?'

'Blimey girl, you what? It was bedlam in here at midnight. Maureen was here and that Daniella.'

'Oh that! That was nothing really. They were just helping me get rid of the evil spirits in the flat...got loads of 'em I have.'

I was struck dumb; my dumb has never been struck harder!

Nelly continued 'they were very kind. They promised if I paid them, they would help and drive out those horrible things.'

I looked at her with a really quizzical face on. 'Let me get this straight, you paid Maureen to clear your flat of evil spirits?'

'That's what I said. What are you, mutton? Now if you don't mind, I've got to do me hoovering and then a bit of shopping, so come on...out...Ta la love.'

"But, but'. But it was no good, she was shooing me out of her flat rapidly and as soon as I was out, she shut her door firmly in my face.

I couldn't really work out what exactly was going on here, but it all sounded very much like another Maureen moneymaking scheme to me.

One thing I really detest in life is a bully and I now had Maureen down as one of the worst kind of them, making it her business exploiting old and vulnerable people.

I left Nell's flat and I stormed round to her office on the ground floor and sat on one of the blue covered fabric chairs outside it. I looked at my watch it was twenty past nine. I was well early, but I had nowhere else I'd rather be.

At quarter to ten, Maureen pulled into the on-site car park in a silver Range Rover, as big as a bleeding tank. Nice motor I thought and on her wages.

She saw me sitting outside as she went into her room and smirked.

Ten minutes she later she asked me to come in.

Her office was pretty small, with a wood effect desk and a computer and keyboard on top of it. All over the walls were tourism posters extolling the virtues of South Africa. Looks like she was missing home.

I sat down by her desk and she looked at me for a few seconds and then began talking at me.

'Mr. Hawkins, thanks for coming. You're new here Mr. Hawkins, not used to our ways of working; you really shouldn't have come in to Mrs. Elkins flat, it was not your business.'

I just smiled at the bare face cheek of the woman.

'Hang on, hang on.' I said, barely able to wait to jump in. 'Lets have it right Maureen. It's midnight and all I'm hearing is screams and I naturally think someone is in trouble and that had to be checked out. I have spoken to Nelly this morning and she has told me some cock and bull story about evil spirits in her flat and a story of you helping her, for a fee of course, and if I'm honest I find that hard to believe and I'm not having it.'

Maureen surprised me, by laughing. 'Oh, I see. You're not having it? YOU"RE not having it ha ha, silly man. Let's get one thing crystal clear here, I run this home, my way.'

'Listen.' I continued 'I know I might have only been here at Benhill for five minutes compared with all the others here, but I've worked out what goes on and it aint right. Exploitation is the only word for it.'

Maureen looked down at her files and then at me.

'Strong word that, exploitation. Can I deduce that you are thinking of reporting what you saw last night, along with these, these other bits of nonsense you claim to know about'?

'Yep, too right. That's about the nuts and bolts of it.' I said.

'Well in that case, you leave me no option. I will counter that with a claim that you have been inappropriate with a couple of my ladies and believe me, you'll soon be shown the door. I would suggest you think on Mr. Hawkins.'

'You what?' I said. 'That's outrageous that is.' I was shocked to be honest. I was struggling to get a breath what with I had just heard Maureen say.

'Sounds …like… like blackmail that does?' I stuttered.

'Tut tut Mr. Hawkins. That is another emotive word.'

She was cool, too cool.

She'd been here for years, and it was sounding like she'd been at it for years. She had it all sewn up. I quickly worked out she had me by the short and curlies here.

'I have to say Mr. Hawkins, you didn't appear to me to be a stupid man when we first met. But now I am beginning to have my doubts. Think about your circumstances Mr. Hawkins. Seriously think about them.'

It was obvious I'd be out of of here in minutes, once that story was put about. She knew that. The thought that I'd be slung into some poxy hostel or worse out on the streets crossed my mind and caused a shudder down my spine. The London pavement is no place for a seventy year old. Come on Vinny son, grip something firm mate!

I had to box clever here. I stood up and smiled. Time for

the white flag.

'Maureen. You don't mind me calling you Maureen do you?'

She smiled, so I took that as a sign to carry on.

'Obviously, we've got off on the wrong foot here. To be honest, I'm still finding my feet. Maybe I've been hasty, too hasty. Made too many presumptions. Listen, I've taken in what you have said. Believe me, I have.

Shall we say I've mis-judged certain elements here? I shall say no more'

She smiled a self-satisfying smile, knowing she'd won.

It was killing me inside being so nice to her.

'You know what?' I continued 'I'd even go as far as to say, if you ever need a strong pair of hands around the place, you know where to find me.'

Maureen's smile got even wider.

'Ok, Mr. Hawk…Vincent, we'll say no more about it for now. Thanks for the offer; I'll bear it in mind. Why not settle yourself in and then we'll see.

I'm so glad we are friends again…'

3

Wimpy and Chips

In reality, I felt dirty in Maureen's company, tainted in fact.

It was obvious she was a wrong 'un and she needed exposing, but the way she used her position to completely control what went on in Benhill, was plainly wrong, but she was clever and horribly devious.

Sadly it appeared the Council just let her get on with. I'm sure she would concoct some old rubbish if someone reported her for something. And if anyone from the Council bothered to come along and investigate the complaint, after chatting to Maureen, they'd soon go away again happy till the next time.

She was a master of her game.

I now had plenty of food for thought as to my next move, but one thing was for sure, I wasn't finished with her.

After what I had seen with old Nelly, I thought a good start would be to get to know a few more of my fellow residents. I want to pick their brains and hear what they thought about Maureen and her little 'ways'.

I left my flat and wandered down the main passage, walking on the threadbare and tattered carpet and made my way into the communal lounge area.

It was a big room, stuffed full of high backed sturdy chairs all facing towards a big television, which was in a wooden cabinet on wheels in one corner of the room.

A few of the really elderly were gathered around it being bored silly by that orange faced antiques fella whose name escaped me but his 'cheap as chips' catch phrase didn't. They appeared to be so bored in fact, half of them were sound asleep.

I noticed the general décor for this big room was pale blue in colour. Pale blue paper on the walls, pale blue doilies on the back of the pale blue chairs and a pale blue carpet that completed the look.

I had a quick shufty round and tried to make eye contact with a few of those gathered there in front of the telly, and that were still awake.

None were taking the bait though.

They were doing their best to pretend I wasn't there, or so it seemed.

A group of four, three women and a man, who were sitting away from the television area and who I had noticed were in a heated debate when I walked in, had now stopped talking, but at least they were looking my way.

"Hello all' I said as cheerily as I could as I looked their way. I knew that my very presence had been the conversation stopper though I wasn't sure why.

'Please, crack on, don't let me stop you' I said and made my way over to a high-back chair, near to where they were sitting.

The eyes of the group followed me to it. They hadn't started talking again, in fact they looked at each other and seemed unsure what to do or say.

A real uncomfortable, eggy, feeling had come over us all.

'Nice day innit. Bright...sunny for a change...' I said as breezily as I could muster.

A couple of them gave a weak smile and looked down at the blueness of the carpet, but no one spoke. I smiled a weak smile back.

I was feeling very uncomfortable by now, but knew I had to plough on to at least try and make a friend or two here. Time to shit or get off the pot.

'Look, this is silly isn't it? Believe me I've no wish to get in the way. I just thought it was time to come and say hello to you all. 'Do you want me to leave or something? Is there a problem?'

Again, I got the minimum response to this.

I was getting a little narked if truth were told.

They all looked at each other and the only fella among them nodded in my direction but still without saying a word.

One of the two women furthest away cleared her throat, as if she was about to spout forth. She was sitting next to a younger version of herself, so I was guessing they were related, probably sisters.

The throat clearer finally spoke.

'Well...hello, yes, we're sorry about that, but we find ourselves a bit of a difficult spot and we've got to be er...we've got to be careful. Walls have ices if you know what I mean.'

She smiled as she delivered that line.

I also smiled on hearing that comment , which was spoken in an accent that had a heavy Scottish tinge to it.

'Look, we've obviously got off on the wrong foot here aint we? Not really sure what is going on, new boy an all that, but can't we start this again?'

I stood up and stretched out my hand to shake the hand of the one that had spoken.

'My name is Vincent, Vinny to my friends, Vinny Hawkins. You may have noticed I moved in a couple of weeks back. Been getting the lay of the land since, but as I say, thought it time I came and said hello.'

The lady who had spoke to me, looked at the others in the

tight knit group for reassurance, but then finally reached out and returned the handshake as politely as she could.

'How d'ya do. I'm Dorothy Cotter. Everyone calls me Dot for short.'

She then nodded over to her look-a-likey sitting in the next chair.

'And this is my younger sister Margaret - Margie to all in here.'

The other lady nodded and smiled pleasantly.

'How d'ya do Mr. Hawkins' she said.

'Call me Vinny, please… I knew you two were related; there is a very strong family resemblance if you don't mind me saying so.'

And the two of them, laughed somewhat girlishly.

'Erm, excuse me if I'm a bit blunt here.' I said smiling. 'but I couldn't help feel a certain chill when I walked in just then. Aint that frightening am I, eh?'

They all smiled too, but looked a little bit embarrassed at the same time.

'Heavens above, no, no, no' said Dot, 'it's just….'

'It's just…' The elderly black gentleman, sitting next to Margie, interjected. 'We got to be sure who it is, how shall we say? We welcome into our little world.'

He still had a large slice of his homeland in his accent, but I guessed he had been over here for a few years. He was stick thin, and had long legs. He was going bald on top and he had on thick half tortoise shell rimmed specs.

One other thing I also noticed was that though he may be marching on in years, but he was very smartly turned out. His black brogue shoes were highly polished and he had a solid crease in his grey flannel trousers. His white shirt looked fresh and his waistcoat, though from a different suit from his trousers, was clean and nicely cut. He also had on a cheery, floral tie.

His sliver watch chain was glinting in the mid morning sun which was shining through the white net curtains hanging up at the big front window, which faced onto the communal gardens at the front of Benhill.

I nodded in his direction.

'Yeah, I can understand that, fair enough.' I said. 'You don't know me, nor I you, but I can assure you, you've got nothing to fear from me, I'm just a regular fella. Scouts honour.'

The old gentleman looked me up and down and then continued to speak.

'That's fine, we hear you. Actually we have been checking. We've heard all about you.'

I smiled as I thought I bet you aint heard it all mate...

'Oh yeah? What exactly have you heard. Please, go on, I don't blush easily?'

The elderly chap smiled at me.

'Well, for instance we heard through the grapevine you tried to help Nelly last night with her bit of nonsense, and then, you are seen going into the office of Maureen this morning and then...here y'are now.

I know you have only been here a short while, but an intelligent man like you would have seen, certain things, not only last night, but that which go on in here in general.'

I nodded at him 'I have. Yeah, I've seen plenty. That's part of the reason I'm here actually.'

I could sense the caution among these four people, they were very suspicious.

'Think it's about time we introduced ourselves, don't you reckon? As I mentioned, the name is Vincent.' and I reached out my hand to his.

The old chap creaked as he stood up and reached out his shaky paw to touch mine.

'And I, I'm Grenville. Grenville Isaacs.'

'Pleasure to meet you Mr. Isaacs' I said, and I hope I sounded like I meant it, cos I did.

My instincts were telling me I was going to get on with this fella. Straight talker and well dressed, not a million miles from a bit of me that

'These certain things you mention Mr. Isaacs. Have they been going on for long?'

As he sat quickly back down into his blue chair, he wiped his head with a white handkerchief, which he had pulled from his tight trouser pocket.

'Not so fast sir. How do I know you is kosher eh? For all I know you have been planted here by the she –devil 'erself.'

She devil I thought? That would sum Maureen up quite nicely, as I guessed that was who he was aiming that barb at. If so, I had to agree.

'Me a Plant? No way, my friend. Though, not easy for me to prove that one way or the other at this stage. Guess, there's nothing else for it Mr. Isaacs, you either trust me or you do not. Your call at the end of the day squire.'

I finished that sentence looking at him squarely between his eyes.

We sat looking at each other. Me expressionless, and him not so, until old Grenville cracked and his face burst into a broad wide grin.

'You win man; you have a good poker face y'know. Anyways, truth is, if you is working for Maureen, I don't really care. She knows I have reported her before, so I'm down in her black book anyways.'

And with that he grinned

'I was wondering if anyone had done that?' I said.

'Well, I have on a couple of occasions in the last year or so. I've been here five years now and at first it was all sweet, we were well looked after and the place was spotless. But then the council tendered out the day-to-day running's to contractors and since then things been steadily getting worse.

Their penny pinching has brought nothing but bad times here.

We also used to have inspectors who would come and check up that everything was in order, but they don't come as often as they did do, so things have got a little, shall we say, slack.

So I had a word with the council people when I went to pay my rent recently. A couple of people came down a week later and must have mentioned my name, cos Maureen looked at me like I had, if you excuse the phrase ladies, shat in her hat.

It was obvious to all, that she knew who had spilt the beans.'

'So, nothing changed then?' I already knew the answer to that.

'No sir, if anything it got worse, it was months between each visit instead of week's from then on. She and her staff then started to exploit the old and infirm among us, which continues to this day, as it sounds like you have seen for yourself'.

'Ummm... Got it sewn up aint she.' I said. 'What I have seen already with Maureen and her staff is bang out of order and I'm guessing you know of a lot more going on?'

'Yeah man, we've all seen it, even been the victim of it meself. All of us have thought about reporting it again, but it's useless man and I know she'll get rid of us out of here sharpish if we do, so…that's that .'

Mr. Isaacs sat there shaking his head.

Dot suddenly coughed. She was obviously uncomfortable in this situation, as they all were, or that is how it appeared.

She was quite squat, fat you'd call it I suppose if you

were being unkind, and I guess was in her late seventies, early eighties. She had a mauve rinse in her grey hair and a matching twin set on of the same shade.

'I fear we may be saying too much, Grenville, oh dear…'

It was obvious she, and it looked like her sister Margie, were really frightened of what we were talking about. Maybe it was best to slow down a bit. I mean I hardly know 'em and this conversation was obviously unsettling them.

'Tell you what, why don't we all introduce ourselves properly? At the end of the day, I'm like you, you have to believe me, I don't want any fuss or bother. That's why I came to live here.

I hope you're ok with that? You never know we might have something in common, apart from a shared dislike of David Dickensian'

They all looked at each other again, this close band of friends, and one by one smiled and nodded.

'Aye, right enough. You seem ok. S'pose it comes down to trust and you've got caring eyes, so I'm gonna trust ya. But if I'm wrong and you let me down, boy, I have ways of making your life a misery ha ha.'

Blimey, with women like Dot on the premises, there was no need for a guard dog!

'Ok, I'll go first then, eh?' she said, everyone nodded.

'Dorothy Cotter, that's me, born in Glasgow, bonny Scotland, and if you don't mind, I wont reveal exactly when!' she said laughing.

I liked old Dot already, seemed a real livewire. Once she was talking, I doubt much could stop her!

'I studied nursing straight from school. All I ever wanted to be was a nurse, and I ended up as a Matron in various London hospitals for many years, after coming down to the big smoke in the early 1960s.

I had started my career back home, but wanted to spread out after a few years, and London seemed the place to be. I ended up at St Thomas' for over twenty years in the end. Good times, happy times. I had found my calling alright.

And, jeez, London was on fire then, not that us student nurses had too much money to get too involved, but I had some good times socially.

What else is there? Aye I know. Men!'

We all laughed at that, especially sister Margie.

'Never married, no, not me. I went out with plenty of suitors, but…well put it this way, I never found the right chap. No, nursing and the theatre became the love's of my life.'

'So, a surgical matron then? I asked.

Dot looked confused.

'Sorry, I thought I heard you say theatre there, I was guessing you got involved in operations and that?'

'Ha ha. No son.'

Blimey, been a few years since I was called son, but I liked it.

'I mean Amateur Dramatics, you know acting and that? Me and a group of other young nurses joined a nearby theatre group for a bit of cheap fun. I took to it like a duck to water. I've done it all over the years, from The Bard to Alan Bennett. What joy it's brought me, well, us. Both my sister and me were very keen on the Am Dram for years. Eh Margie?'

Margie smiled as the memories of those days came flooding back and she then continued the conversation.

'Aye Dot, that's right. We joined initially in the hope of meeting suitable gentlemen for marrying purposes, but sadly most of the men involved with the company were already married or you know, liked hitting the shuttlecock from the feathered end, if you get my drift.'

'Margie Cotter!' yelled Dot.

The rest of us sitting there laughed, though Dot looked a little uncomfortable if truth were told.

'Dear me, you're a terrible woman Margaret Cotter and no mistake.' She shook her head at her younger sister.

'Now, where was I?' Dot was keen to take over and continue.

'Alan Bennett.' A woman who was sitting amongst us, but who I hadn't been introduced to yet, suddenly piped up.

'Ta Pauline love' said Dot.

I looked at Pauline and smiled, and she shyly smiled back, but she broke eye contact quickly.

'Och, after a wee while, the smell of the greasepaint won me over and I became hooked. I'm extremely partial to Gilbert and Sullivan as a result.

My Margie's story is similar to my own, only she's younger and never made Matron, no, Staff Nurse is as far she got to.'

I looked at Margie at the mention of this, and noticed she was getting redder and redder, looking really flushed and ready to boil over.

'I can tell my own story Dorothy Cotter, if you don't mind!'

Classic case of sibling rivalry here I thought. Margie was obviously fed up playing second fiddle to her older sister, a role, I guess, she had played since they were kids.

'Hello' she said looking directly at me. 'Margaret Cotter, as introduced earlier. It's true I'm younger of the two of us, and always will be...'

She then smiled a very satisfactory smile.

You didn't have to be an expert in human relations to realise you had a classic case of love and hate on display here.

'I too loved my job and settled on becoming the best staff nurse I could. I never had any aspirations to go higher, I knew my place on the ladder if you know what I mean.'

She had a fiery look in her hazel eyes. Again you wouldn't mess with her. Margie was the darker in complexion of the two, and I found myself staring at her thinking how much she would have looked like a young Elizabeth Taylor in her younger years. I began to daydream about black velvet bags of gems…and, had to snap out of that sharpish!

'Nice that you have each other though, as you get older ' I said.

They both smiled weak smiles at me, which said more than a million words would ever do.

'I've been here nearly twenty years' said Dot and Margie joined me, when she retired five years later. Thankfully I had a double bedroom, so she could move in with me.'

'Seemed like the ideal thing at the time.' Margie said and then left that statement hanging in an uncomfortable silence.

I looked at Mr. Isaacs sitting opposite me for some help.

He smiled a knowing smile and straightened his tie and patted down his thinning hair

'My turn I guess?' he finally said, which came as a big relief to us all I reckon.

Funnily enough, since he had first spoken, I had already thought of a nickname for him. I've a real fever for giving people nicknames, and have done so for years. It's mainly cos I really struggle to remember their proper names and after years of prison and being on the road in the lorries I've just found nicknames easier to recall.

Therefore I find I give most people a name and old Grenville here, though he wouldn't know it for a while yet, would be forever known, by me at least, as Tubby.

You worked it out yet?

Come on, its easy. Tubby Isaacs innit. The king of the seafood in the East End of London. He long claimed his jellied eels were a powerful aphrodisiac and had a great catchphrase, which he shouted from his barrow, parked down by Aldgate tube station for years.

It went…

'Ere ya are lady. Take some eel's home today. Every basin a baby!'

As it happened, looking at old Isaac again, the name worked on two levels, seeing as that he was so skinny too!

Mr. Isaac then continued, unaware of his new moniker.

'I came over in the late 50s from Trinidad and Tobago with a couple of pals, looking for work and we soon found it when we settled on the buses.

Man, those were tough, cold, hard days. It's an old cliché that we thought the street was paved with gold, well we knew that was wrong, they were most certainly not.

But we expected a warmer welcome than what we got!

Oh Lord…It was so ROUGH!

I had got that job pretty quick, so I had money coming in, but the way I was looked at, and spoken to…Jeesusss, I'm amazed I didn't took the next boat home.

'Heard it was tough then.' I said 'all that no black, no Irish or dogs stuff eh?'

Grenville continued as he nodded.

'Yeah saw many of those notices on doors, when I was looking for digs. Too many. Eventually we bunked down with some fellow Trinnies over in Notting Hill, which was a real slum area back then.

Seriously I'm telling ya, if it weren't for the church and my strong belief, I would have crumbled there and then.

Mind you, in truth, I had little to go back to, so I knuckled down, and in time, I settled.

I managed to find a room in a house where some of fellow travellers, who had been over here already for six months, began to show me the ropes. It was all a mystery to me, but slowly I worked London out.

It was through a friend of a friend who also flopped at my house, that I got the job on the buses. As ever in life, it's always who you know and hardly ever what you know, that helps you get on in life.

I worked as a conductor mainly on the number 12's all the way from then to till retirement in the mid 1980s.'

I was listening but I was also really studying how dapper he was. This man was immaculate. His barnet was trimmed to perfection.

This was a man who could afford to let his standards drop at his age, but he weren't having any of that. I remember me being like that forty year back, but as I've got older, I find I'm not so fussy – but him, you could tell from the cut of his jib, he don't come out of his flat unless all that is attended to.

"What you looking at sir?' He had noticed I was checking him out.

'Er, nothing, really. I was just admiring your turn out. Very smart it has to be said.'

He seemed surprised and I guessed quietly pleased.

'Oh, thank you. Each day that I wake up on the right side of the dirt, I think I should make an effort. Always liked to look good. All us Trinny boys did back then.'

'Well, you are putting me to shame. I'm gonna have to shape up, I can see that.'

Grenville smiled. 'As I mentioned, I am also a God fearing man and still attend my church every Sunday, never miss it, that can't be done. I am a spiritual man. Yes sir.'

A reflective look came over his face and he went silent for a moment.

'It was at my church that I was blessed to meet the lady who was to become my wife, my Priscilla. Oh gosh, we caused a rumpus with that little episode...oh my.'

I was now very curious.

'Oh yeah, what'd you do?' I was struggling to think what this straight-laced man could do that would shock people.

'Well might you ask sir. Well, my Priscilla happened to be a white lady And please remember this is the late 1950s and this just was...not...done.

This was a scandal!

 Of course, looking back now, we were forerunners for today. Always been ahead of my time I'm pleased to say'.

I had to smile, who would have thought old Tubbs as a rebel.

'Priscilla and me though. We never saw colour. We saw love.

But it is fair to say, we was in the minority, because everybody else, well, Praise The Lord!

You would think we had committed MURDER! Fire and brimstone came from all angles, all of it, raining down on me head!

But, I stood firm. I loved that lady.

I called her Cilla and she was a local girl. Man, times were so different back then.

People were blatantly racist, so you knew where you stood. And a white woman with a black man, well, that was a rare thing to see and we were very easy targets. Her family disowned her immediately, the minute they found out.

'Be gone they said, be gone out of our lives! You are bringing shame and embarrassment to this family.' They said.

Man, I was so vex, but I just kept my counsel, just didn't rise to their bait. I decided we just had to get on with it. We were in love, nothing we could do about it anyway.

So, we married in 1958. None of her family attended the

service. To be honest, they weren't missed.'

I looked down at my feet on hearing that. This country was so backward then, uneducated really in many ways. I found from my time travelling all over Europe on the lorries, that fundamentally, we are all very similar. We just happen to look and sound different.

'Well, we had many young black nurses back then, working with us, lovely girls they were. But I have to be honest, we did hear the comments from the patients, about how they wanted an English nurse and "not a blackie". Sorry to have to say that Grenville.'

This conversation had also stirred painful memories for Dot.

'Don't take on so, Dorothy. They were different days wasn't they? And thankfully things got a little easier as time went on, but it was years before it settled down. But me and she, my Cilla, through it all, we never had any doubts. We were strong in our convictions.

Despite all of it that came our way - the hurtful name calling, the being ignored in shops, and look of disgust on some of their faces, we were happy. We truly were. In our own house, in our own company, we were fine.

Praise the Lord and Amen. He bless us with three pickney, two boys and a girl. All good kids and I'm proud to say, they're all doing well. Don't forget it was also very hard for them too. They were light skinned and shunned by most of their white family, but also by a few of my brothers of a darker hue.

Man, praise the Lord, it was coming from all sides as I said, but we struggled through together, with the Lords help, you hear me?'

Oh I hear you Mister Tubbs I thought, I hear you.

'You know what? I know my Cilla and me gave those kids the best we could. Education, clothes and a lifestyle I could only have dreamed of, when I was their age. My eldest boy

Denzil, is 52 and is in property, buying and selling all over Europe. He's now got two kids of his own. My middle one, Barratt is 48 and is a social worker in this area, he's got three children and our baby Carla, just turned 40, qualified as a lawyer when she was 27. She's a senior in her practice, so busy, busy, and doing very well, so very well. Most importantly, they are good people y'know.

And I love being a grandparent, yes sir!. So proud, SO proud am I, as was their mum.'

Sadness came over him as he spoke. Something painful had occurred here. He took out his white cotton hankie again and dabbed his eyes after raising his glasses on to the top of his head.

'Sadly, I lost my sweet Cilla when she died six years ago. Breast cancer got her . Which is how come I'm in here. It was thought best for me.'

I expressed my condolences upon hearing that news

'Thank you, thank you Vinny. Sad, very sad, but you know what, the one good thing is that but she had lived long enough to see a lot of changes in our society. And they were generally for the better on many matters, I'm pleased to say.

I smile now when I see how many of the youngsters today are in mixed race couples, especially round here. My wife and me were pioneers. We took on the slings and arrows first, so other's can lead a happier and healthier life together.

We weren't deliberately trying to be radical though, no, no, no, we were simply in love.

As it turned out, it was a love we suffered for sometimes, but the strength of it and the power of Jesus Christ got us through. Amen.'

I looked at him and could only imagine the grief they must have gone through together. And yet, he remained the politest man I had met in years, there's a lesson in there somewhere.

'Wow, some story there Tubbs' I said absent mindedly

'Eh? Tubbs? Whose this Tubbs?' Grenville was quick to pick up on my new name for him.

I smiled. 'Well, it's you, you're Tubbs. Everyone gets a nickname from me eventually and that's yours mate.'

Tubbs laughed and shook his head playfully.

'What about me?' said Margie. 'I mean us?' She then glanced at her elder sister, not wanting her to be left out.

I rubbed my chin. 'Bit too early to say just yet, but I'll work on something, you won't miss out, believe me.'

'Why Tubbs though?' asked Dot. 'There's not an ounce of spare meat on him.'

'I'll explain all one day, that is, if you don't work it out in the meantime girls.'

I then smiled at the lady in the corner.

Everyone else then looked over and she blushed because of all the attention. This was the one they called Pauline earlier.

She looked around my age, maybe a couple of years younger and therefore a good few years younger than her mates sitting with her here. I looked closely at her and she looked uncomfortable, very uncomfortable.

'Ooerr. Don't all stare at me!' She said laughing. 'Blimey, you look like a firing squad! Haha.'

'Go on then, we've all had a go. Your turn Pauline, lets have it. This Is Your Life.'

Dot was enjoying this

'Oh bli, I don't know. I've got nothing to say really.'

Pauline was not used to this sort of close attention, that was obvious.

'I've got some more about me I could tell you about' said Margie, trying to be helpful

'We've heard quite enough from you missus'. Big sister

Dot wasn't having any of that though.

'Come on Pauline.' I said 'Just to stop these two fighting if nothing else eh?'

'S'pose so...alright then. (Cough) Well, hello, my name is Pauline. Well, you heard that earlier didn't you, silly me. Anyway, it's Pauline, Pauline Davis. I've been at Benhill just over two year, since I lost my poor Bill.

Some days I still wake up and wonder where I am.? After two years, I still wake thinking I'm at my old family house. Loved that place I did. But once Bill went, no don't want to talk about him yet, still get. (sniff) upset...'

'There, there Pauline.' said Dot. 'We don't want any of that.'

She gave Pauline a tissue which appeared from up the sleeve of her cardigan.

'Ta Dot (sniff, sniff). Right. (cough) Anyway, in this new place that I wake up everyday in, there's this old lady who follows me around the flat, it's really odd. I look in the mirror and she's there. Wherever I go, she appears. I look at her closely and then slowly I realise that the old lady is actually, me. I have no idea how or when I turned into her.'

She suddenly looked at me, which caught me a little off guard.

'One thing is for certain though, that without these three people sitting here with us today, I would have been completely lost, they have been great to me'

She smiled as she looked at her friends and they smiled back. She was slowly getting more confident talking to us all and I could hear it in her voice.

'Aah bless you Paul, we don't do anything.' Said Dot smiling.

'Shut up Dot, you do plenty mate.'

I smiled when I heard that feisty remark. She might have

been shy getting started, but Pauline seemed to be getting into her stride nicely.

She sounded local, proper local. I'd known and grown up with hundreds of women like Pauline over the years, in fact I had married one very similar.

She was a good-looking lady for her age, which I thought was around the late 60s. She was a small woman, grey hair, cut short, but stylishly. I took her to be a knitter too, well at least the cardigan she had on looked hand knitted, so reckoned she made it. She seemed the type that would.

'Where was I? Christ, I hate all this' she sighed half smiling.

'What talking.' I laughed. 'I think you are doing fine, really. My turn next, that'll be so boring, it would send a glass eye to sleep.'

She smiled politely and continued.

'Well, I'm getting better at it, sort of. Not so much the talking, but all the making introductions stuff. When my Bill was alive, I didn't have to do any of that, we just knew everyone around us. Our friends, and all our neighbours. But now, now they are all gone, dead or moved away and I find I have to tell the new people that I meet, who I am, and where I'm from and all that, and I find it hard to be honest'

I sympathised with her. I know the world she was from well, very well. It was all mapped out for you at an early age. You married young, someone local, someone you had probably known since school. You had a couple or three kids, brought them up and then spent your spare time and holidays with your close friends and family. You got some poxy job and did your best to stay in it and earn a crust.

And funnily enough, that was exactly what I was trying to avoid with my antics back in the 1960s.

With Pauline and her old man, if they got lucky, they'd get ten years of retirement to enjoy each others company before bang, one of you goes and the other poor sod is left has to start all over again.

All of a sudden you have to make new friends and go to new places. Some take to it like a duck to water, others, like Pauline here, and me to a lesser extent, find that very daunting.

I started off on the same path, and then took a detour. With me though, after being on my own for so many years since, it's something I have adjusted to, never getting too close to people on purpose, so they can't hurt you when they go. Grief, as Pauline was finding out, was the price we pay for love.

She looked hard at me and then at the others and then she was off and running again.

'Hard to believe its come to this really? I mean, our old house was always full, especially weekends. Bill, the boys, my Dad Sid and sometimes that woman he was seeing, old Vera, all there for dinner.

Every Sunday I would be up early, get the meat on, and then I'd pop out into the garden. Dead -head a few Daffs, sweep up, do a bit of weeding. Loved that garden I did. Loved to see the new growth, fresh life popping through the soil. Mind you, thinking back, I seemed to spend half my time getting our old dog off the bloody plants.... bless old Duke, lovely dog he was, soppy as a sack load.

I sometimes think, blimey, where did they all go? Eh? Where?

Don't know about you lot, but I find Sundays the worst. As kind and nice as you lot are, I still find I can't stay in my flat, or at Benhill for that matter, on Sundays. I have to get out even if it's only for an hour's blow.

Can't do too long on me own at the best of times, find it so quiet sometimes, its horrible. During the week I handle it better, but Sunday, no chance. I tell myself, you're being silly Pauline, but I'd be climbing the bloody walls if I stayed in. Got to get out, even though I really aint got nowhere to go.

Most of the time, I make my way up to the Green and get on a 36 to Lewisham. I don't want anything up at Lewisham either, but it's a nice long ride on a bus and I can lose an hour or two.'

There were one or two knowing smiles from Dot, Margie and Tubbs as if to say, yep, we've done the same thing.

'He's gone then, your Bill?' I asked as nicely as I could.

'Yeah (cough).... Yeah bless him, died couple of years back. We was together fifty years, forty-five years married.'

She went quiet and looked down.

'Hard to get used to that is.'

She pulled out that white tissue and sniffed into it.

I felt a right tosser for bringing up that question now, it was obviously still painful to think of him.

'He was a fruit and veg wholesaler, worked at the old Covent Garden for a few years and then…'

'A what? An old sailor? Didn't know your Bill was at sea ' Said Margie.

I had to laugh, the old girl must be going mutton.

'Och you giddy kipper. She said Wholesaler! What we gonna do with you eh?' Sister Dot wasn't impressed.

Margie looked a little confused if truth be told, but her outburst made us all smile, which also helped Pauline at that precise minute.

'Thinking back, they all had routines on Sundays. Bill and my eldest Terry would go round the pub at 12 with strict instructions to be back by half two, murders otherwise I'd tell 'em with a smile.'

'Heard you mention the boys…' I smiled as I asked and she brightened.

'Yeah two of 'em. Terry coming up to fifty and Chrissy, forty five. Still call 'em me kids. Kids! They're grown men now. Where did that time go?

My Terry's got two kids, Jake fifteen and Jade twelve, so I'm a Nan too.'

The smile on her face when she spoke that word was a picture.

'I've got a boy myself, Matthew' I said. Again, being in relaxed company, I had let things slip without meaning to.

'Yeah, he's fifty now. Me and his mum parted a good few years back.'

Pauline looked like she wanted a longer explanation, but I wasn't in the mood for that to be honest, not yet.

'Long story Pauline, for another day mate, if you don't mind.'

She slowly nodded. Thankfully, she wasn't going to push it and I appreciated that. She continued.

'Back then, our young 'un, Chris, would be still in bed at mid-day, the little sod. He was always out late on a Saturday, down the Old Kent Road or wherever he went, him and his silly mates. You would hear him roll in at three in the morning. Creeping up the stairs, stumbling and coughing, stinking of fags, cheap perfume and one of them kebab things.'

The thought of all that made her smile.

'I would be sitting in the garden, having a cuppa and I'd hear him snoring his bleeding head off up in his room. Talk about a window rattler!

Y'know, I loved that garden so much. I never had so much as a bit of dirt as a girl, let alone a garden, so not sure where my love of gardening came from, but as soon as I was out there, I would lose track of time. I would be half way cutting through an old clump of green stalks or whatever, when I'd catch the smell of something sort of burning. Funny I'd think, what's that, next door on fire is it?

Then Blimey, I'd realise. It's the bloody meat! I'd rush

in and turn the oven down. I'd look at the kitchen clock and see that three hours had gone by since I went out there. Unbelievable that was. Three hours…Felt like three minutes. Loved it. I now realise how therapeutic it was.'

'Good that you are on the ground floor here then.' Dot said, and Pauline smiled.

'Oh yeah, very lucky with that Dot. Got a nice little plot out back.'

'Me too' I said 'I had a little garden in er, a er, previous place I stayed at and began to really love looking after it. Like you Pauline, I found it good for the mind. Great therapy.'

Pauline, smiled and sighed, her mind wandering back suddenly to her bus trip to Lewisham.

'Oh yeah, I was on about a bus, wasn't I. Now then, I always sit on one of the downstairs granny seats at the front.

I've tried to smile at the young girls with their babies who sit down there with me, try to have a chat, but they don't really want to talk.

I find they just smile a sort of pitying smile that makes me feel like I'm being a nuisance. I want to say 'Oi you, listen. I've been there, where you are.

I had two at not much older than you, I know how hard it is, but they don't really want to know. I look at these young mum's, who looks so young and think, blimey my love, what have you done?

You thought you were being all grown up and now, well you've got the baby wrapped round you for the next sixteen years at least.. And most of them you see have never got a bloke in tow. Nope, never. No doubt, he's had his jollies and buggered off and left them both.

These girls, they always seem alone, or at best, have a silly mate with 'em, who looks even younger and will probably be next.

The cycle will go on and she'll cop for one. I hear they do it mainly to get a flat of their own? That right?

'Some do aye, we had a few when I was nursing. Only sixteen years old a lot of them, silly young things. Petrified when it came to the day of delivery. They simply went back to being a wee young lassie, asking for their mum.' Dot was shaking her head.

'And they say romance is dead.' Smiled Tubbs.

'At least in my day, I had a man like my Bill, who married me and who stuck around to share the load, or that was the theory. Different days back then eh?'

I smiled. For someone who said they found it hard to talk, Pauline wasn't doing too bad. I looked at Tubbs and he winked back, like me, he knew this was as good therapy as her garden for Pauline.

'Them other young 'uns that get on, with their music buzzing in their ears or blasting from them mobile telephones, they go upstairs and tend to get even louder once up there. They'll all be deaf by the time they get to twenty-five...'

'Eh?' I said

'I said they'll be...' and then she laughed 'Oi you Vincent, cheeky sod'

I smiled at her. 'Must be getting old Pauline. We were like that once girl.'

'Eh? No, I wasn't. I was a good girl me. '

Once again, a blush came to her cheeks.

'Well, I can't lie.' I said 'I was a right tear away, bit of a Jack The Lad as it 'appens when I look back, a real right pest.'

'Somehow, I can believe that.' Dot was smiling as she let me have that.

'I sit there and watch the shops and flats and cars and houses flash by as the bus makes it way past New Cross. Once in a while I see a house that looks like our old one in Cleveden

Road and my mind goes back. Ere you sure you want me to go on? I aint half rabbiting?'

'Listen Pauline. What's that advert say? It's good to talk. You carry on madam. Am I right everyone?'

Tubbs looked at us all and we all nodded in agreement.

'Ok, if you're sure? Where was I? Oh yeah, that's it. I'd be back in the kitchen preparing the spuds and the greens, having now come in from the garden. I would try and time it all to be dished up at just after 2.30. My Dad would come round at half one. He'd come to me once a month and do the others in the family - my two sisters, Vi and Esther and my brother Gerry in between. Each week, I'd go round with Esther and hoover his place and do his washing and ironing.

Poor old sod he was, he wouldn't do it otherwise and he'd get terribly scruffy. He had lost my Mum in 1967 and he wasn't ever the same really. We didn't mind going round, and I always got on well with Et, used to have a laugh round there to be honest. Things changed a bit when his 'friend' old Vera came on the scene though. To be fair, he was lonely, so to have a bit of company was nice for him, but blimey she was an old dragon!

'Ha ha, sounds a right charmer' I said.

'Oh you don't know the half of it. She was very opinionated too, nothing was ever good enough for her and she was expecting to be waited on hand and foot. Had to be grateful they only came round once a month really in the end. My two boys weren't having her at any price though, suffered her really for their Grandad they did.'

She was laughing at the memories flooding in, no stopping her or them now.

'My Terry was the worst. He struggled to hold his tongue and would make remarks like how she was a greedy old cow and that. I'd say "Terry behave yourself" but at the same time actually agree with him! I think him and his Dad went round the pub and got drunk, so they could fall asleep after their dinner and not have to talk to her...the pair of sods.'

'I had a couple of relatives like that when I was a boy. They'd come round and I'd be off like a shot, out with me football, getting right out of it .' I said as I laughed.

'They've both gone now they have, everyone goes don't they...?'

Pauline was off daydreaming about all of the faces she no longer saw. She was staring into the distance and we all waited for her to come back to us. She snapped out of it and caught us all looking at her.

'Sorry, went for a bit there...ahem.

You know, the funny thing is when I finally get to Lewisham, I don't know what to do with myself. I wander off to have a look round Marks' first, might see something, you never know? Last time I was in, I bought a pair of slippers in the sale for a fiver; my other ones had gone home a bit... Retail therapy they call it don't they?

Usually once I'm fed up with the shops, I'll then make my way to the Wimpy Bar on the high street. This has become a bit of a habit lately to be honest. It's clean enough in there and well, the food is ok. I try and get a two-seater table to the side, just to get out of the way really. There's a nice waiter who is there on a Sunday.

'Ello love' he say's 'back again then?'

'OOOOH! Is he your fancy man then?' Exclaimed Margie.

'No, he's not Margie Cotter!' Pauline cried out all indignant 'It aint like that, it aint like at all, he's a nice boy is all.'

'Sorry Pauline, I though you had a fella.'

I saw Dot then pat Margie on her knee, as if to say, there, there, no damage done. Dot caught me looking at them and then looked to the carpet.

'I'm old enough to be his grandmother Margie love.

Turkish or something like that he is, got lovely olive skin and black hair, only about twenty-five I reckon. Good looking boy, somehow reminds me of my Bill when he was that age.'

'IS he her boyfriend Dot?' asked Margie, still not really understanding.

'No sister, just a friend' and she looked at Pauline as if to say sorry.

It was becoming clear, poor old Margie was struggling to keep up.

Pauline looked concerned, but Dot nodded for her to carry on.

'I order the burger and chips and a nice cup of tea.'

'Fries.' he always says. 'We call 'em fries.'

'Don't come it.' I say. 'Chips in my day they were. As I take a look around the Wimpy Bar though, one thing strikes me, it aint Lyons Corner House. Remember them?'

'Ooooh.' Said Margie, suddenly getting hold of the conversation again.

'We used to love those in the 1960s. We always went to the one in Coventry Street, remember Dot?'

'That we did, Margie. Touch of class there' said Dot.

'Oh lovely them. I nearly became a, er...what were they called Dot?'

'What were who called' Said Dot, her patience becoming paper thin.

'The waitresses at Lyons, they had a special name.' said Margie, oblivious she was beginning to really annoy her sister.

'Nippy's, they were called Nippy's' said Tubbs

'That's it!' exclaimed Margie. 'Thanks Mr. Isaacs.'

"I should know that, what with my Cilla being one back before I met her.'

'Ah bless her.' said Margie, who was then suddenly aware

of us all looking at here. 'Oooh sorry Pauline, I'm getting in the way of your story.'

'Ah no Margie, I think I'm hogging the limelight too much as it is.' smiled Pauline.

'Well, you've got to finish now, we want to know how the Wimpy romance turns out' I said laughing.

'Don't you start Vincent! Anyway, nearly there. I always see the same young couple with their toddler in there when I've been in and they try to get their kids to eat the food, which makes a change from throwing it at each other, which they usually end up doing. I always notice that all four of them have got hoodies, jogging bottoms and them trainers on.

I always feel over dressed, sitting there in a blouse, skirt and the cardi I knitted myself.'

Knew it! I nod to myself.

It's becoming clear to me, that Pauline has bottled a lot of this up and for a good while. I guess she wanted to say all this for ages, but didn't feel comfortable in doing so, but today... well today she's found someone to listen, so she's getting rid of it. I don't mind to be honest, I'm used to listening, another trait I picked up in the shovel, which looks like it'll will come in useful here!

'Last time I was in I also noticed a young black boy and his girlfriend I guess, eating burgers on another table. They are eating but not talking to each other though. Just nodding their heads in time with whatever music they are listening to on those headphone thingy's they are plugged into.

I don't look for too long though; don't want them to think I'm staring or being nosey.

I slowly eat my dinner when it arrives and always find myself looking out of the big glass window at the front of the shop in between mouthfuls. I watch as people hustle and bustle by and notice one or two old souls, like me, among them. They all look a bit lost, again like me, leaning on their shopping trolleys for support.'

'Despite the Sunday's continuing to be hard for you, you did the right thing moving in here Pauline.' Tubbs said. 'People in here of your own age, shared experiences and all that.'

'You're right Mr. Isaacs. Believe me I know. Took some doing though. As it happens, this isn't the first move, since I lost my Bill.

My Terry first moved me in to the flat above him and his missus Sue, good girl she is, very caring. Everyone thought it was for the best. They could look after me and I would feel safe, knowing they weren't far away.

But I became lonely… It was actually worse when I could hear them downstairs laughing and joking. I mean they'd pop up for a cuppa most evenings after work, but only for twenty minutes and then they had to get back to their own busy lives.

I understood that.

Good luck to 'em I thought and I meant it, but the noise they'd make when they laughed or rowed, or…loved each other… just made my own flat seem even quieter.

Despite all that, it was still better than living in our old family home. I just had to get out of that once I lost Bill. It was so big; it was like living in a mausoleum, unbearably quiet, especially after having a house full for so many years. Especially quiet on Sundays…

One day though I gave myself a good talking too.

'C'mon Pauline Davis' I said 'time to get your life back. So, at seventy six, the time had come.'

'You aint seventy six!' I said. 'I aint having it!'

'I am y'know.' Again, the blush.

'Never. You don't look a day over 65 girl.'

'Flatterer.' and with that she laughed.

'I called my Terry at work and told him I want to talk to him when he got home.

'Wassup Mum.'

He asked straight away. I never usually rung him at work, so he's panicking thinking it's an emergency.

'Nothing boy. I just want a word that's all.' and laughed to make him feel there is no problem.

He's a good boy and does his best to take the place of my Bill, but he knows it aint the same. My Chrissy also does his bit too, but I think they know they are only papering over the cracks, no matter how hard they try. Their Dad and me were together for nearly fifty years, which is a flaming lifetime. You can't replace that can ya?'

'They sound like good kids Paul. Sound like they would do the best for their mum.' I said.

Pauline smiled. She knew I was right.

Her eyes welled up again.

'Alright Terry, alright I said. Thing is see, I'm ok up here mate, but...but.' I was struggling to complete the sentence to be honest.

'You're lonely aintcha.' He looked straight at me and it turn's out he has read me like a book.

I told him, it's not his fault or Sue's. I tell him it's really quiet up in that flat and I need to change that. And then he broke my heart in two.

'What's he do? Asked Dot, slowly being dragged right into the story.

'He said – "Aint got a fella have ya Mum? Y'know I'd struggle with that.'

I smiled. No way I'm thinking. I know women like Pauline. They are one-man women.

'Eh?' I said and laughed. She then continued. 'No son, no one could replace your dad you know that, don't be silly.

No I'm thinking of going into sheltered housing is all. Well, he wasn't expecting that!

'No mum.' he said 'I can look after ya, you just need more time and...'

The sound of the sheltered housing was obviously worse than me having a chap!'

And she allowed herself a faint smile.

'Told him. Terry, stop it love. No ones blaming you mate. You've done your bit. You couldn't do anything else, couldn't do much more. Or Chrissy, you've both been smashing. No, I'm doing this for me love.

I looked at him standing there and he looks crushed. '

'He was only being true to your Bill, Pauline, fair play to him for that' I said.

'Yeah I know Vincent, I could see it hurt him, but I had to move. I mean, I was just sitting there with the telly on most nights, not even noticing what was on the screen, just daydreaming about what it was like when my Bill was here and then tears would come to my eyes and I'd cry and hold my hand over my mouth so they couldn't hear me downstairs. I had to get away from that.

No, I had already made my mind up. I was going into Benhill House no matter what they said. It was a done deal. I had been up here for a lunch or two and a game of bingo, with a couple of ladies I had met. I thought then the place was a bit shabby, but I met Maureen and she showed me round and she seemed alright... well, she did then.

Anyway, listen, I've gone on far too long, and we aint heard about you yet.' She nodded in my direction. 'Come on you. Spill the beans.'

So, over the next half hour or so, I told my three new mates a few tales about me, Brenda and Matthew and me being on the lorries.

What I didn't say was anything about Liz Taylor or prison. That story, my friend, was for another time.

4

That Takes The Flaming Biscuit That Does...

The shameless exploitation of those in her care, by Maureen and her numerous dodgy staff could be seen on a daily basis now. Her cronies were strutting about like they were untouchable, which I suppose at the end of a long day they were.

Maureen had clocked me looking on and watching, but she knew I wouldn't say anything. She had me over a barrel with the threat of getting me thrown out of Benhill.

I had really began to notice the general state of the place too, which was getting worse by the day.

Everyday things like hoovering, mopping floors and dusting just weren't getting done. The rubbish chutes, piled high with bags and bags of food waste, were beginning to hum on warm days. I noticed a couple of mice running around the skirting board of the lounge one morning, but chose not to say anything to Pauline or the Cotter sisters. Last thing they needed to hear I decided.

We did have a cleaner, a young Polish sort called Marina, but she seemed to spend most of her time collecting up the tenners and twenties on instruction from Maureen. The poor little cow had been totally corrupted.

Consequently, the communal khazis, lounge and passage

carpets were dirty and the whole place was starting to smell.

I suppose some of us residents could have wiped a couple of things over, but when you consider most of us were paying service charge on top of our rent to cover cleaning, and the fact that they were pretty old, meant they would have struggled anyway. The whole situation was hard to endure and stay silent about.

Of course, I had no option but swallow all of this and found myself winking and smiling when I sometimes bumped into the staff as they were going about their activities. I could see that it was upsetting for these old 'uns to part with the hard cash as was expected of them, but they were also resigned to the fact. No dough, no help. I had to bite my tongue on a couple of occasions each day. Bloody nightmare.

I had also noticed old Tubbs was none too happy with me. After our chat in the lounge, I think he thought I would challenge Maureen, take her on so to speak. But, he had now seen I wasn't doing that, despite all that was going on and I found him giving me a couple of dirty looks. It got so bad, that in the end I could feel his stare through my back. The man wasn't pleased with me at all. If his looks were words, that word would be traitor in BIG capital letters.

I looked him straight back in the eyes and shrugged my shoulder's as if to say 'sorry old son, what can I do?'

I hoped he would work out that I had got to look after number one here. No time or room for any old sentiment, despite how much I actually liked Dot, Margie, Pauline and Tubbs.

The headway in making new friends with these four, was now in danger of falling to pieces. I was slowly being sent 'To Coventry'. It was as if they were blaming me for not putting a stop to Maureen. But I mean, what could I do? I was still a new boy finding my feet. But they had decided I had let them down.

I bumped into Pauline one evening when arriving to put

my weekly wash on, in the laundry room.

I walked in to the white painted, square shaped space to find her talking to herself, as she looked for some lost garment in the right hand machine.

'Flipping hell... I know you're in there' she said as she plunged her hand deeper into the aluminum belly of the washer.

'Alright Paul?' I said, making her jump and lightly bang her head on the rim as she pulled her upper body out.

'Jesus Vin, scared the wassnames out of me there mate.'

She looked flushed as she gently rubbed her head with her right hand.

'Sorry Pauline. Didn't mean to...' I tried to speak, but was cut off in full flow.

'Shush you.' she replied. 'Shouldn't be talking to you anyway.' she did her best to look stern, but I could tell her heart wasn't really in it.

'Oh listen. This is crazy. You're blaming me for Maureen and its got cough all to do with me, has it?'

'We aint blaming you for her. We're just disappointed you aren't taking her on. I mean you are the youngest bloke in here, so if you don't do it, no one will.'

She was almost pleading with me.

'Look, Pauline, I've got to look after number one love. Just got here, can't afford to lose this flat. And...'

'Don't you love me, Vinny Hawkins.' she said, once again cutting me stone dead. 'It's alright, don't you worry. No, seriously, we know where we stand. I'll have a word with my boys; see what they can do, So, if you'll excuse me...'

And with that she scooped up her washing into a bright orange plastic bowl and walked out.

I stood there for a few seconds, shaking my head trying to take it all in, but I knew I didn't have the answer's my new friends were looking for.

So, on and on it went. The skullduggery getting worse by the day it seemed. Word would reach me that one or two of the staff were now walking into rooms and taking money out of purses or wallets if they saw them lying about. People complained and went to see Maureen, but she would work her flaming charm and talk them round. There was no doubt, she had an iron tight grip on the place.

Towards the end of that seemingly never ending first six week's in Benhill, I one day found myself sharing the lounge area with Maureen. She was in there drinking a cup of tea and writing in what looked like a ledger book, with hundreds of figures being entered onto lined pages. I could see she had a smug smile on her face and why not I thought. Queen Bee weren't she?

She'd won the war, with the complaints seemingly being ignored by the council.

I actually hesitated at the doorway when I first saw her sitting there, but she had clocked me, and beckoned me in, so there was no turning back. I swallowed something hard and jagged and walked in as nonchantly as I could.

'Alright Maureen.' I said 'all good with you?'

'Mr. Hawkins. How nice to see you. Yeah fine actually. And you? Are you well?'

I sat down on a large blue covered chair near to hers and nodded.

'Not too bad Maureen, you know what it's like. Some days it's rocks, and some day's it's diamonds. No complaints, really… well, I have, but nobody listens ' and gave out a week laugh.

Maureen smiled a weak thin-lipped smile back me, acknowledging what she took as my poor attempt at humour.

'Noticed that you have taken my advice then Vinny?'

I tried to look like I didn't know what she was talking about, but of course, I did.

'Eh Maureen? Advice? I said.

'Oh you know, the little mis-understanding with Nelly and the subsequent events since.'

She wasn't in the mood to be letting go.

'Oh that.' I smiled…'Yeah, I had a think and decided to do what was best for me in the end. It's me that has to come first at my stage of life. Look after number one and all that. Besides, you obviously have your way of working here, and who am I to interfere with that.'

She smiled from ear to ear knowing she had done me, broken me if you like. No matter what, I couldn't lose the flat, so I was now putty in her hands.

'Glad to hear it Vinny. We've operated this way for years now. Many of the old ones here never have anybody come to visit them, so at the end of the day we are providing a service. So what if one or two have to pay for that service? Is that so unreasonable? I don't think they really mind in the end and well, what choice have they got?'

I nodded and cocked a small smile.

'I know what you mean.' I replied. 'Pathetic really innit, y'know, when you look at the state some of them have got themselves into.

Got to say though Maureen, it was a shock to me at first, you know, your way of running things. Didn't know it worked this way, so, yeah, I reacted badly I suppose. But the longer I have seen it all go on, I now appreciate it's your little, er… perks shall we say, a nice little buckshee bung if you will.'

'Uum, not sure about the word bung Mr. Hawkins. I see it more as a present, a gift, a reward if you will, for services rendered shall we say.'

I nodded. 'Yeah I can see that…'

Maureen continued her voice getting louder and louder.

'I suppose it's understandable that not everyone knows it goes on. We have kept it quiet really to spare the blushes of the respective resident's and their families to be honest. I mean no one wants to be accused of not doing enough for their loved ones, do they?

So, as I see it, what we do is pick up slack, help where we can. And then if the resident decides to reward us, then what's the harm in that, eh? We have so many of you in here now with no family visiting, that I have had to use the cleaning operative to help. Do you know what has happened? A couple of people, people you know personally I'm afraid, have actually complained the building wasn't getting cleaned. I mean I ask you, how can they do that? To me? To my staff.'

I slowly shook my head in sympathy.

'We are helping the more unfortunate and that still isn't good enough for some people, sheeeshhh...'

I just smiled at her and nodded. She was a powerful woman once she got her dander up, I could see how she could intimidate those sent to investigate her. They wouldn't stand a chance.

'I know the bible says pride is a sin, but I'm proud to say this extra care and attention is something I personally introduced and with the help and dedication from my loyal staff, it works for all concerned.

So, if one or two of our guests get upset at first, so what? That's natural. But they soon realise they have no real option. And besides, a lot of these old ladies and gents here have plenty of money, so they hardly miss it once they have paid us.'

'Er, yeah, I guess that is fair enough Maureen,' I said 'and you know what, I suppose if it wasn't you doing it, it would be someone else exploiting the situation.'

Maureen winced at the word exploitation.

'Tut, tut Mr. Hawkins, horrible word. That is a word I do not recognise.' A broad smile creased her face.

She then looked around to see if anybody else was in earshot. Finding no one was there, she leant forward, looking me directly in the eyes.

'Keep this between me and you and I'll let you into a little secret Mr. Hawkins. In most cases the money is just laying about in their homes. If it's not in a purse or a wallet, it's in jars or glass bowls or at best stuffed into cushions or down the back of a sofa. None of them it seems have bank accounts, so it probably safer with us anyway. We take it upon ourselves to look after their money. We like them to think of it as an investment for the good deeds we provide. No, this is not exploitation, no, no no. That is the opposite of that, this is actually caring...'

'Of course.' I said nodding. 'I can see that now you've explained it.'

'Now, Mr. Hawkins I have no wish to be rude, but I have to do my book-keeping, and need to keep everything in order, so if you don't mind...'

It had been made very obvious. This was my command telling me I had overstayed my welcome. This lady didn't do subtle.

'Of course Maureen. Yeah, well, I can see you're busy. I'll be off then, ok, good to see you as always.'

She didn't even look up as I began to leave. She had her head down and was studying the books intently.

This conversation was over. I got up and walked out from the lounge into the main corridor.

I did a sharp right towards my flat, almost knocking Tubbs over as I did so.

'Fuck me Tubbs!' I whispered as I narrowly avoided him.

'What you doing mate, you'll give me heart failure?'

I grabbed him by the elbows and tried to steer him away from the door area .

'Man, get your hands off me!' he said has he jostled my grip away from him. The man was upset. Very upset.

'Don't touch me, I'm warnin' you Mr. Hawkins! You ask me what am I doin? What am I doing? Ya damn fool and traitor. I 'eard you man. 'Good to see you Maureen. Char!'

It turned out, he was just a couple of paces from the door hiding and had heard almost everything from the previous ten minutes.

'MAN ALIVE!' He exclaimed.

'How can you be laughing along with that, that bloody SHE DEVIL! I tell you something. If I was thirty years younger I'd, I'd.... How dare you.'

Then, this church going, good hearted soul, kissed his teeth as hard as he could in my direction.

'Oh Tubbs.' I whispered. 'I love yer mate.'

In truth at that very moment I could have kissed him, but decided against it, I was in enough grief with him as it was.

My last comment had left this old citizen of Trinidad and Tobago, not knowing what the hell was going on and his confused face looked near to tears with the frustration of it all. I could see I needed to act fast.

'Listen Tubbs.' I said. 'keep the vocal's down, something I wanna show ya. Come with me, come...come on!'

'Nah man, I've seen and heard enough of your foolishness to last me two life times. I've still got a bit of go in me, so watch yourself.'

Tubbs wasn't having it, bless him.

I smiled. 'Look mush, stop being such a drama queen and come over here will ya...' and I nodded in the general direction of my flat.

He had a quizzical look on his face and despite his better

judgment, I obviously had him intrigued.

'Why should I, eh? We have already let you into our little fraternity and now I hear you betray me and those fine ladies, Dot, Marge and Pauline.'

'Shush, will ya and come here you old plonker.'

I could see Tubbs was taken aback as to how I was now behaving.

'Hang on. What you up to Vinny man, eh, c'mon tell me man?'

I simply put my finger to my lips to indicate I needed him to stop bleeding talking and start bleeding walking, and that we needed to get a shift on and lively. I then bent the self same finger into a 'follow me' gesture.

Tubbs finally did as he was told and we walked towards my flat.

I motioned for him to come in and then to sit down. Once he had, I made sure my front door was shut tight.

I looked down to my right trouser pocket. From that I took a mobile phone and put it down on the wooden coffee table between us as I sat down opposite him.

'Right. Know what that is then, do ya?' I said.

'Do I know what that is? Yeah Vinny I know what that is, I aint no damn fool! Its a mobile telephone.' He said indignantly.

'Well, technically you're right Tubbs, good spot mate. But, this my old friend, also becomes a voice recorder in the right hands.'

'So?'

And then the smallest of smiles kissed the lips of Tubbs as copper coins began to drop his way.

'You mean...'

'I called my Matthew, the other night, told him what's been

going on here and about all the bloody grief I was getting off you and Pauline. He told me he had an idea, so I met him yesterday in his lunch break at work.

He lent me this thing in front of us, his smart phone as he called it. Told him, it looked like a computer compared the old thing I've got. He quickly showed me how to use it too. I was then up all night, practicing with it.

Now, if I did everything right, and please God I did, I might just have some decent footage of our beloved leader, that might, just might, be the end of all this nonsense going on here.'

I plunged my hand into the breast pocket of my light blue button down shirt and pulled out a bit of screwed up notepaper on which I had written the instructions from my Matt. I pressed a few buttons on the phone, following the wording on the note and then we - Mr. Grenville Isaacs and me, suddenly heard the vocals of Maureen Wiloch filling my flat.

'Keep this between me and you and I'll let you into a little secret Vinny. In most cases the money is just lying about in the flats or at best stuffed into cushions...'

I pressed the pause button and looked up at the face of Tubbs, who was sitting there, with his smile getting wider and wider.

I let the pause button go and we once again heard Maureen...

'I know the bible says pride is a sin, but I'm proud to say this extra care and attention is something I personally introduced and with the help and dedication from my loyal staff, it works for all concerned. So, one or two of our guests get upset at first, so what, that's natural ha ha... but they soon realise they have no real option. And besides, a lot of these old ladies and gents here who have plenty of money, so they hardly miss it once they have paid us.'

I was now smiling more than Tubbs.

'Got her mate, got her bang to rights...' I whispered at him.

'Sweet Jesus – hook, line and blasted sinker, what a CAPTURE!' exclaimed Tubbs.

We both laughed out loud and shook hands, which led to an embrace.

'Ah Vinny, you is a bad man sir. You really had me worried there. I was saying to myself, 'Grenville, you are a good judge of a man after all those years of dealing with the great unwashed on that damn bus, so you KNOW Vinny is a decent man, but here he is cosying up with that horrible person! What gives I thought? Man, I just couldn't work it out'

And we both laughed again. It was the laugh of men who had been underestimated and who were now going to have their revenge.

I stood up and poured us a Scotch each from a half finished bottle of Bells. We touched glasses and then raised them in front of us.

'Right, lets have a proper listen to everything on there.'

We settled back and sat and listened to the conversation I had had with Maureen in the lounge in its entirety. You could hear the boastfulness in her voice, and I hoped that, that very same boasting would now be her downfall. Surely, once this evidence got out, she was finished. Done and dusted.

'That should do it.' I said as the recording ended. 'I'll get this to my Matthew and let him work his magic and then we'll see what happens from there. Now only me and you know about this in here, so lets keep it that way. Just got to play this like the best hand of poker you have ever had and we've got her.'

Tubbs stood up unsteadily and shook my hand.

'You can rely on old Grenville. Thank you, yeah. Actually, I'm sorry for shouting at you earlier, but...'

I just smiled at him.

'Don't be silly. I was dying to tell you, but wanted to see if it worked first'

Tubbs suddenly looked tired, as he replied 'Oh, it worked alright.'

Vinny, I've got to give it to you, you played that well. Really well. Devious mind at WORK! haha!

He suddenly looked very tired.

'Listen Vin, I am done in. I'm going to have to have a lie down.'

All this adventure has worn this old man out. He drained his glass tumbler of its contents and then stuck out his right hand and shook mine, smiling all the time. He turned and made his way out of my flat, cackling all the way.

'See you Vincent, you devil you, haha.'

I walked over to my sideboard and reached for the Bells. I poured myself out another decent measure and settled back on my sofa. I raised my glass to just below my chin and then closed my eyes in satisfaction.

Job done Vinny boy, you've still got it son. Still got it.

Matthew popped round to mine after he had finished work, bringing his laptop with him. Within half hour, he had uploaded the five-minute clip onto that YouTube. He told me it might take an hour or so to be viewable, so we sat and caught up. Hadn't seen him properly for too long, so I enjoyed that. Matt sat there shaking his head whilst I recounted what had been going on.

'How long she been at it then dad?' He asked.

'Well old Tubbs said she actually started out alright when she first got here, three years back or so, but the greed got to her and it got steadily worse, until we ended up with how it is today.'

I mentioned to him how I was having worse trouble than

usual in sleeping, having had Pauline and Tubbs on my case.

'Well, you've won them over today mate.' Matt said as we took off the tops of the last two bottles of Peroni he had brought round with him.

About an hour later, he looked at his watch and mentioned that all systems should be go, and he tapped in his password into his laptop.

Sure enough, up come the link entitled

'Maureen Wiloch – Benhill House – Exposed!'.

We sat there, supping the remainder of our beer, each listening to Wiloch burying herself. The cocky, stupid mare just couldn't help showing off to me like that. I just sat there smiling.

Gotcha!

Before he left my flat, Matt emailed the YouTube clip to the news desks of local papers - The South London Press and The Southwark News and he told me once they got hold of it, the clip would 'go viral'. Didn't really understand that bit, but it sounded horrible.

Well, it turned out I was right. It was horrible.

Well, horrible for Maureen. The next day all hell broke loose once the footage went around. The Southwark News run with the story on-line straight away, and flagged up they would running it in their next edition, same as The South London Press. The story would be on both front pages.

Then the local London BBC and ITV TV stations were showing the clip on their evening bulletins. Matthew rung me and said the clip was up to twenty three thousand views in twenty-four hours, and rising rapidly. The genie was well and truly out of the bottle.

I dwelled the box that next day, staying in the flat, not answering the door to anyone, but keeping in touch with Matt by text.

By the day after however, I was developing cabin fever, so I popped out into my garden and cut a few dead heads and that. Before long though, I could hear people shouting at me from outside our main gate, which my plot backed onto, asking me for a quote.

'Mr Hawkins!, Mr Hawkins! We know it's you Vinny! We'd only take five minutes of your time.'

I quickly went back indoors and decided to go out the back door to the betting shop, which also turned out to be a big mistake. I was only 'papped' as I emerged! Flipping hell, didn't expect all this.

'Are you Vinny Hawkins sir? SIR! We only need a couple of shots and a quote or two if possible. Come on mate, you've done well here; lets have one for the morning papers. I'm from The Metro, do you read that? Sir?'

I hustled on. 'Nothing to say Gents' and the reporters at first followed me, but gave up within a couple of hundred yards, though the snappers kept chasing me, firing off their flash guns. Inside the bookies, I got a bit of sanctuary, but even in there a couple of faces came up and said well done. I knew if it had reached inside here, the story was well truly out.

I later found out that Maureen, on being confronted with the evidence I had gathered had told a couple of reporters my name, door number and a rough description of me and before long they were on my tail. It looked like she was getting in a bit of revenge, even though the game was up for her.

The next edition of The South London Press had found an old photo of me taken at my retirement do a year or two back and had printed that with the headline.

'HOME HERO SAVES THE DAY FROM GREEDY TYRANT"

That image was used alongside a new one of me hurrying into the Ladbrokes. I looked at the paper and then put it down. I decided there and then I didn't like all this attention.

I tried to remind myself that all this would be tomorrows chip paper and in a day or two some other poor bugger would be going through it instead of me. But I still felt sick.

Thankfully, so far, it appeared no one had dug back far enough to find out about my time in the boob and that was just how I wanted it to stay, please God.

Back in my flat, the bloody phone rang non-stop. I answered a couple of times, but they were shouting down the phone at me.

'Mr. Hawkins, lets have a few words. Mr. Hawkins, you're a hero sir, our readers really want to read about solid citizens like you. Come on Mr. Hawkins, speak to us.'

I just placed the receiver back each time without speaking, only for it to ring again and again. I finally took the receiver off the hook.

I really didn't expect all this attention. When you've got a past like mine, you tended to keep a low profile. But with all this, there was a danger of me being exposed as much as Maureen.

I decided to ring my Matthew, as I wasn't too sure what to do.

Got to say, it was good to hear his voice.

'Dad.' he said 'you're best out of it mate. Let the authorities deal with it now, you've done your bit. Why don't you come and stay with us for a few days, keep your head down.'

He was right; I should do that. I should go down to his gaff in Whitstable and get out of town for a while until it all calmed down. I had no need to get involved any deeper than I was already. It was simple advice, but welcome. Yeah that's it, I would lie low for a couple of days.

I felt a lot better after having spoken to Matt and I felt comfortable for the first time in a couple of days as I replaced the receiver. The bloody ringing started up again immediately. It just kept ringing and ringing. I was I trying my best to ignore it, but it was no use, it was driving me mad.

'Oh for fucks sake, will you leave me alone' I heard myself shouting aloud.

Brrng -Brrng...Brrng-Brrng...

'Oh bollocks to it.' I said as I finally snapped and picked up the receiver.

'Look, will leave me alone!'

'Vinny? That you?' A timid voice, one I didn't instantly recognise was on the other end.

'Yeah, yeh, who's...? Pauline that you?'

'Thank God for that, been ringing you all afternoon" Pauline sounded a little frustrated.

'Sorry mate, been besieged on the dog for hours. I was trying to blank it. Anyway, what's up love?'

'Grenville's Carla showed me, Dot and Margie the film you did on Maureen, on her computer thingy. Bloody hell! You caught her lovely didn't you eh? Just wanted to say it's brilliant Vin is all. Brilliant.'

I was smiling back at her on the phone, she sounded all excited like a young girl.

'Ah bless you Paul, bless you love.' I said.

'Oh Vin, old Mr. Isaacs had a tear in his eye and well, Dot and Margie were laughing and crying at the same time. Magic, really. You really had us worried. We thought you were crossing over to help that cow Maureen. You devious sod!' and with that she laughed out loud.

It was nice hearing her laugh like that. I'd wager it's been a while since she's been as happy as this.

'Well Pauline, as long as old Maureen gets the old heave-ho before too long, it will have worked like a flaming charm'.

There was suddenly a ring on my doorbell.

'Pauline, look got to go love, someone at my door. Yep, bye love...yep I know, I know, yeah, we did good. Bye mate, bye.'

I left the receiver off the hook and walked to the back of my front door and peeped through the spy hole.

Two women were standing there. One looked like an office worker, all power suit and sensible shoes, the other more casually dressed, stripy rainbow coloured hand knitted jumper, and a her hair in dreadlocks. Looked like a right old soap dodger in fact.

'Yeah, hello...who's that?' I shouted from behind my door, deciding not to open the door it, in case they are were the Press.

A refined voice came back my way.

'Mr. Hawkins? Is That You Mr. Hawkins?'

'Yeah might be.' I said. 'but who wants to know? Cos if you are from a newspaper, I'm not talking to ....'

'Mr. Hawkins, Mr. Hawkins – please, we're not Press. My name is Laura Trotter, I'm from the council and I'm with my colleague Wendy Hammond. We tried ringing first to let you know we were coming but...'

I looked back through the spy hole and saw the suit look over to her mate who had a friendly face underneath that mop of un-ruly hair.

'...there seemed to be a fault on the line, it was constantly engaged.' she said 'Mr. Hawkins? Mr. Hawk...Vincent isn't it?'

I decided they seemed alright and sussed they weren't Press because they were too polite.

'Well yeah, technically that's my name' I said as my front door swung open 'but most people call me Vinny.'

'Ok, Vinny it is.' The hippy drippy shape of Wendy Hammond had finally spoken and she was now smiling at me face to face.

'Do you mind if we come in?'

I asked to see and checked their ID cards and then beckoned them in. They both took a look round my flat and then settled onto the sofa.

'Thanks Mr. Hawk...Vinny.' said the one called Laura. 'Good to say hello in person so to speak.'

'One lump or two.' I said and made my way into the kitchen.

'Biscuits?'

'I can see we will get on well.' Wendy said cheerily.

'Oh yeah? You gonna be around here for a while then?'

Curiosity was getting the better of me as I plugged in the kettle.

'Well that remains to be seen,' Wendy replied. 'but maybe. I guess you've been kept pretty busy since the YouTube incident.'

'Seen that have ya?' I said smiling, as I re-entered the front room. 'Well, yeah you could say that. I seem to be in demand for some reason.'

Laura had taken out a few sheets of A4 paper from her briefcase.

'Right, ok. Vinny. I'll cut to the chase. I'm from the housing office and I have been called in on this situation we have here. First off, I've got to say we at the council cant really condone your way of dealing with this, but well, the evidence can't be denied. We would have preferred you to have contacted us direct in the first instance though.'

'Well Laura.' I said clearing my throat. 'I was planning on doing that, but Maureen Wiloch made it pretty clear to me, that I would be removed from Benhill so fast my feet wouldn't touch the pavement if I did so. She as good as promised that I would be sleeping rough, if I made a complaint to you people.

News of anyone making a noise to the Town Hall always got back to her.'

I heard the click of the now boiled kettle and returned to the kitchen and proceeded to make them a cup of tea each. I opened a fresh packet of biscuits and poured a few on a blue and white edged serving plate. I then made my way back into my front room.

'You know, you really should look into that if I was you, there's definitely a Bertie Smalls working with her higher up.'

I placed their drinks on the coffee table and asked 'Custard cream?' as I did so.

'Thank you.' said Laura 'I shouldn't really, but have never been know to resist one.'

She bit into it and continued talking, spitting a few tiny crumbs over her suit.

'I have to say, I don't know of anyone called Bertie Smalls, but I'll look into that.'

I couldn't help but smile.

'As you might have guessed, we have removed Ms. Wiloch from her post with immediate effect and Wendy here, will now take her place for the foreseeable future. There will be other changes too, but first things first. Wendy will take the reins.'

Wendy smiled and her pretty face lit up.

'We'll be calling a meeting on in the next few days,' she said 'at which I will lay out all the changes and ideas I have, and I would really welcome yours and your friends input.'

I nodded. That all sounded ok. So it was now official. Maureen was gone, that was all that mattered.

Next contestant please.

'Well,' I said. 'I'm off to stay with my boy and his family for a few days, but my good friends Mr. Isaacs, the Cotter sisters and Mrs. Davis are the ones to talk to Wendy.

They will set you straight, all good, good people.'

'Noted Vinny.' Wendy said confidently 'Really hope you have a nice time with your son. Erm, there is just one last thing,' she said smiling.

'Can I have that last Custard Cream?'

5

Back In The Naughty Square Mile

I was sleeping.

What's more I was sleeping well. Like a baby. Out cold.

It must be this sea air. I laid my head on a pillow and I was fast asleep before the count reached six. For the last thirty-five years or so, I have rarely been asleep before two in the morning. I will just lie there, whether in a bed or more often than not in an armchair and then dissect my past. Examining the mistakes I had made and the relationships I had lost. I would spin and mull things over and over, before finally snatching an hour of restless kip at some point.

Not here though. Not here in Whitstable. No, down here I was relaxed and it was doing me the world of good.

It was lovely to spend a month down here on the coast with my Matthew and his family.

They have a lovely house here, with its garden backing onto the beach and then nothing but the sea. It had three floors and its rooms were quite small, but it felt like a home.

It's outside walls were painted a stylish shade of pink and it had been tastefully decorated throughout by Matthews wife Trudy.

My daughter-in-law was looking after me like I was royalty and my granddaughters, Bella and Evie made a right fuss of their granddad. Got to say, I found myself welling up a couple of times at their love for me. I really didn't expect any of this.

It was all new to me and in truth they hardly knew me.

But it was obvious that their dad, my son, had brought this family up well. He had been the father I never was. He had the devoted love of a strong woman and they had two wonderful, vibrant girls. I worried that Trudy would be carrying some hate for me, for the way I had treated Matt, but I couldn't detect a trace of it. Whatever Matt had told her about me over the years, it must have been positive. Trudy had naturally blonde streaked hair and the life she had with Matt obviously suited her. She looked great and hardly ever wore any make up. She was just simply a natural beauty.

'What you looking at granddad?' Evie asked me one day after catching me staring at her with the biggest smile on my face.

'Don't mind me mate,' I said 'you're beautiful is all. And I like looking at beautiful things.'

She blushed at that, and I felt instantly sorry for embarrassing her. But she was lovey and I was so proud to be part of her life.

Bella too, is also a really pretty girl. At twenty-one she is at Reading University. A very bright kid, it sounds like she's going into the property developing world once she finishes this, her final year.

'I won't be buying boring old office blocks though,' she says 'I'll be looking for the quirky buildings in London and transforming them into art galleries and flagship stores for the big clothing brands'.

I believe her too.

Evie is more individual in character, not so studious as Bella, more of a real creative type. She's just turned nineteen and at art college, studying sculpture.

Both the girls were blonde like their mum and though different in temperament, and they seemed to get on great.

At Bella's age I was already married with a kid and then inside not long after. Never mind different worlds, we were from different planets.

I couldn't help but laugh at how far a family could come in a couple of generations …it's funny when you look at it like that.

All credit must go to my Matt and Trudy; they have provided a solid family unit and done the girls proud. I just wished I had done the same with Matt.

As it happens, his Mum should be very proud of herself too, she did a great job with the boy, whilst I was nowhere to be seen.

I'm more than a little ashamed looking back as to what I put Brenda through back then, I was such a selfish pratt.

Bella came home on each weekend of my stay down there, so she could spend time with me. Evie was home every night from college and she was forever asking me about my old life. I resisted for the first few days, but then Matt said 'Tell her Dad' so I did and she lapped it up. That girl loved hearing she had a naughty granddad back in the 1960s! I didn't touch on my biggest robbery, not even Matt knew about that, but the little schemes and scams I had got up to, kept her enthralled for hours.

All of us spent many happy hours having barbecues in the back garden, or going for long walks along the front, stopping off now and then for a nice bottle of wine or two. Idyllic is the word that sprung to mind.

As I came to end of the month of my stay, I began to plan my journey back to SE5. I really didn't want to over stay my welcome and truth be told I found I was missing Tubbs, Pauline and The Cotter Sisters.

As that wise man once said, always know when to leave a party.

On that last weekend we had a lovely pub lunch on the

Sunday and

I told them all, it had been wonderful getting to know my son and his family. Sounded wrong somehow that did, getting to know your own son and his people…Jesus, what a statement that is.

After the roast, a few tears flowed and they all seemed genuinely upset that I was going back. However, it felt right to be going back. I had to get on with my life and leave them to theirs.

Unbeknown to any of them, I had nipped into town during the week and bought them all little gifts to remember me by, as I wasn't sure when I would doing this again. I had bought them all silver bracelets, with the name 'Hawkins' engraved on them. For the first time in years, that name had a family to be proud of and I wanted them to know that.

Bella left that evening to get back to her digs in time for Monday morning lessons and once again, we had the waterworks as we said our goodbyes and her gift was opened.

In the morning, after an early full English, I bid farewell to Trudy and Evie, wiping my own eyes this time. I promised I would come back and see them real soon.

Matt was travelling into London by train, so I went back to Victoria with him. He had managed to get a couple of hours off work that morning, so wasn't rushing in, which meant we missed the early morning commuter madness.

'How's yer mum?' I asked him as we settled into our train seats, each of us carrying a coffee and a croissant each.

'She seem's alright actually dad. Well, she never complains about much, put it that way. I have invited her down here a few times and she came once, but she didn't repeat the visit. Think she missed the local bingo hall too much.' he said smiling.

I smiled too. Brenda always loved a game of bingo, even when I was with her.

'She'll get a lifetime achievement award in the shape of two little ducks in a few years.' I said 'She must have spent thousands down there in that place. Wonder if she ever won any of it back?'

'She didn't remarry then?'

'What mum? no mate.' Matthew laughed out loud at the very thought.

'As far as I know, she went out with a couple of fella's here and there, but nothing serious. I think you were her ideal man dad, God help her.' and he then gently smiled at me.

'Always had good taste in men, ya mum' I said smiling back.

We didn't really speak much more on the train after that, we didn't really need to. We had made our peace a few years ago and done a whole bundle of talking over that previous month. Often we would stay up with a couple of scotches, after the girls had turned in, and sit and put the record straight on a few things.

Don't get me wrong, it was hard to hear him talk over the last four weeks about growing up without a father, but I explained as best I could about the life I was leading back then, and he knew it was a different time and a place. I was young and where I was from; if you wanted to better yourself, there was only three ways of doing it, boxing, music or robbing.

I took it as a good sign that we didn't have to talk further on this rattler back to town. We were now comfortable with each other, letting bygones be bygones.

'You know Dad, you can come down to us anytime, mean it, anytime.' Matt said as we approached Victoria Station.

I smiled at him. 'I know mate, I know and bless you for that. Thanks for the best month I have had in years. Done me the power of good that has.'

I bid him goodbye at the station, kissed him on the cheek

and within minutes I was on a number 36 bus and half hour after that, I was walking back into the solid brickwork of Benhill.

As I walked through the green iron front gate, and up the concrete paving path, through the flower beds of the front gardens and into my part of the housing block, I could see a group of people with Margie and Pauline among them, sitting on the big chairs in the lounge and waving their feet around.

Those two caught sight of me and waved with their hands in my general direction, and I waved back, but it was obvious they were concentrating on whatever it was they were doing. It did all look very strange to me, but the entire room was doing it, whatever it was?

'What has been going on in my absence.' I chuckled to myself as I walked in to the main corridor.

I put my key into my front door, put down my suitcase and picked up the mail as I walked in. Among the pizza leaflets and supermarket vouchers, was a couple of scraps of notepaper from the Press trying to get me to call them about Maureen Wiloch.

All of it went straight in to the kitchen bin. I plugged in the kettle and got a cup out of the cupboard above the sink. I splashed a few granules of coffee into the cup and then went back to get my case and then into the bedroom and rested it on the bed.

No sooner had I done that, then there came a ring on my doorbell. I opened the door and found Tubbs staring at me grinning from ear to ear

'What you smiling about?' I said as I beckoned him in.

'Man! – Good to see you back,' he said as he shook me warmly by the hand 'we missed you, yes sir, we did. Seems like ages since you were here.'

You could say he was pleased to see me, nice to be missed.

'Missed you too mate and the girls. Been good though Tubbs.' I said. 'Spent some quality time with my son. Got a great family I'll have you know'.

Tubbs smiling continued, as I went back into the kitchen. Seeing the kettle had boiled, I began to make him a cuppa too. Seemed like he might be staying for a while.

I had a sense he was dying to tell me something.

'Go on then, tell me whatever it is before you burst something.' I semi-shouted from the behind the kitchen door into my front room.

'What?' he said unconvincingly.

'Oh leave it out Tubbs, you look like the cat who got the cream mate. Come on spill.'

Tubbs burst out laughing. 'Oh Vin, what a change has come over here at this place. Man, I tell you. This Wendy woman is an angel compared with that, that, swindling merchant we had before'

I had to smile. Old Tubbs hated that Maureen so much he now couldn't even say her name!

I handed him his tea and a plate of bourbons as I re-entered the room.

'In the month you've been gone, Wendy has worked out a new rota of activities we can all take part in. She really keen for those that can to do a bit of walking and to do more exercise, get us off our blasted backsides and move around a bit haha. Here take a look.'

Tubbs pulled out a folded up sheet of white A4 paper from his trouser pocket and handed it to me. Written on it, were various activities. I could see old Tubbs was a happy chappy and going by this piece of paper, this new bird Wendy wasn't messing about. I carefully sat down, and after searching and finding a coaster, put my cup on it in front of me. I pulled out my reading specs from my jacket pocket and read aloud, once

I was focused.

'Right, lets have a look here…. Monday…Pi…Lates. What the flaming hell is Pi…Lates?'

'Pilates man, it's pilates. You not heard of that. All the celebs do it. Gentle, stretching exercises. You must have seen Pauline and Margie out the front doing it on your way in?'

I grinned at the memory from not fifteen minutes earlier.

'So that was what they were doing? Thought it some sort of contortionist torture.' I said smiling.

Tubbs gently burped.

'What was that? Sounded like a drop of thunder.' I said smiling his way, upon hearing it.

He took a sip of his tea, pretending nothing had happened and continued to cradle the plate I had just given him.

'Want one of your biscuits?' he asked all innocently.

'Cheeky sod. Gis one here!' I smiled and then continued 'Ok, Pilates in the morning with a teacher on-site.'

'Wendy says that'll get em all moving again after a weekend of sitting around, good idea I think'. It was obvious, old Tubbs had converted to the Church of Wendy and no mistake.

I couldn't argue, I too liked Wendy's thinking. She had obviously come in to shake things up, and for the better it seemed. She had kept the costs down as much as she could, with some of the teachers only charging a stripe for each session. Between sips and bites, I carried on reading.

'Bingo on Monday afternoon with Wendy as the caller – fair play to her.' I said.

Clever that. One way of getting to know the people she was looking after and having a bit of fun at the same time.

'Then it's art classes Tuesday morning. You going to that Tubbs?'

Tubbs looked up from the plate of biscuits he was slowly

devouring.

'Yes sir. I always liked drawing as a kid, so I got me some pencils from the Pound Shop and I'm going tomorrow. You should come Vinny man.'

'Not yet mate, still settling back in, aint even unpacked yet. Besides I can't draw to save me life, well apart from drawing me pension that is...'

I continued.

'Then knitting at 2pm - well I will be swerving all that 'knit one, pearl one cobblers' but you never know, I might get a winter jumper out of it if I ask Pauline nicely.

Hold up, hold tight...now this looks more like more a bit of me mate. Wednesday we will have a quiz, or crosswords in the afternoon, with a fella called Archibald coming in to set it all up. Now that's right up my strausse.'

I always got five or six right on that Mastermind programme. You know on the general knowledge questions. My best ever was eight one week, nearly applied to go on it after that.

'Welcome to Mr. Vincent Hawkins. Specialised subject - 'The Motorways of Europe' 1974 to 2008'

'I'll join you for that' Tubbs smiling a smile that soon turned to a frown as the bulk of his last bourbon, which he had been dunking enthusiastically, suddenly dropped off and into the cup. He sucked what remained of his teeth.

'Damn and blast it.' he scowled.

'Serves ya right,' I said laughing 'bleeding biscuit bandit you are mate.'

'Ok, Thursday - we will usually have a day trip out to a museum, garden centre, or a pub lunch and Friday is games in the afternoon.'

A list of old pub games was also written down, like - cards, dominoes, rummy cup, shove ha'penny, that sort of palava.

'Well' I said admiringly 'I've got to hand it to her Tubbs, something for everyone there mate. She's definitely got off to a good start.

But who's getting the old un's their papers, putting their bets on etc.?'

'No dramas there Vinny,' replied Tubbs, 'she has got that covered too. The paper shop on the corner is now taking orders and dropping off the papers first thing. The boy they send over is also taking requests for bread, milk, marge and what have you, and then dropping that off in the afternoon with a free Evening Standard for those that want one. The only thing the kid aint doing is putting bet on, something to do with his religion, he aint allowed in a bookies or something, which I guess is fair enough.

In fact, I'm thinking of converting to whatever faith he follows, I could do with being kept out of there too.'

I smiled. I knew the feeling.

Tubbs continued 'I have had gentle a word with Charlie and Sid the new caretakers and one of them is rounding up the bets and taking a stroll round to Ladbrokes and doing it for those who can't get out. Seems to be working fine so far.

Right, seeing as you appear to have run out of biscuits, I'm off. Fancy the bingo this afternoon?'

'Charming you are. We'll see, let me unpack and I'll give it some thought.'

With that, Tubbs bid me goodbye and I sat and reflected on the new regime.

I have to say, I was impressed with what I had seen of it so far. This Wendy mort was like a breath of fresh air it seemed.

To be honest. When I first came in here, I was in essence a loner, but not lonely. I genuinely liked my own company. But as the months went on here at Benhill, I started to like talking to Tubbs and the girls and I genuinely missed them whilst down in Whitstable. Don't get me wrong, it's still strange to be surrounded by loads of old women – and I include Tubbs in that category- but I was pleased to be back.

It was even more delightful to find on my return, that there had been such a positive reaction to the getting rid of Maureen. It would have been a real backward step to just carry on like things were before. We needed someone like Wendy to come in and shake things up, and after reading her new activities sheet, she seemed well on the way to doing that.

However, out of the eighty odd residents in here, I know and Wendy will soon find out, that she will get the same twenty odd faces turn up each day for her new classes. The rest don't want to know, or are house bound and have carers that come in and help 'em. Shame really.

So, obviously if I don't show some willing and turn up for a couple of events every now and then, then I'm becoming part of the problem, and I aint really helping the situation or her.

Thinking about it, I decided there was no time like the present. I quickly unpacked and made myself a lively ham and tomato sandwich.

Couldn't hang about. It was time for 'eyes down for a full house!'

'Welcome back!' Exclaimed Wendy as I poked my head round the doorjamb, and looked into the lounge. The old place had had a couple of coats of beige emulsion from Sid and Charlie and it had really brightened up the place. The carpet looked clean and all the surfaces had been wiped down.

I saw Margie, Dot and Pauline already in position, as well as ten other faces, including one or two of the old ladies who had heard of the new changes and now felt safe to venture out and see what's what. Had a quick head count and totalled up fifteen punters. A good start.

'Hello Vin, good to have you back mate,' shouted Pauline 'like the new place? aint it fancy? Alright at your boys was it?'

'Lovely Paul, thanks, just what I needed.' I said as I looked round at the freshly decorated room, with its new tables, chairs and even a couple of computer monitors

'Seems to be going alright here then?' I smiled.

'Yeah lovely, err, Vinny,' said Margie nearly forgetting my name, 'we like her, Wendy, eh Pauline?'

'Yeah she's great,' said Pauline 'and my hands and feet are lovely after that Pilates this morning, wish I knew of all that years ago. Done me a right old treat it has.'

I could now see Wendy was smiling ear to ear as she handed out the bingo cards. She looked up and caught my gaze and nodded my way.

She then set up the round red wire cage thing, in which were housed the bingo balls on a table.

'Come on then, lets get settled,' she said. 'I reckon a pound a card and we'll have two full houses and two lines and split the winnings to the four winners.'

'Want a dobber?' Pauline enquired in my direction.

'Pardon?' I asked back quizzically

'A dobber. You know, one of these, a fat ended pen, for your card. Aint you been bingo before?' Pauline was clearly exasperated to be having to share a game with amateurs like me.

'Oh do leave it out woman. The last time I played bingo, I reckon I was about eight at a fair with me mum and dad down at Southend. I'll stick with my normal pen here, if it's all the same to you.'

Pauline tutted in my direction and then carefully arranged the multi coloured bingo cards in front of her.

Pauline had four cards. I decided that one would do me.

Once everyone had been sorted out, there was a few bob in the pot, all of which Wendy had collected up.

'Ok, we all ready?' Wendy shouted at those gathered in

front of her. Complete silence had enveloped the room.

'Right, eyes down please.' She then started to turn the handle on the side of the contraption and a ball would then get caught in a trap, which Wendy would then grab and then call the number written on it.

'Tom Mix – Number Six'

'Unlucky for some' – Thirteen'

'Kelly's Eye – Number One'

Despite my best efforts, I found I was just about keeping up with the one card I had. Others were 'dobbing' numbers all over the place. I soon became aware that old Margie was repeating to herself, the number Wendy was calling out.

Tut-tutting could be heard, as people became restless listening to it. It was certainly off-putting, but I also found it quite funny.

I also noticed that poor Margie was struggling with her one card and that her sister Dot was trying to get her to mark off the numbers as they appeared not only on her own card, but also her sister's. Dot looked very flustered if truth be told.

However, after a few more minutes, old Margie seemed to be getting in her stride and Dot left her to fill her own card out. She was crossing off numbers all over the card, most of which I began to notice, hadn't actually been called.

'Three O – Blind Thirty', continued Wendy, who certainly had the 'bingo lingo' down to a fine art.

'Two large ladies – eighty eight.'

'Here y'are Wendy!' Margie stopped Wendy in full flow and was now standing up and waving the card for all to see.

'Well done Marge' said Pauline through gritted teeth. 'They say money goes to money don't they.'

Wendy stopped the red hamsters wheel from turning.

'Ok, we seem to have one lucky winner. Let me check your numbers then Marge, call out what you've crossed off for the full house. At this point, Dot looked down at the table, in a bit of a daze, almost frightened to think about what was about to happen. Marge belted out a succession of numbers, but only a couple of them had actually been called.

'Oh Margie' said Pauline sadly.

A few of the other ladies huffed and puffed and it was obvious they weren't happy at the waste of time that game had obviously been, but they soon quieted down, when it was obvious there was something wrong. Margie looked terribly confused and sat down again quickly.

Bless Wendy's heart though, she said well done to Marge and gave her a couple of quid, whilst all the time looking at Dot a bit puzzled and looking for some help and advice. Dot then nodded to her, as if to say I know, leave it with me.

Dot told Margie that because she had now won a game, she could no longer take part and the poor cow accepted that.

We carried on for another half hour or so, and it was good to see Pauline pick up a couple of quid. I was a complete Joe Loss. I got confused on nearly every game. I found myself daydreaming and then wondering if I had heard a certain number or not? Useless.

After the final game, we all bought teas and coffees from the new vending machine in the communal kitchen area which was another one of Wendy's innovations that had gone down well.

I took the opportunity to sit down and catch up with Dot and Pauline. Margie was with us, but seemed very vague. A dramatic change in her had taken place in the last few weeks, she wasn't her old self at all.

There was only one real topic of conversation that anyone wanted to talk about, and it was Margie.

'Sorry about all that,' said Dot, careful not to let Margie into the conversation 'she's been like it for a while now. Its steadily getting worse though.'

I suddenly had this overwhelming urge to laugh. I tried desperately to stop myself, but couldn't help it.

'Sorry Dot, really sorry.' I said, but found that she was too smiling and even Pauline gave out a little giggle.

'Oooh sorry Dot, but I can't help it.' said Pauline.

Dot was now struggling to hold back a combination of laughter and tears, which were as much from the relief of it being out in the open I guess, as much as to actually finding it funny.

'Terrible isn't it (sniff, chuckle) och, you're wicked you are Pauline and you Vinny! This is no laughing matter you know.' Dot was by now chuckling her head off, caught up in the infectious laughter.

I held my hand up. '

'Ignore me, really. But Dot, love, you've got to admit, that was ...quite... funny, haha.'

'It's not, it's not!' Dot shouted with now a huge smile on her face, 'it's really not....ha ha.'

Gallows humour I think the learned call it.

Once it all calmed down, Dot explained that Margie had been diagnosed with the early stages of dementia. Some days, she was fine and quite lucid. But on others, well, she completely derailed and episodes like the bingo game were becoming the norm.

I thought back to when I was inside at the start of my sentence. I once shared a peter with a bloke who was on the badger game, you know, using porn photos and films for blackmail purposes. Although I was in there with him, I wasn't him, that wasn't my world at all.

I tried to distance myself from him and he knew it. He knew I was judging him, thinking my crime was cleaner than his.

'Don't' look at me like that, you hear me. You aint much

better than me son. A criminal is a criminal.'

Dark days they were, very, very dark. I used to lie awake on that top bunk and think, how did I end up in here?

Funnily enough, I was having those same thoughts at this very moment.

If you had told me then I would be one day living in a sheltered housing unit, laughing about playing a game of bingo with an old girl with 'old timers disease', I would have said you were as stark staring potty as the Badger Man. But, here I was. Never really saw this lot coming.

'Actually all joking aside, it's been murder,' Dot continued 'Margie's losing weight rapidly, because she forgets to eat. I keep saying 'you've got to eat sister' and she smiles back and nods, but I can see I'm not really registering.'

Wendy came over and sat down next to Dot and held her hand. Dot looked at Wendy and seemed to draw comfort from her being there.

'On top of all that, she's also lost all track of time and now thinks that three in the morning, is three in the afternoon and will get ready to go out at that time to do her shopping. Obviously I stop her, but I fear that one day when I fail to wake up, or am just not there, she'll take off into who knows what kind of danger.

She's already lost her door keys more times than I care to remember and I keep finding her glasses in the fridge and her pension book in the freezer.'

'Well Dot,' said Wendy sympathetically 'I need to tell you that old Rosie in flat 28 got the fright of her life the other night when it sounded like someone was trying to open her front door, using a key.

Rosie told me, that she got up and looked through the spy-hole on the door and saw Margie on the other side trying to put the key in the lock. Rosie said it all looked and sounded like Margie had picked the wrong door, thinking it was her home and it was a genuine mistake. Finally, Margie gave in and walked away, but it really upset Rosie, told me she didn't sleep a wink all night.'

Dot looked down into her own lap, wringing her hands over and over again.

'Oh Wendy, I'm so upset to hear that. I'm so sorry...'

We all rallied round and rubbed her hands or her shoulders and said it wasn't Dot's fault and Margie was obviously ill, but in reality there was little we could do or say.

I felt really sad for the pair of the sisters. They had been in each other's pockets all their lives, cared for each other and although they rowed occasionally, there was a lot of obvious love between them.

Sad to see that it would be a struggle for the pair of them from now on.

Before heading home, we told Wendy to leave the tidying up of the bingo stuff to us. She had done her bit for the day.

I felt happy to be back among these people, they were good 'uns and I liked them a lot. I felt secure and content. It was a nice feeling.

I decided to nut into Wendy's office on the way back to my flat and tell her that I hoped that she could think of a solution to the Dot and Margie situation, and if there was anything I could do to help, then to give me a call. I had a lot of time for the sisters and wanted to do my bit.

I knocked on the white door to her office and walked in

I found her sitting behind her desk, surrounded by manila folders with bits of paper spilling out of every one. Wendy looking lost to the world.

I gently tapped on her desk to wake her from her daydream.

'You alright Wendy?' I asked.

I mean, I knew the news of Marge was bad, but I hardly expected this reaction from the person who was in effect looking after us.

'Oh, hello Vincent.' She was suddenly startled by my being there. 'Sorry, miles away there. Terrible shame about Marge isn't it?'

I nodded. 'Its Dot too we've got to keep an eye on too. Terrible illness that. Really hard work for the main carer.

Er, s'cuse me for saying so, but anything else bothering you? You look really concerned.'

She looked me straight in the eyes, and shook her head.

'No nothing, really.'

'You sure, cos you look like you've got the weight of the world on your shoulders mate.'

Once again she looked directly at me.

'Um. Well ok, listen Vinny I guess I can trust you, because you have already sorted this place out once, so I know your heart is in the right place.'

'Bloody hell girl.' She really had me worried, 'What's up, sounds like you've only got three days to live or something...'

She bowed her head and looked at the floor. She had stopped talking.

'Oh Jesus... you haven't only got three days to live have ya?'

She really had me worried here.

Wendy smiled. 'Well, you aren't going to believe this, but in a way you're not too far from the truth. Only it's not me that's not got long...its this place.'

She looked away, obviously struggling to find the words she felt she needed to say.

'Eh? What d'ya mean Wendy, this place?' I could hear the panic in my own voice.

'Shush Vinny, ' Wendy whispered harshly at me 'for Christ's sake, will you keep your voice down.'

'Well, sorry,' I said 'but surely you don't mean what I think you do?'

'Ok. Bloody hell, I know I shouldn't have said anything, but....

'Well you've started so you might as well finish now.'

I wasn't going to be letting go.

Wendy looked really flustered. This was obviously hard for her to do.

'Ok Vinny, listen, I already knew there were spending cuts coming when I took this job on, but I managed to get some funding and spent it on some new furniture and brightened the place up as you have seen for yourself today. But after all the nonsense with Maureen and the papers getting involved, well, the council looked at this place again and by the sound of it, they want to move all you out into other units and sell this off to developers. The area is on the up, and they have plans to build luxury homes on this land.'

I slumped down into one of her office chairs. I was initially lost for words. But not for long.

'Well, that is total bollocks. When has SE5 ever been trendy? And after all that palava with Maureen and you getting this place back on it's feet, you'd think they would give us an easy life, wouldn't ya?'

'Cutbacks, simple as that, Said Wendy 'they say they can't afford to run this unit as it stands anymore. They need to raise money and plots like this are at a premium round here'

If truth be told, Wendy looked resigned to the news.

'Fuck me.' I said without thinking. 'Sorry about the Portuguese Wendy, blame it on stress. Looks like we're in dead lumber here though doesn't it.'

I was genuinely gutted. It didn't seem real.

'Aint there anything we can do here?' I said.

Wendy had her head in here hands, her fingers playing

with the locks in her hair.

'Vin, what can I tell you. It doesn't look like it. It's a real pity. I've got used to the people here really quickly, really like most of em too. They have been so welcoming to me.

I've kept up the pressure on the council every day since taking this job, but it sounds like at least half a million quid is required to secure the lease and a further quarter of million to do all the upgrading on the building that is required. The council isn't going to spend that, not at the minute. I've got to say, I fear the worst Vinny. Vinny? are you listening?'

I was still there, but not really there if you know what I mean. I was thinking, what a day this has turned out to be. It started off all lovely with happy memories of building bridges with my remaining blood family and then later I was re-united with my other family of elderly waifs and strays, only then to find out that we could all be split up, once again, just as we have got things the way we like 'em.

I could vaguely hear Wendy's voice but I was no longer listening to her. No, my mind was already thinking about a once beautiful actress and a plot of land over in North London and what was buried there six feet underground.

As I came out of my daydream, I could once again, hear Wendy's voice.

"You alright Vinny?,' Wendy laughed 'you look like you've seen a ghost.'

'You're not far wrong.' I murmured.

Suddenly in my minds eye, as clear as day, I could see Elizabeth Taylor as a girl jockey in the film National Velvet and as Cleopatra, entering Rome, dressed in gold.

'Vin? Vinny? You still with us?' Wendy was sounding concerned.

I slowly regained my focus.

'So, all about money is it?,' I said 'at the end of a long day, it's all about the gelt, it normally is aint it? Three quarters of a million pounds needed you say?

Tell you what Wendy, don't start packing up just yet will ya' I might have an idea.'

I then stood up and hurriedly made my way back to my flat.

Wendy was up on her feet too now. She shouted after me, as I disappeared down the corridor.

'Vinny, what you talking about? Where you going? What, you thinking of buying a load of scratch cards are you!' and with that gave out a real hearty laugh. I heard her, but didn't want to turn round.

I was no longer listening and I certainly wasn't stopping. No, I was on a mission.

Back at my flat, I poured myself a decent belt of scotch, and watered it down with a couple of ice cubes out of the freezer. I drained the first one straight down; it really hit the spot, with the ice cubes jangling on the bottom of the glass.

I poured another. Quickly.

I sat down and soon I was lost among my own thoughts about what occurred back in 1962.

That tomfoolery had now been in that coffin for so long I had almost forgotten about it.

Notice the word almost...

Every now and then, a small part of my mind would occasionally wonder what it was all worth now after all these years, but I would then just as quickly dismiss those thoughts. I mean I was straight and I was a stand up, solid citizen.

Besides all that, how the fuck do I get them out of the ground?!

As for opening the coffin lid after all this time? That doesn't bear thinking about.

But now, that coffin with a decent amount of dough

wrapped up in the 'tom', would come in very, very handy and would make a lot of good people very, very happy.

To my mind, they had been through enough. They had found a spiritual home here and now it was in danger of being dis-mantled.

I sunk the rest of the scotch.

I mean, old Liz Taylor had now gone up to the red carpet premiere in the sky and the majority of the seven husbands who bought her the sparklers in the first place, had joined her up there.

I reckon she would have had a tidy insurance pay out after my little visit, which would have softened the blow of losing those precious stones, somewhat.

I laughed to myself, when I thought of what I would have wasted the money on, that those gems would have brought me back then on. Probably a dozen racks of whistles, foreign holidays for me and the wife, a Roller and a trip to buy up Hamleys for Matthew.

But I didn't get the chance to do any of that. My collar being felt put a stop to that little lifestyle change.

Well, those days were now long gone anyway.

I was a changed person. I didn't need the wedge anymore, my bit of pension and my savings got me through now. My Matthew had obviously done alright by him and his family, judging by the half million pound house he lived in down in Whitsatble. So he didn't need it either.

So, after all these years, if I now managed to get my hands on the Liz Taylor wedge, I knew it had a better home to go to than before.

A thought then crossed my mind. Maybe I should tell Wendy and my new mates of what I could get my hands on? Sure, it would have meant lifting the lid on my dodgy past, but we were old people now, they would let the past be the past, wouldn't they?

This was now developing into a three-drink problem and I soon sunk that third one too. The taste of the Scotch was lovely, but it didn't provide the solution of should I reveal my story or not.

Would anyone believe it anyway?

By now, the combination of a long day and the drink was making me feel very weary. I decided to sleep on it.

See how I feel in the morning, yeah that's it. If I felt the overwhelming need to tell someone what I could get to, then I'd do it.

Not surprisingly, I had a terrible nights kip.

I laid there for what seemed like hours, but in reality was only half an hour. When I did nod off for a bit, I kept dreaming of me being chased by Richard Burton who was wearing a Welsh coppers uniform and we were running around and around the old Hollywood sign in Los Angeles. Every time he reached out to grab me by the collar, I dodged between the centre of one of the O's and got away.

The combination of a bit of stress and a lot of scotch resulted in these bloody silly dreams.

I gave up trying to sleep at about 6am, just as the light began to creep in from behind my curtains. By this stage, I was sitting in my armchair, having vacated the bed hours before.

It was useless. I decided I might as well get up. I had a quick wash down, threw on the first set of clothes I lay my hands on and then set off for a walk. Didn't really have a destination in mind, but like a homing pigeon, found myself on the way into the West End.

It's about five miles from our gaff to the centre of town, so I thought that was long enough to clear my head.

I headed off down the Walworth Road. At this time of

the morning, it was mostly buses on the road, with very few cars and even fewer pedestrians about. On I went, past the entrance to East Lane market, where I had my first job aged fourteen, pulling out the barrow's for old Ernie Mossop's flower stall.

I then trotted up round the Elephant and Castle and through the roundabouts. Up by the Old Vic, over Waterloo Bridge and then cut through Covent Garden into Cambridge Circus and there, finally, I was on the verge of entering Soho.

The 'Naughty square mile' was all in front of me.

Even at this early hour, Soho had plenty going on. Cafes, and paper shops opening up, spielers and clubs emptying people out into the early morning light.

I wandered into Bar Italia on Frith Street, and though I haven't been there for far too long, I immediately noticed it hadn't changed too much over the years. The photos and memorabilia hanging all over the walls, made it feel like a place you could rest in.

The unbeaten heavyweight champion of the World from the early 1950s Rocky Marciano was still in pride of place on the wall behind the counter.

I used to come in here in the very early 1960s, when it was mainly filled with Italians who had landed in England for a bit of work. Back then, with the main door closed and the air filled with tobacco and cigar smoke, you could find waiters and dish washers all catching up on news from back home. It was all men then too, no sorts ever came in. Couldn't really blame them.

That's one of the few things that has changed here over the years, now having the front door open all the time and no smoking allowed on the premises.

I ordered up at the counter and then told the good looking fella, dressed in a crisp white shirt and black skinny tie, pulling the lever and frothing up my cappuccino that I would be sitting outside.

The darling little sort who brought my drink out to me, was a little brahmer, as acknowledged by all the early morning cleaning geezers all hanging about outside on the pavement. All of them to a man watched her every move as she came and went, in and out of the Bar.

I had perched up among the row of small, round, silver metal tables and chairs out front. The perfect place to sit and watch the world pass by.

'Grazie.' I said as the beauty put my cup and saucer on the table in front of me.

At that precise moment a young junkie bird walked past us. She had all her hair cut off and she was wearing little metal round National Heath type glasses. She was very disheveled and tatty looking and smelt like a rancid camel. She had with her a small staffy dog on a bit of rope and was wearing odd trainers.

'Scuse me' she said to me.

'Yes love' I replied, already getting ready to fish some change out of my pockets to give to her.

'You French?' She caught me off guard with that.

'French?' How d'ya mean, French?' I was now very confused.

'I heard you say grazie then, thought you were French?'

'Er, no sweetheart, I'm not.' With that I gave her the handful of shrapnel.

'Here ya go girl, now don't waste that on food.'

She quickly pocketed the change and scurried off in the direction of oblivion.

I sat there, sipping my drink, looking across at Ronnie's. This place, Soho, used to be my playground. A small smile crossed my lips as the memories tumbled in. Jesus, what times we had back then. Game of dice up on the second floor near to where I'm sitting now. Have an afternoon drink in one of the dive bars, and then take refuge with a decent looking brass when her Maltese ponce wasn't looking.

Mad old times here then maybe, but you felt like you were really living, know what I mean?

One of the by-products of being out and about in the swing of it all was that there was always plenty of news on the street as to who had what and where you could nick it from.

That's how I heard about Liz Taylor and her jewellery in the first place.

I was on my way to my corner street bookie, when I bumped into an Italian hotel porter called Guido who I knew from Bar Italia. He told me Liz was in town, staying where he worked. He told me she was in the habit of leaving her 'tom' all over her bed, something he had personally seen with his own minces when he took her up a decent bottle of claret for her and her film agent on room service one afternoon.

'My facking eyes, they nearly popped out my head Vincenzo! Sparklers all over the kipper,' he said in his best Italian Cockney banter ' Madon! If only....'

I was sitting there thinking you may not be able to, old son, but I certainly know a man who could.

Namely, ME!

I quickly got her room number from him and he confirmed the floor her room was on. She was staying at The Barbury, an exclusive, small hotel whose drainpipes I had previous with.

Present time now stood still as I visualised my life back then.

I seriously haven't thought of those times in a long while, so I was shocked at how clear my memory was.

I slowly finished up my frothy coffee and then left the young bird waitress a decent tip. She was out like lightening and scooped that up before any other street life took a liberty and got their hands on it.

She was a fast mover for a sweet kid.

I decided to stay in the area and have a mooch around for an hour or so. I even popped down a couple of streets hoping to find one or two old faces about, but, of course, they have all gone. Stands to reason don't it. It was all a very long time ago.

In fact I didn't recognize anyone or indeed most of the shops for that matter. It had all gone, except in my memories.

All of a sudden, I began to feel the early start and long walk in my legs. It was time to head back to the ranch.

I got on 'The Orient Express' – the 176 bus used by the South London based Chinese workers, which stops close by Chinatown – and headed back to Camberwell.

On the trip back I made my mind up, I had decided to tell the others of the Elizabeth Taylor caper.

Now that would be a conversation stopper!

6

The Michael Aspel Fan Club

Having made my mind up to tell the others, I actually felt a great sense of relief. This had been something I had carried around with me for many, many years. Only a handful of people knew about the crime and the stir I did for it.

Of course, it was all a long, long time ago, but the whole episode still felt like a ton weight whenever it surfaced. Now, just the thought of telling others the story, made me feel elated. It was a strange, but exciting prospect.

On returning to our communal abode, I made straight to find my little mob and tell them the news.

I looked in and around a few of the regular places they usually congregated, like the kitchen area, and laundry but there was no sign of them. My ears then picked up on a sound and I then found myself being drawn towards really loud music.

As I got nearer I found myself singing along to a song as I got nearer to the source of it. It was 'She Wears Red Feathers' by that old crooner from the 50s Guy Mitchell. He was a real favourite with the teenage 'bobby soxer' type girls back then, when boys like me were out trying to find a clock to rock around.

The music was getting louder and louder until it was almost deafening by the time I got to the door of the communal lounge from where the music seemed to be emanating.

'And a hooly hooly skirt, she lives on fresh cokey –nuts and fish from the sea.'

I poked my head round the wedged open door and found Marge and Isaac doing a little jig to the song, whilst Pauline had her hands to her ears, her face physically wincing from the noise.

'Blimey! That aint half loud.' I said as I walked in. 'You can hear that in bloody miles away.'

Pauline mouthed the word 'What?' back at me, but I couldn't hear her, nor she me.

I SHOUTED 'I SAID!...THAT FLAMING MUSIC! ...IT AINT HALF LOUD!'

She smiled and nodded and then went to speak and then waved her hand at me as if to say, oh this is useless, I'll tell you about it in a minute

Thankfully the song was coming to an end, just as well, as my lugs couldn't take much more

'A rose in her hair, a gleam in her eye

And love (and love) in her heart (in her heart) for me'

'Man, that was great.' Tubby huffed and puffed as he spoke, when the song came to an end, at exactly the same time as his doddery old two step did with Margie.

'My Cilla used to love Guy Mitchell. Me? I'm more of a Jim Reeves man myself.' He then proceeded to sing.

'I Hear The Sound of Distant Drums...tune sir. Ha ha.'

Marge had just flopped herself on the nearest armchair and was struggling to speak at all .

'I...I ...bought ...that...when it first...came...out' she wheezed.

'Reeves fan too then?' said Tubbs.

'No, not that Vic Reeves, can't stand the man, I mean him, Guy Mitchell!' She too began to sing.

'She lives on fresh cokey-nuts' eh? don't write lyrics like that anymore do they?'

I decided to let the 'Vic' slip of the tongue go, because it was great to see Margie enjoying herself, after what she was going through at present.

'Glad you enjoyed yourselves,' I said 'you were both very tidy on the dance floor you was, pity about the warbling after though. But for Christ sakes, why have it so loud?'

Pauline, who had slowly let go of her head with her hands, then piped up.

'Bloody hell, thank God that's finished. It's them two Vin.'

Pauline said, pointing to our very own Fred and Ginger.

'The pair of 'em must be as deaf as posts. Mind you, we've had a lovely morning, all been playing our favourite records. Taken me right back to when I was a girl, it has. I used to dodge about to most of these songs at Marc Antonio's Ice Cream Parlour up the Green, back then.

Been lovely it has, has really, but these two will insist on turning the flaming volume up. I kept saying, I like this one an' all, but for chrissakes turn it down, and they'd suddenly say, 'Oh we LOVE this one' and turn the bloody thing up and up again. Mutton, the pair of 'em.'

I had to smile too, for it did me good to see them all so cheerful and happy again, after all that nonsense with Maureen. It felt like the prefect time to tell them my news, only one of our tight little gang was missing.

'Where's Dot?' I asked as casually as I could.

'She's in the wotsit,' said Pauline 'won't be a minute. Why?'

'Er, nothing really...' I must have looked shifty or nervous or something, cos as soon I said that I could see they were all looking at me rather curiously.

'What?' I said, trying to style it out, but failed miserably by the look of it.

'Come on Vinny man, what do you mean 'what?' – it's obvious you've got something on your mind. Man, I can read you like a book.'

I smiled. Tubbs had me. I actually felt my face flushing a bit. I felt on the spot. I hadn't really told anyone of my past over the years. Well, that's not exactly true, there were a couple of old flames over in Europe in my lorry driving days, that I might have mentioned it to. Well, the red vino would have been flowing, so I loosened up a bit, but their English wasn't too clever so I doubt they understood what I was going on about to be honest.

But this, this now, was different. Those sat in front of me now, I had grown to really like, and I wanted them to like me. Got to be honest I was worried they might take against me once they heard of my dodgy past.

I had run this scenario over in my mind quite a few times in the past and I never really worked out the result. Even talked it out loud once or twice, just me facing a mirror. At the end of the day, others had done much worse, and committed terrible crimes compared to mine.

In reality, I was only a tealeaf with expensive taste. Yeah I had done wrong, but no one got physically hurt. Maybe a little upset and inconvenienced, but in the majority of cases, they could afford to lose what they had.

I found myself pacing the floor in front of them. Up and down I went, to and fro.

'Christ Vin, what's up with you, you'll wear a hole in that bloody carpet if you aint careful?'

Good old Pauline was worried about me, like she worried about everybody else in the World. I doubt the poor cow could ever really get any rest at night, as the range of her worries went from the war in the Middle East down to the price of a packet of bacon in Morrison's.

"I'm alright,' I said unconvincingly 'honest, Paul, just

waiting for Dot to come back from the Benghazi, and I'll...'

And as I said that, Dot appeared as if by magic in the doorway.

'Did I hear my name then?' Dot spoke as she came back in to the lounge and sat in one of the high backed chairs.

'At least we know there is nothing wrong with your hearing then mate,' I said laughing and nodding over at Margie 'unlike your skin and blister '.

Marge then flicked me a glorious two-fingered salute. She had heard that all right!

'We were talking about ya, not to ya' said Pauline laughing.

'That's alright then' Dot smiled.

Then silence, as they all looked at me. Straight at me, right into the whites of my eyes. Well, that's how it felt.

'Come on Vinny, shit or get off the pot young man. There's repeats of Antiques Roadshow on in twenty minutes, want to watch that and have a sandwich' Marge was getting impatient.

'You and that bloody Antiques Roadshow,' puffed Dot 'I wouldn't mind, but it's repeats from 1989, and all the prices will be wrong and out of date now anyway.'

But Marge wouldn't have that. 'Leave me alone, it's my favourite programme.'

'We all know why you watch it and it isn't about the Georgian silver. It's that presenter on it. You fancy him you.' Dot had hit Margie right between the eye's'.

'Och, I won't have word spoken against that man! You know that...'

Marge had gone a very bright red colour.

Ding ding, here we go again I thought. Round one, come out with your guard up. The sisters were at it again!

'Ok, Ok, listen, listen... If I could just shut the Michael Aspel Fan Club up for a minute,' I said, looking sternly at

Marge 'there is something, I've decided to tell you.'

Silence enveloped me, all eyes were now on me. It was time.

'It concerns something I did over fifty years ago....'

I then regaled them for the next hour or so, with the tales of my earlier life and what Wendy had told me about Benhill being under threat. As the story unfolded, I was met with faces in awe of the story. Mouths were left gaping wide open with expressions of 'well I never' all over their boats.

Talk about stop people in their tracks.

Marge even forgot about Antiques Roadshow and the price of an eighteenth century piss pot!

'...and that brings you all up to speed,' I said as I finished 'so, you can see, I did my time and came out the other side. Went as straight as a man could be. I won't lie to you and say I wasn't tempted back into that life, especially in the early days, but I resisted somehow and kept out of it.'

'Man, I have heard some tales in my time,' said Tubbs 'but that one is an absolute belter. What a thing to happen! I've got to ask Vinny, why you feel you have to tell us know, after all this time.'

I rubbed my chin and told them.

'Well, as far as I know those jewels that are still in that coffin.

There is no getting away from it, I'm an old man, so I'm going to need some help in getting them out to be able to put them good use.'

'To good use? Whaddya mean, to good use? What you going to do with them?' I smiled at sweet, naïve Pauline, who still hadn't worked out what I was thinking.

'Bless you Paul,' I said 'sounds like we need money right, to save this place, right?'

'Right' she said 'Well...'

You could physically feel the penny dropping as she and the rest of them worked out my idea.

'Ere,' said a wide eyed and startled Pauline 'surely you don't mean, you're going to go and get those diamonds out of the coffin, and then sell them to somehow pay...for...this ...place.'

I just nodded in her direction.

'No, Vinny. No, no...let's have it right, that is so wrong.' Pauline was now beginning to go a funny shade of white as the colour drained from her face.

'Sweet Jesus up above.' Exclaimed Tubbs, rubbing his hands together, as the thought of it all, hit home.

'Dot, I'm a bit lost sis, what is Vinny talking about?'

This was obviously all too much for Margie, who also looked very worried.

'Don't worry your little head about any of this sister dear. It's just one of Vinnie's tall tales.' Dot never took her eyes off me when she was talking to her younger sister. 'Isn't it Vincent?'

She was looking for me to reassure Margie.

I decided to play along and must have acted it out well, because soon enough, Margie was smiling again.

'Come on Marge, lets get you away and settled indoors. We'll find something for you to watch. Give me five minutes,' she said looking sternly at me 'and I'll be straight back.'

Dot lead Margie by the hand to their flat, and that left Pauline and Tubbs looking at me.

'Well, who'd have thought it,' said Pauline finally 'seen you in a different light today aint we?'

I just smiled at them both. I didn't really know what to say to them.

Tubbs just sat there tapping the tips of fingers together, his hands forming a sort of pyramid shape.

To tell you the truth, it wasn't that much of an awkward silence whilst we waited for Dot to return.

I could sense that these two were intrigued as to what happened next. I felt I had them hooked in with me.

After five minutes, Dot returned. She looked a flushed and a little stressed if truth be told.

"Alright Dot? Margie all settled?' I asked.

'Och, don't 'Alright Dot' me, Vincent.' She had the right hump.

'Look, Dot...all of you. Listen, I know it s a lot to take in, and I aint looking for any rash decisions. I really don't expect any of YOU to get involved.

It just so happens that I've got a way out of the mess this place is in. I know it might be a mad old plan, but it's better than just sitting here and accepting the council decision isn't it?

Yes, I agree, it's not strictly kosher. But really, who has to know? All I've got to do, is get the gems and then find someone who won't ask too many questions to give us folding for them.'

'You make it sound so simple don't you. But the fact is, now that you've told us about the theft and the story of where they are, it makes us accessories to the crime, even though it was half a century ago. Well, doesn't it?'

Dot wasn't a happy camper. She continued.

'I mean, I haven't ever done anything wrong in my life. I haven't stolen, robbed or conned anyone. Not my style. And now this...well...'

I could see, and hear, she was very upset.

'Dot, I'm sorry to have dumped this on you. But I did it, cos I trust you, all of you. Listen, I did time for the crimes I had committed, but also for some things that were planted on me. I finally had to take it all on the chin and I'm proud to have done the right thing since.

Now, I suppose I'm looking to make amends in a way and what better way can you think of, to put right the injustice of those in authority closing this place down and moving us all out to be here, there and everywhere.

Feels like the right thing to do, that's all. I aint making any of you help, but just wanted to let you in on it all, for support I suppose. And, then, well, see where it takes us.'

There was silence for what seemed like hours, but was probably no more than thirty seconds.

Finally, Pauline blew out her cheeks.

'Blimey, what a turn up this is and no mistake.' She gently shook her head.

'Well,' said Tubbs very assertively 'I'm in with Vinny. Whatever it takes, whatever I can do to help him. I'm in!'

'Eh?,' exclaimed Pauline, nodding in my direction 'you're as mad as he is'

'Mad? Me? Yeah I'm mad,' said Tubbs 'I'm mad at being treated like a damn idiot. First Maureen, which don't forget Vinny sorted and now the council. Tell you I have had enough of constantly feeling like I'm under threat. We older people should be having it easier, not harder as we get on in years.

'Y'know, I reckon I've got more chance with Vinny than anyone else.'

I smiled at this good-hearted old gentleman, and nodded my appreciation.

'Oh Tubbs...' sighed Dot 'don't you think you should think a bit longer about it, what about your Carla and the boys, what they gonna say?'

'Hush up now Dot,' said Tubbs somewhat sternly 'I'm an old man, always been on the right side of the law, never even fiddled the bus company. Not my style. But even with me being such a good boy, my Cilla, she still died. Had a pain in my heart ever since. I reckon I've got one last year in me, before this gives up.' He patted his chest and his heart within. 'I want to get it racing again one more time and when my time comes and I face St Peter at them gates, I'll tell him, I have no regrets sir. I did what I felt was right. Amen.'

I gave out a small laugh when I heard this. I was delighted my old mate would be joining me on the next leg of our journey.

'Thanks Tubbs, good to have you on board mate.'

He nodded back to me with a big toothy grin. His face then turned into a bit of a frown.

'Anyway, as for my kids, they aint got to know anything, have they? Not if we all keep our traps shut eh?'

Tubbs looked accusingly at Dot'

'Och, listen Mr. Isaacs, I'm many things, but a tittle-tattle is not one of them. I'll not gab about it to anyone.'

'Ok Dot, I believe you. As long as it stays like that, things will be fine.'

Tubbs seemed reassured, though I could sense that Pauline was beginning to worry big time.

'You're not to worry here Pauline. You really haven't got to do anything. Tubbs and me will have it covered. I'm not even sure how we are going to attack this problem yet anyway.'

I did my best to settle the poor cow down.

'Well, it's not like I don't want to help Vinny, I do, I really do, but this is so far out of my comfort zone, I can't tell ya. And anyway, before I do anything, unlike Tubbs, I want to speak to my boys.'

The look of worry on Pauline's face, creased me up inside.

'Of course love.' I said somewhat unconvincingly. 'It's just if you do, please ask them to keep it to themselves for now, the less people that know the better for all here.'

I gently touched her on her upper right arms as if to

reassure her that it would be alright.

Pauline tried to compose herself.

'Y'know I've not had a drink since my Bill died, just gone right off it, but Christ I feel like I need one right now as it happens. I think I'll go home and pour myself a nice glass of Cinzano and then have a think about what to do next. I feel shattered, I really do...' She had had enough, the poor mare.

The three of us now looked at Dot.

'Now don't look to me.' She said, a fiery look in her brown eyes.

'It's not only me, I've got to think of. It'll be my Margie as well. I can't very well afford to be locked up and not be around to look after her, now can I?'

'Course not Dot.' I said. 'Anyway, if anyone is going to be locked up, it'll be me alone. I'll accept full responsibility for anything that goes wrong. You all hear me?'

They all nodded, but only Tubbs looked convinced.'

'You know what, enough for today. I'm going home and will do the same as Pauline. Time for a drink and a think. Maybe a bit of time to digest it all, eh?

'You're not wrong there mister.' Said Dot, still firing on all cylinders.

I began laughing at the absurdity of what had happened over the past hour or two.

Pauline looked at me in amazement.

'Oh laughing now is it? Mad he is, told ya, mad as they come.'

She stood up, shook her head and tutted as she left me and Tubbs sitting there.

'Y'know, she's possibly right.' I said to Tubbs, who was smiling his head off.

'Sweet Jesus...'

I went back to my flat and sat in front of the switched off telly, revving up all over the thoughts in my swede. It was good to hear the silence. Too much talking today, time now for some thought.

Got to say though, I surely felt a weight off my shoulders.

It felt good to take it off at last.

I woke up still in the same chair eight hours later. I must have dropped off there and then. Just didn't realise how tired I was. I guess the relief I felt had overpowered me and I nodded off where I sat.

I woke up with such a crick in my neck that I couldn't walk upright at first. This age thing is a brute!

I wandered out into the kitchen, but my mind wasn't really on it. Bollocks to cornflakes this morning. I know what I'll do, quick shower and a then a trip to Bully's Café. I think I need something more substantial this morning. A good dollop of stodge should sort me out.

I slowly walked the ten minutes it takes to get to the Istanbul Café, all the time trying to correct my posture and to get my neck working properly again after that nights kip. As the name suggests, the people that own the Istanbul are of Turkish extraction. It was originally the present owners father who ran it, but since he sadly passed away, his son, Bulut, and his family have run it. Over the years, his name has been corrupted to Bully and that is what he answers too. His lyrics are pure local, with an accent as thick as his gravy.

I've been coming in here off and on for the past thirty years, and knew Bully's old man, Mehmet, really well, may his God rest his soul.

I tried to look in, before entering, but the windows that looked out onto the street, were all steamed up, with droplets of water running down in pairs. Tattered posters advertising a local fun fair were roughly sellotaped on the outside of the window. A fairly large black 'A' board, that sat on the pavement outside, told passersby the prices of that morning set breakfasts, all written in different coloured chalk. A large Pepsi Cola advertising sign was situated over the entrance.

'Alright Vin, how's yer luck?' Bully was on me instantly as I walked through the red painted door into the cafe.

'Allo Bully boy, all good mate. Family well? I replied.

'Fine mate. Usual is it son?' He asked, as he wiped down one of the small yellow formica'd table tops.

'You got me.' I said smiling to him. 'I'll tell you what; I'll have an extra dog with it today and two crusty slices. Hank Marvin mate. Do us a cappuccino an' all.'

Bully nodded and whistled as he walked behind his counter and shouted down the order to his missus Tash, who was in the kitchen rustling up the pots and pans below. I grabbed a newspaper from the pile on the side of the counter. Bully gets all the red tops every day for his punters, which is a nice touch, and then I plotted up on one of the aforementioned tables.

Funnily enough, these tables are tiny. I think Mehmet got them cheap when he first came over in the late 50s, and I don't think Bully has the heart to get rid of them.

I just about get my knees under my one and then look up for the first time to see who is about. I take in the sight of the slightly retro feel to the place. Now understand, this is not done in some of 'knowing, style magazine ' kind of way. No, this has happened in a purely organic way. The fixture and fitting and décor of this café has been pretty much left alone and gradually come back into fashion over it's life span of forty plus years. It had ten big white globes lighting the place up and a black and white tiled floor, which had, in truth seen better days.

It was as I scanned the room, that I spied Tubbs and Pauline on the other side of the café.

They had seen me walk in and it appeared had been

holding their breath ever since.

'Hello you two.' I said as our eyes met. 'Don't often see you in here. I deliberately tried to keep the chat as light and frothy as the cup of cappuccino Pauline was holding.

'Mind if I join you?' I enquired.

In truth, before they could really answer, I had broken free of my table and was now struggling to take this one on. Within a minute I was sitting with them, with there now being even less space with three of us round the seven dwarves furniture.

'Not a usual haunt of mine if I'm honest,' said Tubbs 'but Pauline comes in from time to time, and well today, neither of us felt like cooking so we met on the way here. What you sitting like that for?'

'I somehow fell asleep in the chair I plotted in after our chat yesterday. Then I woke up all bent over like this this morning. Getting too old for that kipping in a chair palava, I really should start going to bed like normal people do.

And funnily enough, I felt like something more substantial this morning than my usual cereal, so here I am too.'

'Vin.' Pauline, who had been quiet up until that point, and who now looked completely worn out, suddenly spoke. 'Can I ask you something?'

'Of course Paul, anything' I said as kindly as I could.

'Look, no point lying to ya. I've been up half the night, mulling over what you said. It weren't a pack of lies was it? It's all-straight innit?'

I smiled.

'Blimey Pauline. I'll admit, I've got a furtive imagination, but even I would struggle coming up with that story. No, it's all true girl I'm afraid.'

'Thought so.' She half smiled at me, now knowing she had a serious decision to make.

'Well, I was just saying saying to Mr. Isaacs just before

you walked in, my life for the past coupla years has been like someone pressed the 'pause' button on me. I've hardly done anything, y'know, since the old man passed away.

But when I was younger I was anything but mundane and boring. We were all lively, always out and about.

I mean to say, I'm not old now. I know everyone who see's me in the street thinks I am, but I'm not, not in here anyway. I'm twenty five up here.' She tapped her head as she spoke.

'Funny story. I went to a meeting and a talk about old Camberwell the other day up at the library, just to pass the time really. Well, some silly old sod came in and started spouting about what it was like round here in the early 1900s. Telling us the history of the old shops and streets and all that. He then asked if anyone there knew any stories from those times.

Well.

I said to him, just how old do you think we are exactly?

I mean, I was a child of the 1950s. Johnnie Ray and Nat King Cole. Hand made suits from Bettys Band Box. Up The Palladium we were every other Friday, and here's this, this, silly old twit asking me about Marie Lloyd and all about that Music Hall, all of which was in my mums day, God bless her soul. I think they are trying to bury us before our time. I really do.'

Both myself and Tubbs smiled at her. She was very entertaining when she got her dander up!

'Then yesterday, you come out with your thunderbolt of a story and it got me thinking. When I got home and had that Cinzano and thought about how we might be able to save the Benhill, well it actually made me feel alive again, got me thinking how would we do it, and would we get away with it and all that.

I realised there and then, that I actually felt twenty-five again, all over this time, not just in my head.

So, I've decided, if you'll have me, count me in. I'll do whatever I can to help with ya, though God knows what I can do.'

I reached over the smallest café table in London and squeezed her hand.

'What about your boys though? I asked.

'I'll have to tell them still, but will tell them I've made me mind up. They can like it or lump.'

'Ta Paul,' I said 'that means a lot that mate.'

She then started blushing, just as Bully brought over our breakfasts and my coffee.

'Right, what's the first step?' asked Tubbs stirring his cup of tea. 'No time like the present to crack on. Besides if we think about it too much, we might lose our nerve!'

'Aye aye captain' I said smiling. 'Ok, tell you what, what you two doing today?'

'Well nothing really. I was going to get a bit of shopping up the Green, but that can wait, why?' Asked Pauline.

'What about you Tubbs?' I enquired.

'Nothing man, just planning on listening to the cricket later on, maybe stick a pony on a pony, but that is all.'

'Alight, how about this then. As Tubbs quite rightly says, there is no time like the present, so how about we all jump on a tube and head for the Northside Jewish Cemetery and go and see the grave where the jewels are?'

'Eh? What now?' Pauline began to panic.

'C'mon Pauline,' said Tubbs 'you just said you want to live again. Well a tube ride aint going to kill ya.'

Pauline looked concerned at first, but forced out a smile and finally nodded her head.

'Hang on though, what about Dot and Marge?' she asked.

'Not sure.' I said 'From what I saw yesterday, I think old

Dot will need more time to come to terms with all this, and as for Marge, well lets be honest, she'll do whatever Dot tells her to do.

No, lets not put them under anymore stress. Lets just go and do it and fill them in on what we've found when we get home.'

We set about our breakfasts, and mine tasted fantastic. I was now by this point starving and this hit the correct notes as far as I was concerned.

Tubbs, like me, polished off his plate, but Pauline was doing little more than picking at hers. I'd have to keep an eye on her, make sure she don't start getting ill with all the worry of what was about to come.

We paid Bully for our scoff and bid him farewell. We then went back to Benhill to get our freedom passes, and before long we were heading by tube from the Elephant towards North London, a part of the world none of us knew that well. I had only been over that way once or twice, since my last visit to the grave, just before I was banged up.

As we left the nearest tube station to the cemetery, we found a sign directing us to Northside and we duly followed that. Within ten minutes we had arrived at the main gates.

Tubbs surveyed all that was in front of him. Which was basically hundreds and hundreds of gravestones.

'Man, we are never going to find it among all them. We are going to need a bit of help.'

I couldn't argue. It would be like looking for a needle in a haystack.

I looked around and noticed a one level concrete construction at the bottom of a black tarmacked road and guessed that would be as good place to start as anywhere.

As we approached the building, I noticed a sign above a door that said simply 'Main Office.'

'I would suggest that is our first port of call.' I said nodding in its general direction.

We pulled the door open and found ourselves in a small office. Piped classical music filled our ears, as we looked around for someone to talk to. A late middle-aged woman, who was immaculate in appearance, finally emerged from an inner office.

'Good Morning' she said, looking over her glasses at us, 'how may I help' she asked somewhat snootily

'Morning,' I said 'we're looking for an aunt of mine who was buried here in the early 1960s. Sadly, I lost touch with her family and this is the first time I have been back this way since the day of the funeral, we're from South London see.' I nodded towards Tubbs and Pauline as I finished speaking.

'That's nice for you.' said Mrs. Snooty with a smirk on her face.

I instantly felt like giving her a right dose of the verbal's at that remark, but quickly remembered why we were here.

'Yes, quite.' I said, humouring her for the time being. 'As it happens, I think I, er, we, are going to need a bit of help finding her grave.'

Mrs. Snooty looked me, Tubbs and Pauline up and down, from head to foot and then coughed into a small handkerchief. She then looked at her computer screen, sitting on top of her plastic wood desk.

'Name' she suddenly said quite sternly.

'Whose?' I replied. I'm afraid I couldn't hold back any longer from a little windup.

'Pardon?' She said.

'You asked for a name then. Did you mean mine, the deceased or my good friends here?' I said as I pointed to Tubbs and Pauline.

'Umm, oh I see. The deceased of course' she replied,

slightly ruffled.

'Right, gotcha, finally getting somewhere aint we', I said smilingly sarcastically. 'Samuels, Myra, Mrs.'

'Year?'

'Eh?' I said, at which point, Pauline kicked me slightly in the shins, as if to say, pack it in, just play nicely with Mrs. Snot Bags here

'The deceased?' I replied '1962. September 1962'

She typed in the name and the year using her keyboard and read from the screen in front of her.

'Let's see...ummm yes' she said looking closely at her monitor, lifting her glasses as she did so.

'Yes...yes, here we are. We've got a Myra Samuels over on plot forty-five, section twelve. She's been here since 1962. That must be the one.

Pretty straightforward to find really. Turn left out of this building and follow the path as far as you can go and there will be a row of graves in front of you. It'll be your job to find Mrs. ...er...Samuels.

Think you can manage that, yes?'

'Yeah, I think between the three of us, we'll have a good go. Thank you ma'am.'

I bowed ever so sarcastically.

'Right. If that is all, I'll bid good day to you. You can see yourselves out' and she went back to the pile of papers, in front of her.

I guessed that was all we were going to get out of her, but it was enough. We turned began to walk out of the office, with Tubbs, ever the gent, raising his felt pork pie hat to the demon behind the desk. A touch of class that she wouldn't have been use to. Even if she had been looking.

'Right.' Pauline said as we exited through the office 'Glad to get out of there, thought you were going to throttle her at one point.'

She was now staring at me.

'Well, she was giving me the right old pip, with her superior bleedin' attitude and digs at South London. Got to have a dig at our manor aint they. Like she was the flaming Queen of Sheba. Suppose her farts smell of rose petals?'

'Oh ignore her, come on. Left, she said.'

Pauline was taking control of the situation as only a woman can.

We walked down as far as we could before finding a sign saying section twelve and then we were near our final destination, final being the operative word here.

'Man, I hate these places.' Tubbs, his face slightly screwed up at the sight of hundreds of grey and white gravestones in front of him, looked uncomfortable.

'Think that is the general idea mate.' I said, smiling at his unease.

'And to think, I've heard of some people who visit these places as a hobby? Think I'll stick to my crosswords.'

Tubbs looked like he had enough already.

We decided to split up and carry on the search of this plot, the last resting place of old Myra. Ten minutes went slowly by when suddenly Pauline said softly.

'Vin…Vin…' and then a little louder 'VINNY… found it.'

Tubbs and myself looked round in Pauline's direction and then walked over towards her. We looked at the headstone she was now facing. It had the right details on it, along with a lot of hebrew writing.

'Myra Samuels

Wife and Mother

Forever In Our Hearts

Born 1890

Laid to Rest 1962'

We all just looked at it for quite some time. That was it. This is what we had to come to find.

There was a collections of small stones on top of the head stone, so I presumed it had been visited fairly recently.

I took a little walk around the entire grave, sizing it up, and found that it had a couple of feet gap all around it.

'Plenty of room' I whispered to myself.

'Well, there it is. In there is the answer to our entire problem.

One question remains however. How the bleeding hell do we get it out?'

All that brain power being used in thinking of a way of getting to the 'tom', meant I hit the sack early when we all got back to Benhill at about 7.30 that evening.

I was shattered.

Thankfully this time, I managed to make it into an actual bed and within seconds I was out like a light.

After what seemed like ten minutes, I was stirring and slowly waking up. I picked up my bedside clock, which was laying face down on the floor, and it read 6 am.

Christ I'd been asleep for nearly twelve hours.

All those years in the shovel had the effect of turning me into a very light sleeper. Really it was the result of keeping my wits about me, not allowing myself to fall into a deep kip. S'pose in my subconscious I was thinking that anything could happen, so I had better be ready even if this meant I denied myself a deep sleep. To be honest, with all the coughing, farting, burping noises coming from within a cell to the sound of the warder's boots shuffling on the tiled and polished floors outside, there was very chance of a decent kip anyway.

But not last night. Last night, for the first time since I got back from Whitstable really, I slept like a log.

But even after that, here I was still waking up at the crack of a sparrows fart...

I commenced to shit, shave and shampoo and was out of my front door by 6.30- ish. Soon, I was strolling through the passageways en route to get a paper, and some bacca.

That was another trait I picked up in the nick; roll what little bacca you've got thin as you can to make the bacca go further. Bacca was scarce inside; it was the equivalent of cash. Very valuable. Even though I could now afford plenty of the stuff, I still rolled prison thin fags, with Old Holborn being my choice.

As I sauntered through on my way, I noticed a shape, which looked a lot like Dot as I got nearer to it. She was laying flat out on one of the settees in the communal lounge area. My mind raced as I tried to think of what was she doing there. I walked over to it and to find it was Dot. She was lying there fully clothed. I stood there for a second or two, but she didn't murmur, she was spark out.

What's up here then? I was about to gently shake her awake, but decided in the end to leave her and crack on and get my linen draper.

The way she was snoring, she wasn't going anywhere in a hurry.

It was only a short walk over the traffic lights and back, and all the way there and back I thought of Dot. Poor cow, I knew she was having it tough with old Margie, who was slowly but steadily breaking up with the Old Timers.

That can't be easy to live with I thought, as I walked out into the path of a 12 bus! Thankfully, I just managed to step back onto the kerb as it came speeding by.

Jesus. The Cotter sisters nearly got me browned off there.

After my little scare, I walked back into Benhill and decided it was best to get Pauline. Well, if I'm found shaking Dot, it might look a bit noncey, know what I mean, so better a fellow female do it. Luckily I found Pauline was up, though she was still in her night things. After she put on her toweling dressing gown, I explained to her what I had seen, and we were soon on the way down to the lounge.

'Oh my God,' said Pauline as she saw what I had discovered 'what d'ya suppose is occurring here then?'

'Only one way to find out girl aint there, go on lively her up.'

I was by now, somewhat impatient to find out.

Pauline tutted in my direction, before she gently rubbed Dot on her upper arm.

'Dot…' Pauline said gently,'Dot love…'

Dot slowly began to stir. As she did so, she nearly rolled backwards off the settee, obviously not sure where she was, but thankfully steadied herself.

'Ooh, where…where am I?' she said, slowly rubbing her eyes and then she looked up and clocked me and Pauline, and she looked even more surprised.

'Jesus…och…. hang on, oh dear.' Slowly the events which had brought her here, slowly came back to her.

'Oh Dot love, what you doing here?' asked Pauline sympathetically.

Dot rubbed her eyes again as she tired valiantly to focus on her surroundings.

'Oh Pauline, what a night.' said finally said wearily.

I could see she was parched, so I volunteered to get some teas from the vending machine.

'Ta Vincent, I dying here for a wet. Dear me, where to begin?'

'Might as well go from the start Dot' I heard Pauline say 'always best love.'

I collected the three plastic cups of tea from the machine

and set them down on the coffee table to the side of where Pauline was now standing.

Dot began.

'It's Marge…I'll have to sort something soon, it's getting very bad now, dangerous in fact.'

'Well, guessed it was something to do with her Dot,' I said 'just suspected like. Nothing too bad I hope?'

'That's the problem Vinny' she said 'I just don't know. She went missing last night around 8pm.'

'What!?' Said a startled Pauline, now beginning to get all frantic.

'Aye, I was watching 'Eastenders' and I heard our front door shut. I got up and opened it and looked out to find Margie walking towards this lounge. She had no overcoat or jumper on, so I thought she was off to the laundry or to see one of her friends. I called after her, but she just kept on going.

I gave it ten minutes or so, hoping she would come back, but no, so I set off for the laundry room and passed by here on the way. No sign of her in either place. Strange I thought and went back home and rang her mobile but only got the answer phone. I was now getting a little concerned. It was now coming up to ten o'clock and still no sign of her. I even rang your doorbell Vin, but got no answer'

'Bloody typical that is. The one night when you needed me, I was out cold. Sorry Dot. I'm usually wide awake til at least two in the morning. Must be all that fresh North London air I had yesterday.'

'Not to worry, I doubt you could have really helped as it happened.

Eventually, there was nothing else for it,' she continued 'I pulled the emergency cord and told them I thought my sister had gone outside and therefore considered her missing, what with the condition she is suffering from. The people on the other end of that cord were great.

They told me not to worry, but got me to describe Marge and they then put a call into the local police.'

'Flaming 'ell Dot, you should have called me.' Pauline said.

'Thought about it Pauline, but I knew she wouldn't have been round one of yours that late at night, not without one of you calling me and telling me that news, so I knew there was no point. Somehow, someway, I just knew she was out in the street.'

'Anyway,' Dot sighed 'I had a call from Walworth Police, checking the description and saying their patrols were keeping an eye out for a woman that fitted it. After another hour or so, my phone rang again and God it made me jump, but it was just the pull cord people stationed out in Croydon, saying that they hadn't heard anything yet and then at just after midnight, the police rang me to say they had found Marge wandering around the Elephant roundabouts. She was very cold, and agitated but apart from that, in good shape, if mightily confused.'

'Well, that great news that she is ok Dot. You got any idea what made her go out?' I asked.

'Och, turns out my dear sweet Margie, thought it was 8 o'clock in the morning and not the evening as was the case and decided to go for a little stroll. She told me that she got a little confused as to her bearings after ten minutes and then couldn't find her way back.

I collected her from the main front door and me and the policewoman, who was there with Marge, took her to our flat. Bless my wee sister, she was apologising all the time.'

'Sorry Dottie, sorry. I …I…lost my way' she said.

'Shush' I said, trying to comfort her and then got her undressed and into her bed.

I then escorted the woman PC back out the front door,

thanked her from the bottom of my heart and then sat here on the way back to my flat and cried my eyes out...(sniff)... couldn't help it (sob) I was so relieved she was alright. I must have fell asleep here. I better get back and make sure she is alright...'

Pauline sat down with her and put an arm around her shoulder and did her best to calm Dot down.

'It's ok Dot, dry yours eyes first love. I'm sure she's fine. We don't want Margie to see you like this, do we? Eh?'

Pauline then gave Dot a fresh tissue from her dressing gown pocket.

I just stood there like a right plum to be honest, and didn't really know what to say or do. I tried to think what it must be like to be in a situation like this. There but for the grace of God, go I...

Pauline took Dot back to her flat and I made my way home too.

As I turned the key in my door, my mobile went. In truth, I usually need a pair of glasses on to find my glasses, but today I was lucky. They were laying on top of the telly and looked at the number flashing up on the screen. It was a number I didn't recognise. I hate answering those ones, when you don't know who's calling, usually someone trying to sell you something, so I left it. Whoever it was decided to not leave a message, so I guessed it was an insurance salesman. However, twenty minutes later, it went again. Same number and again I swerved it.

This time however, the caller did leave me a message. I listened back to it and was surprised to hear it was Terry Davis, eldest son of Pauline. He said his mum had given him my number and that he wanted a word if that was alright, and to bell him back to sort that as soon as I could.

Christ I thought, the boy will be well pissed off with me. What with dragging his old mum, who was a bag of nerves at the best of times, into this crazy scheme of getting back Liz Taylor's gems.

I had to think about this. Can't be too hasty, had to think of me in his place. Here I was, someone she hardly knew, getting her into a major caper and her at her age too.

What a rascal I must be, he must have been thinking. So I was prepared for the worse. What that could end up being, was anybody's guess. It might be a right bollocking or a right-hander.

Sod it, only one way to find out. After three rings, a deep voice, with a strong south-east London accent answered

'Hello, Terry speaking.'

'Er...hello er Terry, its me Vinny, you rung me earlier. I'm a mate of your mums.'

I was very hesitant speaking to him, nervous really. He on the other hand seemed very comfortable, which had the effect of him sounding very confident.

'Hello Vin, heard a lot about you mate.'

'All lies I promise ya' I said trying to make a small joke.

'Yeah. I did wonder?' he laughed 'listen, the old girl told me about the little situation you are in, I'd like to know more, can we make a meet?'

He wasn't messing about, the boy. Cutting to the chase. Made him right of course.

'Er, yeah, sure. Where were you thinking of son? I said.

'Somewhere quiet, an out of the way boozer maybe?'

Sounded like Terry knew the coup.

'Well, I use the 'King Louis' on Camberwell Hill' I told him. 'Real quiet during the day, or so many dodgy deal's going on during the evening, that no one takes a blind bit of notice. Know it?'

'Yeah I know it, how about this evening, say 7pm?'

Sounded like Terry was keen to get it sorted it.

'Ok son, you're on, I sit to the left of the dartboard, got grey crew cut... you"ll find me.'

'Sweet, mums described ya. I said, no one can be that ugly with only one head,' and he gave a little chuckle 'see you then.'

Funny, but as I put down the receiver, I was suddenly overcome with a real touch of the nerves about meeting the cheeky sod. Back in my pomp, none of this would have bothered me, but after years of going straight, I was out of touch with the ducking and diving, especially with people I didn't know.

For the next few hours, I run over the various reasons why I thought he wanted to see me. Number one seemed obvious. He was going to stop me getting his old mum involved and I could see that, and I definitely understood that. I mean he doesn't know me and here I was getting her involved in something, well, however you wrap it up, it was against the law.

Then the terrible thought crossed my mind that he might be a grass, but on reflection, no, I couldn't see it. A son of Pauline and her Bill's doing a Bertie. No, that didn't sit right.

And then I thought, say him and maybe a gang of his mates are going to rob us, turn me right over, as I reach into the coffin and ...

Hang on, hang on. Blimey I was getting in a right old state here...I decided to have a belt of scotch to calm myself down, a bit of dutch courage never hurt anyone.

I showered and put on a clean shirt, and decided if I wanted to make a good impression, I would go suited and booted. I used to love a decent suit back in the day, and it felt the right time to revive all that again.

I left Benhill just as it started to rain. Thankfully I had brought my umbrella for the ten minutes walk to the 'King Louis'.

As I got near to the pub, I noticed old Siddy Bennett's dark blue mobility scooter parked outside, with its plastic canopy pulled up and over it. I knew it was Sid's, because of the 'No One Likes Us' sticker on the bumper, denoting his love of all things Millwall.

Only, on closer inspection, I noticed it wasn't Sid actually sitting in it. Strange I thought, as I entered into the warm, dry environment of the pub. I looked round immediately for Sid and found him, engrossed in a copy of The Racing Post.

'Oi Siddy boy. That your chariot out there?'

'Evening Vin,' said Sid 'yeah that's mine, wassup with it? Some cheeky little sods trying to nick it are they?'

'Nah' I replied 'well I don't think so. It's just that there is some mush sitting in it, as bold as brass he is.'

'Little fella, black barnet?' Sid barely raised his head from the paper as he spoke.

'Yeah, sounds about right' I said.

'That's alright Vin, that's Jason, Big Keith's youngest. He said he fancied a fag and asked if he could use my scooter as a fag shelter, due to it raining. He's a good boy, he got me a short for my trouble.'

I could only shake my head and smile, as I got near to the bar and found young Neville behind the ramp.

'You hear that Nev?' I said smiling.

'Does it all the time when it's raining,' he replied. 'cheeky old sod, never has to buy a drink all night.'

I ordered up a scotch to steady myself, took a swig and sunk it in one belt.

I was about to order but I was conscious of this six-foot plus, big man looking my way.

'Vinny?' he asked.

I nodded.

He was good looking fella, about the same age as my Matthew. He held out his right hand and we shook.

'Alright mate, Terry Davis, good to say hello.'

'What you drinking Terry?' I said.

'Oh ta, I'll have a vodka and slim line, trying to keep the weight off' and he laughed as he said it.

I winked at Neville to get his attention and put our order in. I told Terry to find a table and I would bring them over. I gave him my now refolded umbrella to take with him. Seconds later, I brought over the drinks. We both raised them and wished each 'good health' and then we made small talk.

'So, you live round here then Terry?'

'Not far away, got a small flat with my missus up Denmark Hill. Not fallen too far from the tree, what with Mum and Dad both being from around The 'Well.'

'You local then?' he asked.

'Yeah, born here as it happens. Been all over since, but somehow and it wasn't planned, I ended up right back on the manor.'

'Look, Vin.' Terry leaned forward as he began to cut to the chase and spoke as softly as someone like him could manage. 'It's about mum.'

'Nice lady your mum, proper person.' I said, and I meant it.

'Yeah, yeah that's one of the reasons I wanted to have a little chat Vin. When she told me and my brother Chrissy your story, we were impressed. Some tale. At first we had a million questions as it took some believing, but the more we thought about it, the more it seemed kosher. Put it this way, we could find no real reason to doubt you. I mean, you could be a Tom Pepper, but why would you go to such extremes with a story like that. No need really. So, we decided to believe you.

But listen, its all a bit strong innit? I mean, it's fucking grave robbing at the end of a long day mate'

'Hold up, hold up.' I said, a little agitated at the phrase Terry had just used.

'I'm getting back some property that's all. Technically it's in a grave, but...'

Terry held his hand up to silence me.

'I'll be straight with you Vin,' Terry continued 'we've tried to talk her out of it, I mean, it's a bleedin' mad idea, whatever you describe it as.'

'Yeah, I can see you'd think that,' I said 'and it is potty, that we are even thinking about doing something like this at our age. But I think we've all come to realise we aint getting any younger and well, this might be our last bit of life to lead. So...'

'Hang on,' he said 'I aint finished. She tells us, she's made up her mind made her and if there's one family trait we all share it's being stubborn.'

Terry sipped at his vodka and had a twinkle in his eye as he did so.

'So,' I continued 'you haven't talked her out of it?'

'No we haven't. Actually because of that me and Chrissy have decided instead of trying to stop you, we'll actually help you. From what I can work out from talking to Mum, the sparklers are in a coffin at least 6 foot under?'

'Yeah, that's about the size of it.' I said somewhat perplexed at the turn of events.

'Thought so,' Terry continued 'well, my day job is on the sites, driving diggers and the heavy plant. If you can square us getting in on the plot, I'll do the rest. Got to say, you are all fucking crackers, but we insist on coming along and keeping an eye on the old girl, well, all of you actually.'

I sat there and just nodded. I wasn't expecting to hear this tonight.

'And before you offer, cos I know you will, we don't want any cut'

Now, I really didn't know what to say.

'Me and Chrissy just want to make sure our mum is safe and secure for the remainder of her days, and I don't mean in Holloway, know what I mean? Same again is it?'

I nodded to the drinks offer, still taken aback.

Well, that went better than I expected.

Time to crack on with the plan, there really was nothing to stop us now.

7

Dig For Victory!

Thinking back on it now, I could hear in Terry's voice at the pub that he had begun to see me in a different light. What he made of Tubbs, Dot, Margie and even his old mum getting involved, is anyone's guess?

Like a lot of people, he would have had us down for settling for the quiet life, all cribbage and knitting. Couldn't really blame them I suppose. To the outside world we looked well doddery, past it even, but they all conveniently forget that we have all led different lives in our past, before we ended up in this sheltered home.

Some more 'interesting' than others…

In an attempt to give my brain a rest from all the thinking I was doing as to the next step at the cemetery, I had settled down in one of the big armchairs in the communal lounge where I had found a quiet corner. I started to read a Radio Times, I found lying about, but within minutes, my eyes were drooping and before long I was experiencing that strange state of not really being asleep, but not fully awake either.

My eyes were tight shut, when suddenly I heard Pauline's voice enter the room, followed closely by that of her two boys.

'So you've talked to Vin then Tel?' I heard Pauline say to her eldest.

'Yeah he seems alright ma. A bit of a character, I'll give him that. Told him you're all crackers, but that I wouldn't stand in the way of the idea of getting at the, er 'goods' so to speak.

If they existed in the first place, that is...'

'Eh? What d'ya mean, if they existed?' Pauline sounded confused.

'Oh come on, lets face it mum,' said her younger boy Chrissy 'we've only got Vinny's word for it all aint we? He might not have half inched anything for all we know. I mean Elizabeth Taylor? Come on. For all we know he might be telling you a tale.'

It went quiet for a second or two.

'No. Not having it. I believe him. Whatever he is now, I reckon he's been a rascal in his time, I aint got him down as a pork pie peddler'

Thank you Pauline, I thought.

'Well...' said Terry yawning, as he stretched out his big frame in his chair, 'there's only one way to find out aint there?'

They all fell quiet. It appeared they hadn't noticed me in the corner from the way they were talking.

I decided to keep my eyes shut. Playing possum you might say.

I inwardly smiled to myself though as I thought, who could blame Pauline's two for thinking my story was a get up. To the untrained ear, it would sound so far-fetched.

'I know one thing, and let's have it right, if it all falls through here mum, then maybe the time has come to leave Camberwell mate?'

Terry spoke as if this particular conversation was a well-trodden path.

'Now you're talking silly Tel,' said Pauline quickly 'born here, and you both know I will die here. Good enough for your granddad, good enough for me.'

Obviously, Pauline wasn't impressed with Terry's train of

thought.

'Yeah but it was different then mum, times have changed aint they? And so has this manor.' Chrissy decided to take a turn. 'And you've got to say, not for the better.'

'Well you might be right there,' Pauline conceded. 'I know I always say it was better back then, but it WAS. And I loved that old house we grew up in. Number 15 Mansion Street, just round the corner from here. Long gone it has. Put up some poxy tower block on top of it in the 60s. Stupid people that council. Got me out once and they're trying to do it again'

'That's what I mean,' said Terry ' stay on this manor and you are at the mercy of the bloody council. Get down the coast, do you good.'

'Down the coast? Down the flipping coast. Who the hell do I know down the coast? All my mates are here. I go down the coast, I'll be brown bread in a month from boredom!'

The boys went suddenly quiet. I think they knew they were onto a loser here.

'Puuffffttt.' Sounded like Terry was boiling up at the frustration of trying to get his mum out of the area. It also sounded like he'd given up.

'Alright, alright. We'll take that as a no then, shall we? Pity we can't bring Mansion Street back for you really?

I heard Pauline laugh.

'I'd move in today love.'

'How much rent back then mum?' Chrissy asked.

'You know what? I can't remember. Doesn't matter really, your granddad never paid it on time anyway.'

Pauline made them all laughed with that.

'Good days. Happy days. My first school was at Comber Grove. Coal fire in the classroom we had and we were put to bed in the early afternoon. Yeah! Laid us down for a little kip. Don't seem possible now does it?

My schooling was terrible, well I had bloody Adolf trying to kill me every night, plays havoc that does when you're trying to do your homework.'

'Can't have been easy.' said Terry and the boys laughed.

'Your Nan wouldn't let us go to be evacuated. "No" she said 'if we get bombed, we get bombed together. She wouldn't even go down the shelters. We hid under the bloody railway arches. You'd be having a wash, one leg in a tin bath and the siren would go off. Bleedin' nightmare and the sound of that wailing when I hear on it on the old films, still gives me the horrors it does. We had one one terrible night in particular, we knew they had bombed close by. When we woke up next day, well, half the bloody next street was gone. We weren't half lucky that night. Others were less so.

Now you know why I still can't spell for toffee. Reckon I only did a year and half in total at school, rarely went.

It was embarrassing sometimes when I had to wear your uncle Gerry's clothes to school and in the street, because mine were too small.

My poor old mum couldn't afford to borrow any more from old Gertie the moneylender to gct me new stuff. No Social then. The kids today don't know they're born.'

'Jesus,' said Chrissy 'can you imagine that now?'

'You'd have that Esther Rantzen round like a shot,' said Terry ' I reckon if all that kicked off again, half of London would be bloody empty.'

'S'right Tel,' said Pauline 'kids today wouldn't stand for it. Of course, we had no option, we made the best of it. Your Granddad even had chickens in the back yard and he made me a lovely dolls house before he went in the army. Which I wish I still had...'

For the first time Pauline since sounded sad when telling the stories of her youth.

She brightened up quickly though.

Come to think of it, I think the chicks ended up living in that dolls house, bless 'em.'

Obviously, the boys talking of her leaving the area had stirred up old memories for Pauline. They, wisely, decide to let her get on with it.

'Probably told you, I left school at 15. I found work straight away as a seamstress. On 17 and 6 a week I was, which was good money then. I was making blouses and pyjamas.

I loved having a couple of bob in my pocket. Once I paid my keep, I still had enough to go to the pictures in the daytime on a Saturday and we sat there and watched the main film at least three times and come out in the dark. I used to make all my own clothes all based on the styles coming out of Hollywood. Tinsel town in SE5, what must we have looked like, eh?.'

'You were the start of the first proper teenagers mum, Teddy boys and all that.' said Terry.

'That's right love. We was, your Dad did a bit of that, well he had hair then!

We used to go to The Camberwell Playhouse and The Brixton Empress. Saw 'em all up there we did, old Max Miller, The Crazy Gang, Lonnie Donnegan. When I speak to some of the youngsters who volunteer here, very few of them ever go to the theatre now. One of them said it was too expensive for them, besides her Dad paid forty quid a month for Sky telly, so that was their theatre and cinema trips all rolled into one. Not the same though is it?'

'Well, its like my two mum, hard work getting them out of the house sometimes, always on the bloody computer, playing games and that.' said Terry.

'Blimey, you two were never indoors were ya? Always out playing football or cricket in the summer. Could never get you in for your tea. Shouted my bloody head off calling your names out I did…little sods.

Where was I? Oh yeah, I also started buying a few 78's. Guy Mitchell, Johnny Ray and that Frankie Laine. Liked the Americans we did. My old Dad made the record player.'

'What?' said Chrissy, somewhat surprised.

'He did, telling ya. Clever old stick he was. Think he found an old washing machine or something and used the parts from that.

When you think about it, all those Yanks we had over here at the end of the War left a big legacy didn't they? I mean we used go round saying 'Give Us Some Gum Chum' and all that.

We had the American Shoe Shop just off the Green, run by old Bertie Smith. About as American as me he was, silly old sod.

My favourite shop though, was the Marc Antonio's. Lovely ice cream that was. So classy.

As I got older, I then started going to pubs, The Rose was our favourite, that's where I met your dad, bless him. It was all dart matches and charabanc trips down to Margate. The Rose had a great football team. Me and old catholic Mary made all the numbers for the shirts out of old vests and sewed them on.

They even won a cup once, funny it was.

Some fella brought out a great big table to present the prizes from, only the cup they won turned out to be the size of an egg cup, haha Didn't half look silly sitting on that table. Oh we did laugh.

The team broke up when we lost a lot of the boys to National Service, though some of them went AWOL and got away with it, hiding up in roofs and that. Think old Ronie Loveday might still be up there!

Oh here, talking of the army and that, have I ever told you about old Doo Lally Tap?'

'Doo Lally what?!' said Chrissy laughing.

"Oh, he was mad as a hatter he was. We would all be hanging about on the street corner and every night at the same time, he would walk past us dressed in loads of different uniforms.

One night he'd be an American soldier, then he'd be a St Johns Ambulance man, then a Japanese army one and the next night, he'd be dressed as a sailor… soppy bleeder he was.'

'You're joking. Would have paid good money to see that. I mean, where he'd get the clobber from?' asked Terry.

'Funnily enough, I haven't thought of that before? He must have got it all from all those army surplus stores that sprung up, bleeding awash we were with war clothes, kitted himself in all that I suppose. Shouldn't laugh. Probably had a bang on the head in the war.'

Pauline sounded like she was struggling not to laugh and even though I was pretending to be asleep in the corner; I had to bite down hard on a finger not to laugh out loud myself.

'Lunatic the fella haha.' laughed Chrissy. 'One thing I remember you and granddad always talking about, was Hopping. What was all that about?'

'Now you're talking. Loved Hopping, we did.' continued Pauline. 'None of that Spanish fortnight back then mate, oh no. Same place every year, Gibsons Farm down in Kent. Picking the hops for the brewers. Loved every second of it.

No baths, all mucking in, washing from a stand pipe out by the huts. Your father only went once, hated it he did. Too fussy about his hair and clobber. Just like you pair he was, loved his clothes. But me, I was out all day I was, covered in dirt. The sun always seemed to shine. We'd come back as brown as a berry.'

'Not surprised, you just said you never washed!' laughed Chrissy.

'Cheeky little sod' laughed Pauline.

'Seriously Chris, it was good times, really good times...'

'Yeah I know mum, but as we said, it's not like that now though is it? All these little mugs on the doodle bugs, nicking and that. Worry about ya, we do. That's all.'

Her Chrissy sounded genuinely concerned.

'Listen love' Pauline said sympathetically. 'I know. And I know I've painted a pretty rosy picture of the area back then, but I aint silly, it was rough an all, I know that, and there were some flash Harry's about. Some right bad 'uns. One or two who became famous years later, used to stand up the Green, looking all menacing'

'Like who?' asked Chrissy.

'No names, would never do that, but you know of 'em son. But you know what, instead of robbing an old boy for his pension like they do now, that crowd would actually slip the old boy a couple of bob, and actually look after them.

That's what's changed. They never robbed their own, not like now. Too much greed about now. They've got everything now, and yet, in many ways, they've got nothing.

But... I've still never felt like moving out.'

I sat there smiling. You tell 'em Pauline, you tell 'em mate.

Over the next couple of weeks I made the point of going down to Myra's grave as much as possible. I took photos around the site of the grave and paced out the yardage to, from and round the plot.

Felt a bit awkward the first time, all because I had no flowers with me. Blimey, I really felt really out of place. The next time up there, I took a wreath and no one took a blind bit of notice.

I sat and watched how many staff there were milling about as I ate my packed lunch on a wooden bench dedicated to a long lost Uncle Joe or Auntie Kit. I also made a note of the opening and closing times. From September, which was a few weeks away, I noted they opened at ten and shut at four, just as it began to get dark.

It became obvious, this was going to be a morning job. We had to get in there and do the work before the place opened. I didn't want to do this in the dark. Because of the lack of lights at the cemetery, it was pitch black once it closed.

I went on my own on these sorties, preferred it that way and I was careful to wear a hat or a pair of specs on each subsequent visit trying to disguise my appearance.

On my third trip up there, as I was grabbing a smoke in the car park, I saw a couple of the gardeners coming towards me. I could over hear their conversation, at the same time, desperately trying not to be noticed. They were saying something like "poxy building work coming up" and "it'll play merry hell with the winter bedding plants."

I decided to follow them as close as I could with out being sussed and finally heard that this work was planned for a couple of week's time.

Blimey, I thought, this could be it. If they are doing building work on site, we just might be able to sneak in and do the business without drawing too much attention to ourselves.

Only thing I was missing was a date they were starting on. The only thing for it was to go into the main office and talk to my old mate the receptionist and see if I could get any info. from her.

I dogged out my snout, straightened my cheese cutter cap, adjusted my glasses and headed for the office block, bowling in like I owned the gaff.

She was behind her desk, typing furiously on her computer keyboard. I looked down at her desk and this time noticed her nameplate. So she was called Mrs. Hardy.

She didn't look up and I felt sure she was determined to ignore me for as long as possible. What a snotty cow this really was.

I gently coughed, trying to get a rise out of her as much as anything else.

She slowly lifted her head and looked down her long pointed hooter at me.

'Yes. Can I assist?'

'Oh hello.' I said desperately hoping she wouldn't clock it was me from our previous encounter. 'I really hope I'm not disturbing you?'

'Well, I am really rather busy, will it take long?'

I stood there thinking considering her job must be talking to bereaved relatives all day, I don't this one would notice sympathy or compassion, if they stood up in her soup.

I swallowed hard.

'Well, not too long. Its just that I want to bring a coach party of overseas relatives to visit my fathers grave in a couple of weeks time, and wondered if I could reserve a decent parking spot?'

The look on her face was one of disgust.

'No, of course not. Really. You make us sound like we're a theme park or something similar. We are most definitely not a tourist attraction. We have a policy of not reserving spaces, apart from staff, due to the amount of visitors we already have each day.

And, well, besides all of that, your timing is terrible. We have building work starting on-site from the third of next month. The crew on that job will be taking over most of the car park for at least four weeks. I simply can't have you in the middle of all that.

I'm afraid, you'll have to make alternative arrangements for your friends and family at a later date.'

'The third you say.?' I quickly made a mental note of that date. 'Oh dear, that is a pity. The family will be most upset. It's too late to re-arrange their flights. Oh bother!'

Mrs. Hardy then stood up from behind her desk and began ushering me out of her domain.

'Well, there really is nothing we can do now, is there. Now, if you don't mind, I do have rather a lot of work to catch up on'

'But, but...' I protested, but before I knew it, she was escorting me out of the office and back into the grounds.

I kept the sarcasm going up to the last second.

'Thank you so much, really...'

Well, that worked like a flaming charm. Nice. Think I got away with that and I now I had the date.

As soon as I was outside the main gates, I flicked through my pocket diary and wrote D-Day on the third of September, circling entry with my pen a couple of times.

That left me just two weeks to make arrangements.

When I was back at Benhill, I rung the sisters, Pauline and Tubbs and asked them to join me for a cuppa in my flat.

Even though Dot was resistant to my plans, I had decided to keep her on side and make her feel part of it, but only if she wanted to. She turned up, so I had my answer to that, but she had decided to leave poor Margie behind. That poor cow was getting more confused by the day, so the last thing she needed was to hear any of what was to follow.

Once they were all safely gathered in, the tea was poured and biscuits laid out, I told them the good news.

'So,' I said 'we've got a fortnight and then over the top we go.'

'Lord Almighty!' said Tubbs and he gulped down the Bourbon biscuit he was holding.

I noticed Pauline was very quiet; in fact, she wasn't actually looking too well. And she hadn't said a word since I had told them the news.

I looked over in her direction.

'You alright Pauline?' I gently said.

'Me? Yeah, I'm fine, it was just a shock to hear it was all only two weeks away.' She was very hesitant in her reply.

'Listen Pauline, you know no one here will think anything bad of you, if you decide this caper isn't for you. Really, there is no pressure. Besides, I've got your Terry and Chrissy helping me now, so...'

I noticed Pauline smile for the first time since she arrived, at the mention of her boys names.

I continued, '...and they'll help me with the er, digging and that...'

'Sweet Jesus.' Tubbs was off again. He too was also obviously having a touch of the horrors.

'Listen, listen. This is crazy. You two look scared out of your life! I can sense your bottle is going. I suppose I shouldn't really be surprised...'

'Man, I've said I'm in and I'm in!'

Tubbs was sweating up a treat, but he sounded determined to go through with it.

'Ok, relax, relax, ok? Look, I've already decided if you do come along, all I need you for is to keep dog eye for us, you wont be doing any digging of anything up or...having to touch anything remotely, er, dodgy, understood?'

Tubbs gulped and nodded and reached for more biscuits.

Pauline was sitting there wringing her hands together.

'Paul, I hate seeing you like this.' I said.

'S'alright Vinny. Seriously I'll be fine on the day, and I'll have my two there won't I, so, I'll be fine...'

'Well, if you are sure?'

Pauline quickly nodded. I decided to let her be.

Meanwhile, Dot, bless her, just sat there and didn't say a word. But the look on her face, well that said quite enough.

And she was beginning to give me the needle, if truth be told.

'Alright Dot, spit it out.' I said 'I know you are dying to say 'I told you so'.'

'Me?' she said, acting all innocent.

'Yes you!' I said somewhat sharply.

Dot smiled and then summoned up her true feelings.

'It's someone's final resting place, you shouldn't disturb that' she said.

'I hear what you are saying Dot,' I replied 'but archeologists dig up bones all day long, this really is no different.'

'Oh come on Vinny. You are not trained professionals.' With that, Dot had a point.

'No, that's true. Can't argue with that. What we are, is a group of people who will not touch any of old bones, but only remove what is amongst it, namely the black velvet bag, which we hope will save this place.'

In all my life, I never expected to ever say a sentence like that!

'Well Vinny, did I not say you were all mad when this first got brought up? I still think that today, you're all crackers. You'll never get away with it.'

'Oh listen Dot.' said Pauline suddenly, before I got a chance to reply.

'As far as I can see, we've got two options. Do nothing and we lose this place, or have a go and try and change things. I've done the right thing all my bloody life, and look where that's got me. I was saying to my boys the other day, the bloody council knocked down my mum and dads place in the 50s and all these years later, they're doing the same thing to me. Arse'oles to 'em Dot! I did nothing to stop them back then, but not this time.'

Dot looked at the floor. She had been well and truly told.

Pauline sensing that Dot was a bit out numbered here,

then reached over and held Dot's hands.

'Look Dot, we know you've got Margie to look after. That's enough for anyone love.'

'Och, too right Pauline' said Dot 'and that isn't getting anyway better I can tell you. Bless her, she made me a jam salad last night'

'A what?' asked a surprised Pauline.

'You may well ask. We had a salad for our tea last night. Only, she got mixed up with the strawberry jam and beetroot. Ruined it she did, only poor old Margie didn't even notice.'

'Oh Dot…' Pauline looked really sad.

I must confess, I felt a small smile cross my lips.

'Listen Pauline, don't be sad. It is what it is. I just have to cope with it all don't I? Look, I wish you all the best in the world with what you are doing with Vinny, I do. Because from what I have seen in the last half hour, you going to need it.'

Dot then looked at Tubbs and Pauline and then back at me.

'Obviously, I've got enough on my plate, with my Margie. And nothing I have heard here tonight so far, has changed my mind about not getting involved, I'm sorry.'

None of us really could argue with that. None of us wanted to.

'Right.' I said as I stood up.

'Ok then Dot, that's fair enough. Can I now ask you to leave us to it? The less you know, the safer we all, and I mean ALL, will be'.

I could see Dot was a bit stunned by this, but I wanted to make her aware that I was serious in what we planned to do and there was no room for passengers. Might have been a bit harsh but in truth, I was trying to protect her. Dot slowly stood up and looked a little sheepish. She looked at us all one more, and then quickly made for my front door.

Myself, Pauline and Tubbs watched her leave my flat, with Pauline mouthing the word 'sorry' as Dot looked back one last time.

I waited til my front door was closed and then started to speak.

'Right, this is what...'

'Bit rude that, wasn't it Vinny?' Pauline wasn't happy with me.

'Listen Pauline, what we are about to get involved in is serious, no time for personal feelings. I'm doing her a favour in not telling her any more info. It'll do us a favour too, if it all comes on top and goes bandy. Don't want her to know anything that'll incriminate any of you two'

'And you' said Tubbs.

'Yeah, yes, of course, and me.' I said smiling his way.

'Ok' said Pauline finally 'I think I understand.'

I was keen to crack on, we'd spent too much time already talking about stuff, that wasn't critical to the job.

That was about to change.

'Right, as I was trying to say earlier, this is what we are going to do on the day. The builders start there on the third. I'll go down there that day on a little scouting mission. I'll get there really early and make sure I see what time they arrive and that will give me a rough idea of when we can get in, undisturbed. If all goes to plan, we'll dig on the fourth.'

I heard Tubbs gulp, again.

'And the fourth, is where you two come in. On the day, you'll be dressed as a lollipop man and woman...'

'A what?' Said Pauline in disbelief 'us? Dressing up?'

I did my best to plough on '...and we'll put you by the zebra crossing outside the main gate of the cemetery, so you can keep any eye on who's coming and going.'

'A lollipop lady, me?'

'Yes Pauline. I've not see anyone at that crossing on my last three visits, so the position is vacant. We'll get you a long white coat, the high Vis vest and an official looking hat. I reckon you two being of pensionable age, you wont look out of place up there.'

'Lord Almighty Jesus!' said Tubbs.

'Let's hope he is on duty the day mate,' I said smiling. 'We could do with him as back up.'

'Tubbs crossed himself and quietly uttered 'Amen.'

I pressed on.

'If all goes to plan, your Terry will get the digger going, and Chrissy and me will direct him to the grave of old ma Samuels. I reckon we'll only have a little time before we are tumbled...'

It suddenly went very quiet in my front room. It was as if everybody was thinking over the raid and visualising how it would go. It suddenly all seemed very real.

Got to be truthful, I loved the feeling of the on-rushing adrenalin that I felt everytime, we talked about the plans.

It was like I had gone back fifty odd years, and all the juices were flowing again. I couldn't lie. I was enjoying the buzz I was getting every time I spoke of the dig.

Funnily enough, there didn't appear to be any fear of the pinch by the the boys in blue. Now, believe me, I have no desire to spend the rest of my days in the boob, but this caper had the promise of resolving two loose ends for me. Saving this place and sorting out the business I had with my old mate Maury from all those years ago.

It was a risk I was prepared to take.

'Can I get anyone more tea and biscuits?' I asked, breaking the deafening silence in the room and trying to bring it all back to normality.

Pauline looked in shock and Tubbs was mid Custard Cream anyway, so I took that as a no.

I rang Terry and let him know what I had heard from the gardeners at the cemetery and what we had all discussed that afternoon. He said he would ring his brother to gen him up to speed.

He also arranged to come with me on the morning of the third, to the cemetery at the crack of a sparrows fart, to clock the coming and going of the builders arriving for their shift and also to see what security, if any, they had on-board.

Terry was also keen to see what kind of heavy plant they were using on the job.

'I've used most of the current models in my time Vin,' he said 'but always best to be a boy scout about it, you know, prepared eh?' he said laughing on the phone

DIB! DIB! DIB! Indeed, or was it more a case of DIG! DIG! DIG!

Whatever it was, we were all systems go.

Over the next couple of nights, not surprisingly, I found myself dreaming of the caper we were about to attempt and everything went really well until the moment the first bit of earth was dug into and then the dream would stop?

Same every time. In would go the digger and then bosh. End of the dream.

I woke myself up in the end, feeling it spinning around and around in my swede. Truth was, I was in danger of slowly driving myself flaming nuts with it all.

On the Saturday before the Monday the third, I took Pauline and Tubbs to a theatrical costumier in the West End and got them kitted out as close to look like lollipop people as we I could.

They gingerly put on the clobber and laughed nervously as they clocked themselves in the shop's big mirror.

To tell you the truth, Pauline was beginning to worry me. She looked like a frightened rabbit most of the time.

Tubbs, however, he was actually beginning to enjoy himself.

He looked great in his new kit. I think the truth was he actually missed his bus conductor's uniform, so this was a decent second best.

I settled the hire charge and we headed back to Benhill.

As we travelled back on the bus, I spoke to them both.

'Do me a favour and wear the clobber around your flats tomorrow. Get used to 'em, how they feel and that, so it aint strange when you put them on for real on Monday.'

Pauline nodded nervously, and I got the impression Tubbs would have liked to have worn his one home!

It was fresh but clear on the morning of the third when Terry and Chrissy picked me up at 6am in Chrissy's black cab, and we drove out to The Northside. We sped out there quickly, what with the lack of any traffic on the roads. The neon of the streetlights flickered away in the early morning gloom as we sped along. Gradually it began to brighten up as we began to approach the cemetery at just before seven.

We slowed down about a hundred yards or so from the main gates and plotted up opposite in a layby. Chrissy turned off his engine, and then climbed into the back of the cab, with Terry and me.

Looking over towards our target, we could see there was the occasional flash of a torch visible, so obviously there was a night watch man or security guard in the grounds, employed to keep an eye on things.

'Fuck that job for a game of soldiers.' Chrissy said as we sat there waiting. 'Fancy spending the night in a cemetery? Scare the flaming whatsits out of ya.'

Terry nodded. 'Poxy job that...and dead boring too...' a

broad smile upon on his face.

At 8.30, our man with the job of the year suddenly appeared in the open and unlocked the padlock around the black, ornate metal main gates. Terry wrote the time down on the back of his fag packet with one of those tiny green pens you get from a bookies.

We waited and watched further. Around half hour later, just before 9am, a succession of white vans, and bashed up old pick-up's, drove up to the main gate and through to the other side.

'Going by the state of them vans, cheap labour that mob. Probably a gang of Poles. That mob are rarely late, but also never get anywhere early, cos they are all picking each other up on the way into work from all points across London.

Handy that really, means we should get a clear twenty five minutes to do the business, from when he opens the gate and they then turn up.'

It was obvious that Terry knew the habit of a builder after years in the game.

We watched as one by one, the men walked up to a fella with a clipboard, reported in and signed on. They were directed to what looked like an old shipping container and they then each emerged from that , each with a yellow hard hat and a bright high Vis vest. Before too much longer, they had then set about the job.

'I reckon that head ganger is also a Polski.' Said Terry looking closely.

'Don't look like a lot of graft left for the old school British builder then does there? What with this mob coming over and working for cheaper wages.' Chrissie said somewhat bitterly.

'Grafters though bruv, it has to be said,' Terry replied 'I work with them all day long now. They do get stuck in, and love a bit of overtime.'

I was sort of listening to the rabbit, but I was also closely observing the comings and goings of what was unfolding in front of me.

'Terry, make sure you get three hard hats of the same colour and similar vest's mate, we've got to blend in as best we can.' I said.

Terry nodded. 'Ok Vin, no dramas. I do know a few Polish words actually, well mainly swear words, but can say hello and what not, which might come in handy tomorrow.'

I smiled, that could be useful.

Slowly and gradually, I was beginning to get a good feeling about all this.

We'd seen what we had come to see, so it was now time to leave them to it, we didn't want to be spotted at this stage.

We motored on til we spotted a roadside greasy spoon "Nick's Double Double" about a mile back towards the South. The place had seen better days it had to be said, but it smelt spot on and to be fair, we were all "Hank".

The café was basically an old porta cabin, with white plastic garden furniture straight out of the Argos catalogue. No expense spent!

I noted the geezer behind the ramp had a passing resemblance to Mario Kempes, the Argentinian striker, curly black barnet and everything.

Above Mario, was the full menu available to select from. It was your standard scoff for your truck driving types, so I felt right at home. The prices were hard to work out though, because some of the little stickers with the numbers written on had fallen off due to the condensation. So, for example, two beans on toast was priced at

£ -. -0p. Carol Vorderman would have her work cut out in here.

Me, Terry and Chrissy plotted up after all three of us had

ordered up the 'Full Monty English' still not having a scooby at the price.

Within ten minutes, Mr. Kempes served us up three of the biggest full fry up's I had ever seen. Double beans, egg, sausage, rashers, toms and door step thick bread.

'Get that down ya,' he said in a Welsh accent, that caught us all off-guard 'and that'll make your hair as curly as mine, see.'

Silence enveloped our table for ten minutes, as we polished off the lot. Tasty, very tasty.

Once the scoff was out of the way, we started going over the plan for the next day, writing diagrams on the serviettes as we rabbited in hushed tones.

The "lucky dip" bill came to £15, so we settled up with up the 1978 World Cup's leading goal scorer and headed off home.

Once back at Benhill, I headed straight to my flat. I poured myself a large single 2001 Malt, which I had been saving for a special occasion.

A drop of Dutch courage I hear you ask?

Possibly, it tasted very nice all the same.

I was slipping into my old routine from all those years a go, when I was, how should we say? 'Active'

An old peter man told me to always have a decent drink the night before a big blag, because if it all went tits up on the next days job and you had your collar tugged, that might the last decent drink you would enjoy for quite some time.

So, here's to ya. cheers!

Before I got too carried away with the light ale, I put a call in to Pauline and Tubbs and arranged the pick up time for the following morning. I told them to wear the lollipop clobber going out there - except for the titfer - but to make sure they had a change of clothes for making their own way back by the rattler later.

Our phone calls were all matter of fact. Calm, sensible and quick. The realisation that the big day was upon us, meant there was little else to say. It was good to hear that Pauline sounded fine, and Tubbs was raring to go.

I poured one more belt of scotch and then put on an old Sinatra CD I was particularly fond of. For some reason, I kept repeating the track "Someone To Watch Over Me" over and over again. I must have listened to it ten times in succession. Great words and lyrics by George and Ira Gershwin that somehow captured my mood at that precise moment.

Once I was finished with Francis Albert, I put the scotch away and set my alarm for 6.30am as I had told the other's to do.

Before long I had climbed in to bed and drifted off into a light sleep. At first, I kept waking up what seemed like every hour. Finally however, the kip netted me and I had that recurring dream, where everything went to plan and as the digger dug its first hole...bang!

I woke up!

I turned my clock to face me, after removing my night mask and it read 5.45 am.

I decide that'll do, close enough for jazz. I got up and made myself some tea and toast and got dressed in the oldest clobber I possessed. Soon, I was resplendent in old green overalls from my lorry driving days, and my old prison wellingtons, which the warden gifted me when I was released 'for services to the prison garden'. If he knew now what I was about to attempt in them, he might have not been so generous!

I threw on my old man's black and leather donkey jacket, and waited for the call on my moby from Terry to say he had arrived outside.

At 6.30 sharp, the phone burst into life and I was on my way. I met up with Tubbs in the passage way and I must say he looked mighty fine in his uniform. He had managed to pick up a real lollipop sign from a junkyard not far from our dwellings. Tubbs noticed me admiring it.

'The fella said a real lollipop lady gave it to him after being made redundant. Her loss, our gain I s'pose?'

I smiled at and patted him on the back as I said 'good spot mate.'

We found Pauline already in the silver Seat motor Terry had borrowed from a mate at a garage he knew. Chrissy was in the passenger seat, and me, Pauline and Tubbs filled the back seat. After checking everyone had everything that they should have, Terry got us on our way.

As the headlights beamed on the main entrance as we left, we saw Dot and Marge standing there waving us off in the early morning mist. God bless 'em I thought as we returned the wave and Pauline began sniffing into an already soggy white tissue.

'You alright mother?' asked Terry.

'I'm ok, I'm ok.' answered a teary Pauline.

'Nice day for it' said Chrissy trying to lighten the moment, but he had no takers in the banter, everyone now seemed preoccupied in their thoughts.

'Listen,' I said 'been meaning to say this for a while. And now seems the right time. Whatever happens later, if it all goes the shape of a pear, it'll all be down to me. I'll hold my hands up. All my idea.'

'Nah man, can't have that,' said Tubbs 'we all know what we doing. No one is making us do this y'know.'

'Listen!' I said as forceful as I could. 'It's all down to me or we stop the motor here. I filched the sparklers in the first place, so it's my call if the old bill or the cemetery security grab us. Is that understood?'

There were a couple of nods from Terry and Chrissy,

and even though old Tubbs was none too pleased, he finally nodded.

'Ok Vin, whatever you say Vinny.'

It was very quiet in the car from then on, as that conversation was mulled over by all in that car. We sped along and we made good time on the journey, arriving outside the cemetery at 8am.

Terry parked up within inches of where we ended up yesterday, just out of sight of the main gates. As we sat there, all of us strained to look for a flash of a torchlight.

'THERE! What was that?' Pauline made us all jump by suddenly bursting into life.

'Jesus Mum,' said Terry, 'you nearly gave me heart failure there girl…blimey.'

'Sorry love, thought I saw something.'

'You did mate' I said 'that was him, on his rounds'

I looked down at my watch and saw it was approaching twenty-five minutes past the hour. Suddenly we could see him at the gate has he began to fumble with his keys.

'Right, we're on' I said 'Tubbs, Pauline, you know what to do. Get up by that crossing. Make sure you cross it from time to time, even if there is no one needing your help. If you see any builders turn up or God forbid the Lily Law, blow those whistles I've given ya, as hard as you can.'

'Right, Vin,' said Tubbs 'we wont let you down. C'mon Pauline. Show time…'

Those two climbed out and walked up to the zebra crossing. We watched them as they began crossing the black and white stripes painted on the road. To the untrained eye, they looked kosher, so that part of the plan was working nicely.

Terry, Chrissy and me then got out and removed the hard hats and high Vis vests that were in there, put them straight on.

We walked up to and then through the gates, kindly left open by the night security fella and Terry calmly walked up to the main digger. He had a bunch of keys in his pocket, one of which he hoped would kick the bloody thing into life

As it turned out, he needn't have worried. When he got up into the cab, he found the proper keys still in the ignition. We heard him "tut" at this poor security and then saw his face crease into a smile when he gave Chrissy and me the thumbs up.

He fired the machine up and we all looked round to see if the noise had alerted the security bloke. Thankfully, we could see no sign of him, so I guessed he was going on his last inspection of the grounds.

I walked on down the concrete paths towards the gravesite of old Ma Samuels and Chrissy followed me holding what looked like a jemmy, waving it at and directing Terry, who followed us in the digger. In less than five minutes, we were by the grave, which was about 500 yards from the main gates.

I pointed down to it to Terry and with out any airs and graces he plunged the cutting blades into the earth, slicing into it like a knife through butter. We had no time for niceties, so bosh, in he went. He had taken off about five layers of topsoil off, before Chrissy held up his hand.

'Hold up, hold up,' he shouted 'I can see the top of the coffin. Get down the right hand side now of it now bruv.' He then indicated the area which Terry should now be concentrating on.

I was now looking down at the coffin lid and began daydreaming about what was inside.

I hadn't seen the contents for fifty years and I was now really looking forward to the reunion.

I was woken from this trance however by Chrissy waving his right hand about and then pointing behind me.

I slowly turned ninety degrees.

'Bollocks.' I uttered as I saw the security man, dressed in a black rain mac, black jumper and black trousers, topped off with a black wooly hat pulled on his head, coming towards us.

'Chrissy,' I said quickly as I turned back to face him 'carry on and get all the earth moved, I'll keep this mug away from ya, best I can.'

Chrissy nodded to Terry and he cracked away with the digger.

I then turned back and the security fella was now no more than five foot away from me. I noticed he had a gold coloured badge on his coat, which read...

'GCT Security - F. Bracewell'

Chrissy stayed by the digger, whilst I slowly walked towards to our man who had finally heard the noise of the engine and the digging and was coming over to see what was going on.

'Hello mate,' I said smiling as cheerily as I could muster 'not a bad morning is it?'

'Never mind all that,' he said in a thick Birmingham accent 'what the flamin' hell are you lot doing?'

'Sorry mate?' I said. Don't get ya' I tried looking as puzzled as I could manage.

'You three, just what you playing at?' Fair to say he had the major needle.

I had to think quickly.

'Us? We're digging up a few.... Hang on,, hang on. Don't tell me they didn't let you know we were digging up a few whilst we had the kit on site'

'Digging up a few what? ' Mr. Bracewell was now getting very flustered.

'Coffins chief' I stated blankly.

'Coffins?, do you mean coffins here? No, nobody said a word to me. No, they bloody never!'

He was outraged.

'Typical that is. That bloody Mrs. 'Lardy Bloody Dar' in the office, never tells me anything.'

'Who her, the bird in the office you mean?' I said almost laughing. 'I know exactly who you're talking about. Met her myself last week, hard faced cow aint she?'

'You don't know the half of it mate, you wanna work for her.' He had removed his black wooly hat and was now scratching his apparently itchy head.

'Show us the paperwork then. You have got paperwork?' He said narkily..

'Paperwork? No mate, we've got nothing. Just told to report here at just after 8am and start in this corner. Get a couple up and then...'

He was standing in front of me, shaking his head, disappointment etched all over his boat.

'Don't believe this. I don't. They treat me like dirt they do.'

Mr. F. Bracewell was now sulking.

He was also now getting right on my nerves and beginning to eat into our already short time to do what we came here for.

I noticed all the time he was talking to me, he had also been looking over my shoulder at Terry and Chrissy. I looked round to see Terry was still in the cab, with it's engine ticking over, as he "pretend" chatted with his brother.

Chrissy caught my gaze and raised his right thumb and thrust it in the air.

I turned back to the security guard.

'Listen, sorry pal, but we've got to at least get this one sorted before the rest of the workforce arrive. They'll need the digger back, so is it alright with you, for us to crack on like?'

He sniffed and made a strange grunting noise with his throat and finally said 'Well, yeah, I guess so, but I shall have a word with Mrs. Hardy when she gets in. I need bloody telling what's what, I do, it's only right innit?'

'Couldn't agree more old son,' I said 'couldn't agree more. Well, anyway, good luck with her mate.' A smile crossed my lips as I let him have that.

He replaced his wooly hat and turned and shuffled off, I guess back on to his rounds.

I tapped my hard hat with my finger and bid him farewell and walked towards Tel and Chrissy.

As I approached them I mouthed 'Is he looking?' and they both shook their heads in the negative.

'Thank fuck for that.' I muttered under my breath.

By this time, Terry had turned the digger engine off and had climbed down from its cab. All three of us were now looking at the exposed coffin, which Terry and Chrissy had now cleared the earth from, not only on top, but also all down its right hand side.

The digging had left the area looking like a bomb crater. Basically, we had made a right bleeding mess.

Terry was looking at his kettle.

'Come on Vin, get down and open her up mate, aint got all that long left.'

I took the jemmy off Chrissy.

I gingerly made my way to the floor and knelt in the earth, sinking a bit into the mud. I was now on the right hand side of the wooden casket. I then put the thin edge of the tip of Jemmy into the small crack between the lid and the rest of the coffin. I gently eased all the way around it first, and then began making more of an effort on the second lap, in the now widening gap, to prise the two apart.

The cracking noise of timber fibres was all we could hear, drowning out the sound of heavy breathing from the three of us.

'Slowly… slowly…' I said to myself.

I was now getting a good leverage on the lid and it began to lift up.

'WHAT WAS THAT!?!' shouted Chrissy unexpectedly, nearly making me jump out of my wellies.

'WHAT! EH?! What was what?' I said with a real concern in my voice.

'Nothing, it was nothing Vin, he's pulling your plonker.' laughed Terry.

'Fucking need you, don't I?' I said sternly, turning to look at Chrissy.

'Sorry pal. Couldn't resist it.' said Chrissy smiling.

'Dear me.' I said as I shook my head. 'Right, here goes.'

I now used full force to really loosen the lid.

I once again turned and looked both brothers in the eye this time.

They weren't smiling now. Both had serious looks on their faces, nodding at me as if to say to crack it open.

By now, the lid was no longer attached.

I handed the Jemmy back to Chrissy.

'Right chaps' I said 'here we go.'

I slowly, very slowly, lifted the lid, with my hands on either side of it.

I raised it higher and higher, to finally reveal…

That the coffin was EMPTY!

COMPLETELY FUCKING EMPTY!

No piles of old bones and certainly no black velvet bag.

Chrissy, suddenly dropped to his knees down next to me, closely followed by Terry, who slightly nudged his brother out of the way for a better look.

I was just rooted to the spot. My brain was in a state of

total confusion. I struggled to form words.

'What the ffff...?' whispered Terry.

But before he could finish his sentence, a loud, piercing, shrill, whistling noise filled the air. Two old policemen's whistles were being blown by two OAP's dressed as lollipop people as hard and as fast as they could manage.

The three of us looked at each other, panic all over our faces.

We knew we had to move and fast. We'd got company.

Chrissy quickly grabbed the lid off me and slid it back in place on top of the coffin and then the two of them hauled me upright and we hurriedly started to walk out back towards the main gate.

As I walked, I was frantically trying to make sense of what I had just seen. But Terry wasn't in as a reflective mood as me.

'C'mon Vinny, liven it up mate.'

As he approached the group of ten or so workers, who's arrival had triggered the whistling, Terry said a few words of Polish to them. He got a few nods back and a few more curious stares, but they soon went back to their chatter and smoking their fags.

We motored on, walking just fast enough not to arouse too much suspicion. We were soon through the main gates and close to our motor. We could see Tubbs and Pauline looking at us, whilst walking a mum and her two young kids over the crossing.

Chrissy frantically gestured for them to join us and as soon as they had finished the latest episode of the Tufty Club, they walked towards us and the motor, as quickly as their geriatric bodies could muster. They were removing their white coats and hats as they came towards us.

'Well? How d'ya get on eh? WELL?' said Pauline all

expectantly as she approached us.

Terry simply put his right index finger to his lips, as he helped his old mum into the back seat.

'Shush mum, shush'

He then jumped in the drivers seat.

'Drive Terry boy.' I said 'Drive mate. For Gods sake… DRIVE!'

'…And another thing Mrs. Hardy…' Old Bracewell was in full flow… 'I really must protest in the strongest terms that in future you tell me of any extra work that is going on. I really should be made aware.'

'Really Mr. Bracewell, I have no idea what you are talking about, and if this is a waste of my time, I wont be very happy, and…' Mrs. Hardy, was buy now sounding even more grumpier than usual, having been made to leave the comfort of her office by our loyal security man.

However, her mood was about to get ten times worse, as she stopped in mid sentence and walked towards Ma Samuels grave and surveyed the scene of devastation in front of her.

What she now saw looked like a mini Somme. There was piles of earth and mud everywhere, complete with one of her coffins exposed to the elements.

'See, see…see what I mean? What is the meaning of this?'

Old Fred Bracewell was loving this.

For the first time in a very long while, old snotty knickers was speechless. Totally speechless.

'Come on chaps' said Tubbs to us all as Terry sped towards the beautiful South. 'What happened eh? Put us out of our misery.'

Terry and Chrissy laughed together.

'Good word that Tubbs' said Chrissy smiling. 'Misery. Just about sums this morning right up.'

I sat in the back of that car, completely lost in a world of my own. I'd gone from out of the frying pan, into the frying pan!

What had happened here? What had happened to my sparklers?

To be honest, I really had no idea.

But, I think I know a man who did.

8

Round And Round The Garden

I didn't even bother with getting into bed after what I'd seen today. No point, I'd never sleep. I just sat in my favourite armchair and drank the best part of a bottle of Scotch mulling it all over.

My mind was spinning like a washing machine, as I tried to equate what I thought I knew from what I knew now.

I mean, what the fuck had gone on here? I was now questioning everything that I once took for granted.

Had Maury's old girl really died? Or was the whole thing a total gee up?

If it was, it was very elaborate, what with that brass, not to mention that Indian mush and his family.

I knew I had to get a plan together. I needed to know what had occurred.

I NEEDED TO KNOW!

As one drink became ten, I also sparked up a succession of roll ups with my favourite lucifer's and sat and searched deep into my memory, frantically trying to remember any clues from the intervening years.

The one recurring image that flashed across my mind was of Maury coming to see me in the boob. I never really knew if was he genuinely concerned about my welfare, or just checking I was still in there!

I mean, with me in the shovel, did he sell on the Tom? Or did he hang on to it?

Come to think of it, was he still alive? I'd not seen him to my knowledge for over forty years or so. I genuinely had no idea if he still drew a breath. If he'd gone, had dear Elizabeth's sparklers gone with him?

I walked into the kitchen to rinse out my glass tumbler under the cold tap and glanced at the kitchen clock. It was fast approaching 6 am. I'd been sitting there for nearly eight hours and it had felt like eight minutes. Despite all the Scotch I had consumed, it appeared to have had no real effect on me. Don't suppose it had a chance really, too much else on my mind.

There was nothing else for it. I had to get busy. Time to crack on.

I jumped in the shower and was togged up in under half hour.

I decided to try and find the only man I knew who might be able to give me a couple of clues about Maury and his whereabouts…

Soon I was on a 45 double decker bus, seated among the early morning cleaners on their outward journey and night clubbers on their way home. It was a misty morning, a touch fresh and I pulled up my collar on my Aquascutum rain mac to soften the blow.

We were soon flying over Blackfriars Bridge and I looked at St Paul's to my right, standing proud among the modern architecture that surrounded it. That dome, for me, says London more than any other structure and always pleases my heart when I catch sight of it.

A couple of stops on from Fleet Street, I then got off at the top of Shoe Lane.

I crossed over the always busy road and then looked around to find a café. I was too early to find any of the shops open, and for Hatton Garden to yawn into life, so I had an hour or so to kill. This is the centre of London's jewellery trade, gold and diamonds available in hundreds of shops and units. If I was to find out what had happened to my ill gotten treasure, then I could think of was no better place to kick off. There is one main road there, with hundreds of shops on either side of it, as well as plenty of workshops and offices above the retail spaces. It has loads of little turnings, which run off in all directions, some into dead ends and some into the Leather Lane market.

My stomach was now reminding me I hadn't eaten for nearly twelve hours, so a spot of breakfast was now in order. I found a food place called 'Mario's Garden' and walked into the narrow space in front of the main counter and ordered up a bacon sandwich and a large cappuccino. I told the mush taking my order, that I would sitting outside and he nodded and then cracked on preparing my scoff.

It had now become a very bright, but still fresh morning and I found a nice spot outside, which gave me a bit of sun in my face. The sun was so strong it felt like it could split a stone. Lovely and warm on my boat though. I plotted up on a aluminum chair by a round table, on which was placed a handy ashtray and got my bearings and thought about my day ahead.

Within minutes, my food and drink were in front of me and I then decided to read the copy of the Metro I had picked up on the bus. I was a couple of mouthfuls into my sarnie when suddenly, I was aware of the geezer on the next table to my left, looking over my shoulder and at the paper.

He was a brazen fucker I'll give him that. Even though I was now staring his way, he avoided eye contact and carried on reading.

He was very thin man. I'd say in his mid to late 70s, with a swept back head of grey hair. His pinched features and long hooter, and what a glorious schnozzle it was, put me in mind of a Pelican for some reason. He was tidily dressed though. Shirt and tie and a dark blue rain mac and polished black shoes.

Nutty retired office wallah I reckoned.

I gave it a couple of seconds and then had had enough and said sarcastically.

'Alright there are ya mate, I mean, you can see the paper alright there can ya?'

Finally he seemed to get my drift and bristled as he sat back in his chair.

'Bleeding Americans,' he said out of nowhere 'bleeding Apollo missions, load of cocking eye wash that was.'

If I'm honest, I really knew not to engage this one in conversation, but I had an hour to kill, so sadly the curiosity got the better of me.

'You what mate?' I said.

'Them Yanks. They never got up on the Moon. Never. Bunch of fanny merchants. All poppy cock it was.'

I examined his words for a couple of seconds, and they took some digesting.

'What you talking about mate?' I said smiling to myself 'what you mean Neil Armstrong and all that? All cobblers was it?'

'Definitely. All filmed in a Hollywood studio. Oh yeah, well known that is. He got drawn in an' all. Old wassname with the funny eye and barnet all over the shop.'

'Who?' I found myself asking despite my better judgment. I was in too deep now anyway, so yes, I know I should have supped up and run for my life, but in a perverse way I found myself actually enjoying this.

'Him, you know, plays the kids instrument with the sticks. Did the TV programme on the stars an that.'

'Who? Patrick Moore?'

'That's him! Got well mugged off he did. Only believed it didn't he...'

I sat there shaking my head.

'That's cos it was true you silly old sod, they did get up there. Course they did.'

I had decided to argue it out, instead of legging it.

'Cobblers. If they landed on that Moon, I'll eat my head' He said.

You'd struggle to finish that nose if you did, I thought to myself.

He carried on. 'I mean, ask yourself who was their President at the time?'

I genuinely couldn't remember. 1969 wasn't it? Well, I was staying at Her Majesty's pleasure then, so a bit out of the swing of the then US political situation.

'Who was it?' I asked.

'Him weren't it. Black hair, holes in his shoes, tricky Dicky...'

'Jimmy Carter?' I said. His was the only President's name that came into my head.

'Nahhhh, not him mate. Nixon! Richard Nixon. Him weren't it. Watergate and all that. Stands to reason. He was finally caught lying later about all that and had to turn it in. Not up to snuff him? That all started with the Apollo nonsense. He fucked it wholesale...'

As it happened, I had heard the conspiracy theory about the Apollo thing before, they even made a film about it I seem to remember. But I wouldn't admit that to this fella. And I didn't believe all that pony anyway. Of course they got up there. Though old "fly blow" here, he seemed convinced.

'Sorry old 'un. You're a comedian mate. I aint buying any of that.'

'Suit yourself. Got a fag cocker?'

Oh here we go. He'll be on the earhole for a couple of bob next. I pulled my Old Holborn tin out of my jacket pocket, it's gold lettering glinting in the sun as I popped the lid off. I had a couple of pre-rolled in there, so gave him one of them.

'Ta son' he said politely. 'I only smoke OP's hehe.'

Cheeky old duffer I thought, but really, I couldn't help but smile.

In the meantime, I was hoping him sitting there choking on a fag, would shut him up for five minutes and I could make my escape, but I read that wrong.

'Them rockets they had then are the same as them North Koreans have got now. All made out of papier-mâché. (cough) Look great on a launch pad or a military parade I'll grant ya, but you try firing one of the buggers! Don't make me laugh… it'll catch fire and burn to a pile of embers in seconds… (cough)'

Dear me. There really was no answer to that. Time to make a swift exit I reckoned. I quickly munched up what remained of my bacon sandwich, and drained my cup of froth.

'Ta la then guv,' I said 'enjoy the snout. Gotta shoot mate.' and without looking round, I shot into the café, settled my jack and then bolted down the road like a scolded moggy.

I was soon bowling along and on to today's business in hand. Which was to locate and chat to one Douglas 'Spennie' Spencer. Spennie and me had done a few years together when we were up to no good. I first met him in Brixton where we shared a peter for a few months and then same again at the 'Ville, before we went our separate ways.

Like me, he was determined to go straight once he got out. He found the majority of our fellow inmates total idiots…as did I if was I was being honest. Most of them knew nothing else in life, they'd been stealing, nicking and hoisting since they were nippers and accepted the years in their dingly dells without too much complaint – 'An occupational hazard' as

Norman Stanley Fletcher of the Porridge TV series, famously once said.

Me and Spen knew after only a few months in there, that the nick was no place for us when older and wiser. We vowed we wouldn't be coming back at any cost once our time was up.

Spen told me then that he had an uncle in the jewellery game and I laughed out loud.

'Not nicking it like you though ya plum', he said 'I mean making it. A good solid trade, and I'm going to have a basin full of that as soon as I'm out of this pigsty.'

Which as it happened was not that long in coming. He had done his three years for poncing, or 'living off immoral earnings' to you and me. He had a couple of old sorts working the game round Streatham, but one day one of them hooked up with an off duty copper, who took a dislike at not getting the service he was hoping and paying for, so he nicked the brass and went after Spen.

Bang – three years and goodnight campers.

When Spennie got out he stayed true to his word by going into an apprenticeship with his Uncle Eric. He even wrote me a couple of letters, saying he was settling down well and working in and around Hatton Garden. He had met a bird and it looked like wedding bells. Good lad I thought. Keep that nose clean son and that gold shining.

We lost touch as the years went by and I had almost forgot about him, until the early hours of last night, when the Scotch and much reflection brought his face and name back into view.

I kept mulling over who did I know in the jewellery game… who? And then wallop, it hit me like a gold bar between the eyes. My old mate Spennie.

Funnily enough, halfway through my bucket of scotch last night, I thought for some reason, it would be easy to find him. In the cold light of a fresh day, this was now looking like a bit of a 'needle in the haystack' number. I didn't know if he was still on the plot, who he was working for, or if he had a shop?

I spent the next couple of hours schlepping around and in and out of all the shops. As my spirit began to wane, I peered inside shop windows, hoping for a glimpse of Spen, but it was useless.

No sign of even someone resembling him.

Dejectedly I began to walk away from the Garden on the verge of giving up, but I felt a sudden hunger pain strike me again. It was then I looked at my watch and noted it was just after midday and my earlier bacon butty had been well and truly walked off.

I found a greasy spoon, with it's extensive menu plastered all over it's windows, half way down Leather Lane and decided to settle in among the cheery stallholders and sour faced businessmen, hiding from their 9 to 5 hell.

The thought had struck me that I might as well eat here, than go home and cook. I was ready for some comfort grub after the last couple of days I had had.

The waitress came over and I ordered up sausage, beans and chips. Only, I had to repeat my order three times. Her East European, I'm guessing Romanian ears, were struggling with my broad unaffected London accent, but we seemed to get there in the end.

She brought over my cappuccino and I was just looking round at the photos of Elvis and Marilyn Monroe on the walls, when I heard a voice up at the counter.

I knew instantly. It was Spennie.

I looked at his back for a minute or two as he talked football to the chef, so guessed he was a regular in here.

I wanted to shout out, but that would have drawn possibly unwelcome attention to us, so I stood up on the pretence of getting a bottle of tommy sauce from an adjoining table. The ever-attentive waitress came straight over as soon as I got to my feet.

'Ok?,' she said 'All is ok?'

'Yeah darling' I smiled 'Just want a drop of rocking horse for my dinner, so…'

'Er…rocking what?' The poor cow was even more confused now.

Spennie had turned round when he had heard me talk, not that he recognised the voice I don't think, but he was laughing at the turn of phrase.

'Blimey,' he said 'you don't' get many people using that lingo anymore mate.' He then looked me in the eyes, seeing something familiar there.

This was my chance. 'That you Spen?' I said, pretending I hadn't noticed him earlier.

The fella facing me looked shocked. He had greying hair cut short, and he now carried and extra bit of weight, but he was dressed in a very nice grey flannel suit, which was accessorised superbly. Lovely black and white dog tooth 'peckham' held in place with a pearl tie pin. There was the occasional flash of what I presumed were top-notch gold cufflinks and he wore highly polished black Gucci trotters. All in the all, he looked like some one who wasn't doing too badly in life.

'Only certain people call me that. Who…are …you? Hold Up, hold up! I'd know that ugly fizzer anywhere. VIN? Vinny, that YOU?!

'Yeah, it's me son.' I nodded and he burst out laughing.

'What the fuck you doing round here mate? He came closer and reached out to shake my hand. 'Blimey, it's been a few years eh pal?'

By now the other diners and most of the staff were looking our way.

'Not half,' I said. 'Christ on a bike. Look, you got a minute? Come and join me over here eh?'

Spennie joined me at my table nodding eagerly.

'Course mate, course. Blimey, what is it now?' He then racked his brain as he tried to work out how long it had been, since we had seen each other.

'Let me think. Got to be over forty years I reckon. You know what though mate, you aint really changed a bit, a little thicker round the Darby maybe, but...'

'And you my son, eh? Put a bit of timber on there aintcha ha ha.'

I couldn't resist having a pop at his weight gain

'Good living that is mate.' He then patted his finely clothed belly. 'Also, the love of a good woman. The enjoyment of the finer things in life equals an extra couple of stone. Aint you heard that phrase, "love makes you fat" Eh? Haha'

I just looked at him for a couple of seconds.

'Great to see you son, really is.'

'How's your family, seem to remember you had a boy?, Mike...Martin... something like that.'

'Nearly there mate, well done. It's Matthew actually,' I said 'his mum and me split up whilst I was inside. Inevitable really. I tried to sort things when I got out, but she really didn't want to know. Gradually re-built the relationship with Matt though. He's a good lad, fifty-one would you believe, married, got a couple of kids. How about you, any saucepans?'

'Saucepans? You're at it again, remind me.'

'Sorry Spen, it just comes out naturally. Saucepan lids, kids... simple really' I said smiling.

'Haha oh yeah, it's all coming back. Yeah, got a couple of saucepans. Both went to Uni, did really well. Ones a GP and the other lives in Australia, doing my game out there. Buying and selling gold. Doing a roaring trade, what with the price of it at the minute.'

I looked down at my plate of food, which the confused waitress had just dropped off.

'Ta love,' I then looked back at Spen. 'You still grafting though, no retirement plan then?' I said.

'Well, I have cut down. Only do three days a week now. My partner's kids have taken the reins and I only pop in as a consultant and to "glad hand" the older clients. Tell you what, we were lucky to have found each other today boy, eh?'

'Delighted we did mate. Could do with some help as it goes.'

Spen looked at me quizzically.

I continued. 'Ok, one of the reasons I'm round here today is to try and find out some information on a geezer from your trade. We've got a bit of history, me and this fella.'

'Oh yeah, sounds interesting. This geezer you mention, he got a moniker?

'Bit too interesting in some ways.' I said as I looked around at the rapidly filling café and thought it a little too, what shall I say, public.

'Look,' I said 'I know I've got a total liberty, but you got time for a quick one? Want to run something by you?'

'What about your grub? You've hardly touched it.' He said looking down at my plate.

'That's alright, I'll grab something in a bit. More important I speak to you.' I looked him directly in the eyes as I said that, hoping he'd see that I was being serious here.

'Well...what's the time now?' He said as he looked at his tasty kettle, a Cartier by the look of it.

'Ok.1 .15, ...Ummm. Listen, I've got an important meeting at two, but I can spare you half hour if that's any good?'

I nodded quickly 'Great.'

'I'm guessing you're looking for somewhere quiet?' Spennie had begun to read that this was important to me.

I laughed. He had me sussed. I got up and paid at the till for the uneaten food, this action leaving my waitress completely non –plussed as we headed off out in the market.

Spennine guided me to a little back street pub five minutes away, called 'The Hand and Heart.' It had a dark interior of heavy wood, varnished a dark purple colour. A real fire was roaring away and a few candles, sitting at odd angles poked into the top of the top of old wines bottles, whose necks were covered in droplets of melted wax, flickered away as a small breeze running through the rooms hit them.

The pub was quite full at the bar, but we managed to find a quiet corner, and settled down with each of us tending to a vodka and tonic.

Just as I was about to speak, he held up his hand, signaling me to stop.

'Got to make a quick call son.' he said and Spen took out his moby and called what I presumed was his office.

'Bun? Bunny, its me Doug, listen, I've just run into an old pal love… If Mr. Miller gets there before me, text me as I'm only round the corner. Ok…right…yep, I know, I know. See you in a bit love. Ta Bun, ta love.'

Spen then looked my way. 'My secretary. Lovely kid. Can't afford to lose that client.'

'No worries. I wont keep you, promise, I know you are a busy man,' I said 'I just want to throw a name at you. A name from my past, someone who owes me big time. He'll be a senior gentleman like us now, but I need to speak to him badly.'

'Shoot.' Spen was now looking very curious.

I coughed as I cleared my throat.

'Maurice Samuels.'

'Maury?' smiled Spennie – 'old Maurice Samuels? Everyone around here knows Maury. A legendary figure in the buying and selling game. Asks very few questions and makes a decent living by doing it that way. If you want my advice, keep away. Stay away. He maybe old, but he's a wrong un'. Simple as.'

'Ta for the advice,' I said ' but it's bit late for that. Fifty years too late as it happens.'

I then begun to tell Spennie the tale of the gem heist, Liz Taylor, Maury and his mum. His mobile was pinging every couple of minutes and continued to do that every couple of minutes. I guessed it was his secretary Bunny, but he just ignored it and sat there open mouthed, his drink untouched, as he took in the full story.

'What a caper Vin. I had no idea.'

I pointed out that his phone was making all sorts of noises, but he just waved my concern away.

'You sure? I can't walk out on this story now son!'

I had now reached the point where I was about to lift up the coffin lid.

'Oh Jesus wept. Bet that smelt charming, very fragrant, eh?'

When I told him, it may have done, if a body had been in there, old Spennie nearly fell off his chair.

'YOU MEAN…?' He said this too loudly, which got us unwanted attention from the other drinkers around us.

I made a hand gesture for him to lower the volume and he fell into a whisper.

'You mean to tell me, there…was nothing in there…. It was flaming EMPTY!'

I couldn't help but laugh at how he raised voice again.

'I got to say, I preferred the whispering mate to be honest.'

Spennie held his head in his hands.

'Look I've got to go,' he said glancing at his watch 'but, I tell ya, I have heard some tales in my time, but this one. Look take…this.'

He then reached into his wallet and fished out a business card.

'That's where you'll find Maury, well most days. Like me now, he's only part time. But if he's not there, it's where you'll find him eventually. And here's my number.' He handed me one of his own cards.

'You listening? Call me. Call, if you need anything to help with this? You hear me. I mean it.'

We both stood up and hugged like only a couple of lags could.

'I will. And ta for the contact details.'

I wrote down my home number and gave it to him. 'Just in case you need it…'

And then Spennie was gone, out into the daylight, like a greyhound out of trap four, speed dialing as he did so.

I could hear him in the street outside the pub doorway.

'Sorry Mr. Miller, I truly am. Nothing I could do, this woman fainted right in front of me in the queue at the café. Couldn't just leave her could I now?'

I smiled as I sat and looked at the first card Spen had given me. It read…

"Laimbeer and Sons – Buyer and Sellers of all Quality Jewellery".

The address was 35 Princess Street which was one of the roads that filed off from Hatton Garden and down towards Farringdon.

I slowly finished off my drink, ordered up the ploughman's lunch and planned what to do next.

Within the hour, I found myself standing outside the shop. It's main window was chocker full of what I would call 'old style jewellery', rows and rows and rows of second hand rings snuggled into black velvet pads, situated inside emerald green boxes, alongside cuff links, chains, watches, pots and pans and much much more.

This was all good gear. All hallmarked. No rubbish and the prices weren't cheap. Whoever did the buying had a good eye.

I lit up another fag and gave out a little cough as I inhaled – which I took as a signal that I have smoked too many of these lately - and then began composing myself.

I now had the feeling of butterflies in my stomach. It was a feeling similar to the one I had standing by that grave yesterday morning. Nervous at what I might be about to hear, and I was sure that was going to be bad news.

After a few more puffs, I stubbed out the dog-end and pushed at the shop door to get in, only to find it was locked. I looked at the door and noticed a sign saying "please press the buzzer to gain entry" and I tried to focus on where the buzzer was. Having found it, I pressed and then I heard a long bleeping noise as the door release mechanism clicked in. I pushed once again at the door and this time it opened. I had used a little bit too much strength and I found myself stumbling into the front of the shop.

'Hello Sir, how are you today?'

A kindly faced, young woman, with longish brown hair was looking at me and smiling. I scanned her soft features and instantly recognised the same family resemblance on the older gentleman behind the main counter and also on the younger chap sitting at a nearby desk, surrounded by a pile of paperwork.

It was most certainly a family affair.

'Er, hello,' I said somewhat startled 'actually, I'm just browsing at his stage'.

'That's ok,' the young girl replied 'as you can see, we have plenty of stock to be, er browsed. If you need any help, just ask.' A broad smile split her face.

I thanked her and turned round and pretended to look at the trays of silver and gold under the glass cabinets, but in reality, I was really trying to see if there was any glimpse of Maury.

So far, so nothing.

I continued to have a look round and whilst in the silver watch chain section, I felt a tap on my shoulder.

I turned around somewhat startled and found myself looking into a face I hadn't seen for many, many years.

'Hello Vinny, how's yer luck?' This face was now smiling sarcastically. 'Had a sneaking suspicion, I might bump into you after hearing of that bit of business up at Mums grave.'

The voice alone took me back fifty years. I can still recall hearing it for the first time on the telephone, when we were sorting out the fencing arrangements with the then hot tom.

And now here we were face to face again after all these years. My old minces must be going, cos he didn't look a day older than when I last saw him, which was that last day he came to visit me in the shovel.

Looking again, maybe he was now larger than he once was. His three-piece suit was a nice piece of work, but a bit snug on his corpulent frame. He looked like a well-dressed beach ball if truth be told. He now had a mop of black hair where once there was none, so a syrup was now in residence.

An expensive one no doubt, but it was too dark, too noticeable, which I guess defeats it's object. I was thinking of passing comment, but I had more pressing matters to attend to.

One thing I did notice about the Maury of now, was that he had the look of money about him. He looked like he had survived nicely. He looked like he had done well.

I nodded in his direction and smiled a weak smile.

'Had to happen Maurice. Inevitable you might say.' I whispered this as discreetly as I could.

He just chuckled and his ample chins wobbled, as he smiled along with me.

'How did you find me?' he asked.

'An old mate called Spencer, thought I might locate you here' I said smiling as I waved the shops business card that Spen had given me at him.

'Ah. You know Spennie. Nice man, but I find he's a bit free and easy with those cards.'

I nodded behind him. He turned to find the rest of the shop staff were by now looking at us, with a quizzical look on their boats.

'It's ok people. This is Vinny. He's an old friend, back from overseas. Come to say hello. Just saying, been too long.'

He then gestured for me to follow him.

'No good talking here Vinny. Lets go out back. Bit of privacy on offer there.'

I followed him out through a door at the back of the shop and into a smallish kitchen area, which had a table and four chairs from different decades around it. Propped up against the walls were old advertising boards from the shop that were no longer used, along with flattened out cardboard boxes.

'Pick a chair and plot up Vin. Cuppa?'

I sat down on a white wirey looking thing, that I had last seen at the Festival of Britain as a kid in 1951. I bet the authorities are still looking for it.

'Ok Maury – coffee please, black, no sugar.'

Maury made himself busy at the sink, filling up the dented silver coloured kettle and then he arranged a couple of odd mugs on the side. Looking round the room, I noticed a few family snaps on the wall. Days out at the seaside and a couple of what looked like the same children from those photos, now older, in black graduation gowns and hats.

'There you go mate.' Maury broke my nosey trance, as he put my coffee down on the table. It was steaming hot and I followed the steam trail into the air. Maury sat down, taking off his glasses as he did so. He rubbed both of his eyes and then gave the specs a quick buff up on a handkerchief he had taken from the breast pocket on his jacket.

'Y'know, you and your mates made a right old mess of that cemetery.' He said laughing. 'They called me that morning and said there had been a terrible incident and for me to get down there right away. Of course, once I heard the news, I guessed what had happened, it could have only been you. The question is why now Vin? After all these years.'

I had now stopped smiling and looked directly at him.

'That was a real turn up when we lifted up the lid, got to tell you.'

Maury smiled and hunched his shoulders.

'Would love to have seen your face' he said.

'Probably the same one you pulled when you saw the grave later.'

A remark that instantly wiped that flaming smirk off his chops.

Time for the straightener, time to cut to the chase.

'So, Maurice,' I said coldly. 'Time to explain old son.

And, please, take your time, I'm in no rush.'

9

The Shopping Trolley Hard Men

I left the Garden about five and arrived back at the Benhill at around six that evening.

As I walked towards my flat, I could hear Pauline talking to old Vera up on the first floor landing.

'Bloody junkies I bet V. If my Bill was about, he'd give them what for.'

That didn't sound too good, so I decided to investigate. I climbed up the small flight of stairs and found Pauline on her hands and knees looking at the shopping trolley in front of of her.

'What's happened here then?' I asked as I approached them.

'Oh hello stranger,' said Pauline smiling 'It's poor old Vera, Vinny. Been had over. Some toe-rag nicked her pension when she was in "Capri's", getting her lamb chops.'

Old Vera was ninety-four. She stood about four foot two and weighed seven stone soaked through. So, obviously easy pickings for some absolute waster.

Vera had a really bemused look on her face, as Pauline tried to fold back the plastic bag inside the wire frame of her shopping trolley into some sort of shape.

'Looks like that bloody thing has been run over.' I said pointing at it.

'Know what the little berks did, eh?' Pauline almost had steam coming out of her ears.

'They cut the bag inside the trolley open. Must have followed her from the Post Office when she picked up her money and then sliced it and grabbed her purse and that, as she stood there in the butchers.'

'The little bastards confused me when I was getting my meat,' Vera said suddenly 'got me talking and then wallop, all my money's gone. I only popped out for my pension and a couple of cutlets.'

I could only shake me head at what I was hearing. What has happened to these youngsters today, eh? I mean, who would have a pop at a ninety four year old woman? It beggars belief.

"I don't understand them Vera,' said Pauline 'good job really, otherwise you'd be like them I spose. Don't take one of them rocket surgeon's to work out that they were on them pills does it. All bloody mad, the lot of 'em. Mugging an old 'un like you? Oh yes, flaming shopping trolley hard men aint they.

Tossers more like, excuse my Portuguese. They wouldn't have lasted ten minutes back in the sixties, someone would have grassed 'em up and wallop, they'd be off the street and given a scenic railway from ear to ear, to remind them not to do it again.'

I just stood back and let her crack on. Pauline was in full flow.

'But now, now…can't touch 'em can ya? They'd be pleading for their human rights in five minutes through some ponced up Hampstead barrister, all paid for by Legal Aid. Makes you sick, it does straight.'

I looked at poor Vera.

'Come on girl, lets get you home and I'll get your daughter to call the old bill and report it.

Er, you about later Pauline? Want a word with you and Tubbs. Round yours if you like, say eight ish?'

Pauline's eyes lit up at this. 'Oh alright then Vin. You got some news then? Can't wait to hear what's that all about.'

After I settled Vera back at her flat and called her daughter for her, I crept back to mine. I kicked off my shoes and nursed a hastily prepared drink, which went down really well. I considered a second, but thought I had better keep my wits about me, what with the meeting up with the others in an hour or so.

I actually felt myself nodding out and sleep took me. I was dog-tired.

The next thing I know, I'm being woken by my doorbell, which made me jump up with a start.

I quickly straightened up and got to my feet and walked unsteadily to my front door. Looking thorough the spy hole, I saw Tubbs standing there.

'Hello mate' I said as I let him in. 'Sorry, must have nodded out there.

'Hello Vinny. Thought I'd pick you up on the way to Pauline's.' he said.

'Good shout that mate, without you calling, I probably would have slept right past the time.'

Tubbs then looked at me in my disheveled state. 'Yeah she rang me earlier. You coming like that, or putting a frock on?'

'Alright, alright, ya saucy old bark. I'll just throw on a clean shirt and a cardigan and I'll be right with ya.'

Tubbs smiled. 'You look tired Vin. You need to rest up'

'Not wrong there old friend. First things first though. I want to let you all know what is occurring with the gems.'

'Ah man can't wait,' said Tubbs 'thought about little else all day.'

Within a couple of minutes, with me in a fresh bit of

clobber, we were in Pauline's flat. Dot was already there and she waved a fairly cheery hello as we entered.

'Hello Dot,' I said 'didn't expect to see you here?'

'Hello Vinny. Pauline told me about yesterday. I was shocked and wanted to know what happened. Hope you don't mind?' She looked a little sheepish if truth were told.

'No worries Dot, you're more than welcome. Nice place Pauline.'

This was the first time I had been in here actually. It was very tastefully done. My guess would be that her boys, would have decorated it for her. She had a few bits of old pine furniture in there and a photo, I guessed, of her Bill and her boys at a football match in a prominent position. There were also photos of a couple of younger kids, who I took to be her grand kids, Terry's two. Everything in there was spotless.

'Blimey, you look knackered Vin, early night for you tonight mate.' said Pauline.

'Funnily enough, Tubbs just woke me up, so think you are right Paul.'

'Can I use your bathroom please Pauline?' Asked Tubbs.

'Course you can Mr. Isaacs, first on the left my love.'

'Can I get anyone...?' and she gently shook a crystal tumbler in our direction.

Dot declined alcohol, and asked for a cup of tea instead. But I winked at her and told her me and Tubbs would have one with her and she poured us each a decent drop of Johnnie Walker.

'Nice drop of Cinzano for me I think.' She said as she part filled her glass.

Within seconds, there was some serious sniffing noises coming from Pauline's toilet. Seconds later, Tubbs emerged.

'Tell you what' I said smiling as he came into view 'You want to be careful there Tubbs mate, if I didn't know better,

I'd say you was on the wassname mate, the charlie, what with all that sniffing.'

'Get away you damn fool. Don't want any of that rubbish. Just my sinuses giving me gip. Bunged up. Can hardly breathe.'

'Well get that down ya' I said handing him his scotch 'that'll clear your tubes,'

I laughed after pulling Tubbs' chain and raised my glass in the air. 'Cheers all.'

'Cheers yourself...ahh lovely drop,' said Tubbs. 'Right, come on Vinny boy, we're ready.'

I smiled at Tubbs and his impatient ways. 'Ok, ok, I'll get straight to the point. After the "surprise surprise" moment at the cemetery yesterday, I went looking for Maurice the fence, whose mother should have been in that coffin.'

'Right an' all. That's what I would have done. Good on yer?' said Pauline 'Any luck?'

'Well, yeah. The good news, not least for Maury, is that he is still alive. I'm pleased to say we had a good chat. My mate Mr. Tunnel put us in touch. Douglas.'

'Who's Douglas Tunnel?' said Dot.

'Oh Dot, Douglas Tunnel haha. Vinny got you there, good and proper.' laughed Pauline.

'Och, this all too much for me.' Good to see Dot could take a joke still. 'You're a great big Mary Ann, Vinny Hawkins and no mistake.'

'Sorry Dot, just in a decent mood.' I said smiling.

'Bet he was surprised to see you wasn't he, that Maury?' Dot asked.

'Well, funnily enough, no Dot. He had heard about the grave being dug up,' - Dot made the sign of the cross as I said that – 'so he worked out it was probably me, and was sort of expecting a visit.'

'Man, I would have liked to have been a fly on the wall at that chat.' Tubbs took as sip of his drink as he spoke and I smiled in his direction.

'It went alright actually Tubbs. Better than I thought. No screaming or shouting. We just kept it very civil like. Maury come clean and told me he set up the fake burial story, cos he knew the old bill was on his case, so he concocted this pony tale to throw everyone, including me, off the scent.

I fell for it, and then eventually the rozzers let the trail go cold when nothing was appearing on the second hand 'tom' market. They raided a few other fences, but found nothing from the Liz Taylor robbery, so were stumped. Maury said they spun his gaff over four times in total, but found nothing. He had it all nailed up under a floorboard, and somehow they never found it.

He said he was delighted to hear I was then banged up, cos it got rid of me from the equation for a few years. He said he came to visit me, just to make sure I was in there! Cheeky git eh?'

'He had some nerve didn't he,? said Pauline 'bleedin' "Casey's Court" all this. To be honest, I'm still a bit confused. I mean, did his poor old mum actually die the day he said she did?'

I smiled at her. 'Yeah she did. That bit was true. Only she was buried at a smaller Jewish cemetery, but Maury used that fact to cover his tracks. Turns out, he dropped someone at Northside a nice drink, to put a plot aside and put up the stone to Myra to throw me off the scent.'

'So, are the jewels not in the other one?' said Dot, now looking as confused as Pauline.

'Nope. Maury claims he fenced them a couple of years later when I was into my fourth year of porridge. He said that he was trying to put his sons through a decent school, so cashed them in and used whatever he got to pay the fees. So the sparklers have gone. It's all over.'

'Blimey, what a turn up,' Pauline was shaking her head. 'What happens now then?'

'Good question,' I said 'personally, I'm going to have another scotch if that's alright?'

'Ooh you silly sod. All that time you were waiting to get your hands on them, and now you find out they've been long gone. You must be gutted?'

I thought for a second, and pondered that question.

'The old me would have been fuming, going off alarming, you're right. I would hate the thought of being tucked up and would have brooded on it all big time.

But the me of the last few years is no longer that bothered if truth be told.

Maury told me that he tried for a couple of years to forget he had them, but in time all he could think about was selling them, in a way, they overpowered him. He couldn't get rid of them quick enough in the end.

Funny really, I went the other way inside, thought about nothing else for a year or so and then gradually lost interest. And when out, well, then I forgot about them completely, until the past few months.

Think I've realised, and too late really, that money aint that important, not when you look at all the things I lost. The missus, the boy, nigh on ten years of my liberty and all for what? Eh? So as I could be Charlie big bollocks, flashing it up for a few years.'

'Language Vinny!'

'Sorry Dot, sorry. Anyway, now it's all over, but at least I now know what happened.'

That bit hung heavy in the air.

'Oh well,' said Dot 'as you say, it's all over now. I suppose, I'll have to start looking at alternatives. I can't have Margie going into a place on her own, I've got to be with her, simple as that.

Talking of my beloved sister, I really should be going; I've been gone long enough already. I can't leave her too long y'know.

I'll bid you all goodnight, want to make sure Margie is comfortable before I turn in myself. Night all.'

And with that Dot, was gone.

Poor old Dot, the last year or so has been terrible for her. She and Margie were so close and happy and then it all started to un-ravel. Terrible illness that Alzheimer's. I pity the poor souls with it.

The quiet, sombre mood that was beginning to fall over the room was rudely interrupted by the sound of Tchaikovsky's 'Nutcracker' suddenly blasting out. It caught poor old Tubbs so unawares that he nearly spilt his drink.

This musical refrain is perhaps better known to many, set to the lyrics "Everyone's a fruit and nutcase."

Pauline had this as the ring tone for her house telephone.

'Jesus, Pauline!' said Tubbs slowly recovering 'What on God's earth is that all about?'

'Oh, shut yer cake 'ole you. I like it, makes me happy when it rings.'

You couldn't argue with that.

She answered her phone and it sounded like she was talking to her Terry.

'Allo boy. Yeah…Vin and Mr. Isaacs are here now. All sounds very complicated to me son. The upshot is, I might be moving again sadly. Yeah…well what can ya do. Yeah, I'll be alright boy. Tell you what, you ring Vinny tomorrow and he'll explain it all. Probably best. I'll only make a pigs ear of it'

She put the phone receiver down and then flopped down on her settee and blew out a big sigh.

'Right, you know what you two, I think I'll turn in too. Had enough heart damage today, what with poor old Vera earlier and now your story Vin, hope you don't mind?'

'Not at all Pauline, I think we'll have one for the road back at mine and then be asleep ourselves. Had a busy couple of days aint we?' I said wearily.

'Come on old soldier,' I said to Tubbs 'how about a night cap?'

Mr. Isaacs slowly staggered to his feet and with that we bid Pauline goodbye and goodnight.

Within a couple of minutes, we were in my flat and I had the top off the Scotch in seconds.

'Here you go old friend,' I said to Tubbs 'get your laughing gear round that.'

Tubbs held out his hand and gladly accepted the glass.

'Good lad' Said I.

We settled down into my armchairs.

'So Vin – what next?'

'You know what Tubbs mate, I really don't know. I just don't know.'

'Do you believe your man Maury really sold them? Wouldn't you be able to find out one way or the other?' Tubbs sounded like he was still suspicious.

'Got to be honest, the thought he was filling me with lies again, crossed my mind. But gems like that little lot, will go underground pretty much straight away. It would be squirrelled away into a private collection and with all these intervening years, well it's well buried, if you pardon the phrase.'

We both laughed as our thoughts turned to the cemetery and the Scotch began it's magic.

'You know Vin,' said Tubbs between his laughter 'we must have been mad! – I mean digging up a grave. Jesus Lord of all above, I hope you forgive me!'

I smiled. 'The big man will, I'm sure. You tell me this is your one and only misdeamour from over the years. If that is true and I have no reason to not believe you, I'm sure you have a bit of credit in the bank son.'

I turned the bottle upside down and drained out the last few drops. One nip for him and one for me...

This liquid was really beginning to kick in nicely and I felt my eyelids drooping. It was like I had a ton weight on each of them. With me hardly having any sleep for the past thirty-six hours, it was getting harder and harder to keep them open.

I woke up just as the sun was rising and beaming into my front room. I was still sitting where I must have fallen asleep the previous night.

Tubbs was long gone, but he had thrown a blanket over me on his way out, bless his solid gold heart.

I looked down and my glass was on the floor where I dropped it and I caught sight of the empty scotch bottle and winced. I'm going to feel the effects of that all day, I just know it.

I slowly focused and worked out what day it was. I made my way into my shower and before too long, the refreshing water was crashing over me, soon bringing my senses back to life.

I couldn't deny it. I had noticed I was drinking more and more these days. It was almost like I was trying to blank out the memories of what I once was and where they had taken me. I thought I was over all that, but the recent conversations with people from my past had stirred it all up and when I turned to the bottle, I invariably ended up drinking it to the finishing line.

I didn't like the way it was going if I'm honest. This wasn't how I wanted to be. I was becoming a poor, shallow version of the Vinny I once was. I was slowly becoming someone I didn't like anymore. I was drinking every day, and they say if you can't go a day without a drink, well, it's a slippery slope.

The old Vinny wouldn't have just taken Maury's word and accepted it and then got pissed. No, I would have challenged him and his word.

Under that showerhead I began to think up another plan, which was already striking me as crazy. But the idea kept coming back to me, which was usually an indication that no matter how mad it seemed, it was one that wasn't going to go away.

During the course of the day, I tried my hardest to think of other things, to occupy my mind, but I kept coming back to the same thought.

Bloody Maurice had tucked me up once already, and now the absolute truth was that I had no idea if he had sold Liz Taylors baubles or not.

Once again in this never ending saga, there was only one way to find out.

'Help me, please help!! Oh God in heaven, please… somebody, please come quickly!'

The sound of Dot crying out cut through all our sleep and before long those that could get up quick and move towards the sound of Dot, were doing so.

It was freezing cold as I opened my front door onto the passageway and headed towards the voice. I found the back door to Benhill open slightly and the sight of Dot wearing a heavy navy blue toweling dressing gown walking towards the little roadway which was at the back of our block.

I was caught off guard by the headlights of what looked like a BMW car, which were pointing towards me and which were also lighting up the wet, damp road in front of it. In the road, lay a bundle of what looked like clothing, only as I got nearer it appeared to have arms and legs, though one of those legs was at a funny angle.

I was ten foot behind Dot when she suddenly bent down and sobbed her heart out. As I got nearer I could see she was comforting a figure, a person. It was her sister Margie.

What has happened here, eh? I looked towards the young fella standing by the now open front right side door of the BM

'What went on here mate, eh? Talk to me son!' I felt an anger sweep over me.

'Don't know bruv, really, don't know. This figure appeared from nowhere,' he was shouting all this at me 'I swear, I just couldn't stop and …and…then…this.' His voice trailed off as he struggled to put into words what had happened. Instead he just looked down at Margie.

'Dot,' I said gently 'Dot, have you called an ambulance mate?'

Dot just slowly shook her head, whilst still cradling Margie's body.

'Don't worry, I have love.' A woman who was standing on her doorstep in the housing block opposite ours suddenly spoke. She then came a little closer to me, Dot, Margie and BMW man.

'I heard the screech of tyres, come out and saw, this. So I belled 999. Someone is on the way.'

Just as she finished saying that, I could hear a siren in the distance and prayed it was coming our way. I looked back at our block and saw Tubbs was hobbling towards me, closely followed by Pauline. They were both now very close to Dot and me.

'Vin? Dot? What's happ…?' Before she could say much more, Pauline then began to cry.

I just grabbed her tight and we cuddled, as I tried to reassure her.

'It'll be ok Pauline. I'm sure it will.'

Then, all the brick walls, parked cars, the rainy road and

the pavements, suddenly took on a bright blue hue, as an ambulance turned into our turning and towards us. Two paramedics, dressed in green clothing, with highly visible stripes of plastic flashing in the night sky, were soon out attending to Margie, asking questions, as they checked for a pulse, a breath, a sign of life.

Dot stood up and got out of their way and was now holding hands with Tubbs.

'Anyone know what happened here?' The older of the two said.

There was a silence, a deafening eerie silence.

'DID ANYONE SEE ANYTHING HERE?'

The senior paramedic was keen to capture initial thoughts and opinions from the small crowd that had now gathered around us.

'She ran right out in front of my car. I …I couldn't stop, nothing I could do.' The young driver looked like he was slowly going into shock.

'Ok, ok. And how do you feel sir, any bumps and bruises?' The younger medic was now with us too..

'Me? Nah, I'm fine, I'm fine. How she doing?'

He, like me, had noticed they weren't working so hard on Marge, in fact they were just wiping her cuts on her face, tidying up.

'Mel, get in the cab and make sure the police are on the way. Don't worry everyone, it'll be just routine. Just routine.' The older guy was in the process of settling everyone down.

Me, Tubbs and Pauline then stood further back as they manoeuvred to get Margie on to a stretcher, which was then put in the back of the ambulance.

The two paramedics were now in there too. The younger one looked round towards us.

'Any family here?'

Dot nodded in her direction.

'Come on love,' said the kindly faced girl 'get in here with us and you can be with her.'

Dot slowly, walked up the little metal steps at the back of the vehicle and was soon sitting on a small chair. Her hands were clasped tightly together and she was sobbing quietly.

I could feel Pauline shivering as I held her again and it was obvious, I should get her inside.

'Come on you, you'll catch your death out here…and you Tubbs mate.'

To be honest they didn't put up too much of any resistance.

'Take me home Vin, I've seen enough.' Pauline began to cry buckets of tears.

Me and Tubbs put our arms around Pauline and got her back to her flat.

'Do me a favour Tubbs,' I whispered as he settled Pauline down and put the kettle on, 'keep an eye on her for a minute. I just want to make sure Dot's ok.'

'I won't be a minute Pauline,' I said as gently as I could, 'just going to see if Dot needs any help. Tubbs will keep an eye on ya mate.'

'Cup of hot chocolate eh Pauline?' I heard Tubbs say, as I left the flat and made my way back to the ambulance.

When I got back there, the police had arrived and were taking a statement from the driver of the car and the neighbour. The young kid who was driving looked pretty shook up. I kept hearing him say 'She just run into me from nowhere.'

I stood by the back door of the ambulance. Both the doors were now closed. There was nothing I could do, but wait for some news.

Within five minutes, the door opened again and the younger female member of the crew was stepping out.

'Er, how's she er...doing er ...please miss?'

'Are you family sir?' She asked.

'Well, not really, but y'know...' I stammered.

'I can only speak to family at this stage...Do you know the ladies inside well?'

'Yeah, close neighbours. Dot and Marge Cotter.'

The young medic opened the door a little wider.

'Dorothy...Dorothy,' she gently asked 'do you know this chap?'

Dot looked up slowly and her red eyes tried to focus on the pair of us. She finally nodded. 'Aye, That's Vinny.'

'Do you want him to come to the hospital with you?'

Dot looked at me, and again nodded. 'Please Vin.'

The older crew member looked at me 'That ok with you?'

'Yeah, sure, of course...I'll just lock up my place and get some proper clothes on. I'll be two ticks.'

The young girl then looked at me sadly. 'No rush sir, I'm afraid the other lady was dead on our arrival.'

I looked back in to the ambulance and saw Dot holding Margie's hand.

I turned back towards the block and my flat and I'm not ashamed to say, that the tears flowed like water as I did so.

We were at St Thomas' Hospital in a matter of minutes and we were shown into a row of curtained off cubicles.

It was busy in there, with plenty of people milling about. Nurses, doctors, patients, visitors, cleaners, porters, ambulance crews all going about their business. It was a bit of a blur to be honest.

Dot and myself were sat outside a cubicle and told that someone would see us shortly.

'Run out the flat again, she did.' Dot spoke with a far away look in her eyes. Her Scottish accent getting stronger and stronger as she did so.

'Could nae stop her Vincent. She got confused with the time again so she did. Eleven at night became eleven in the morning. I was forever stopping her escaping, but…' Dot looked into her lap.

'Occasionally she broke free and then well, it was all up for grabs.

Somehow last night, she got out. Not sure how long she was gone, but if the car hadnae got her, the cold and damp weather would have, she only had her nightie and next weeks washing on.'

Dot was now holding onto my hand. Her grip was getting tighter and tighter as she went on.

'Only a matter of time…aye…only a matter of time I suppose.'

I spoke to her softly. 'You could do no more Dot love, no one could have done more than you, believe me.'

She looked at me, her eyes beaming into mine.

'Thank you Vincent. Thank you for saying that. She knew you know? She knew our little flat was under threat. She read the local papers in her lucid moments and knew something was afoot.

I'm not saying it influenced her to do what she did tonight, but somehow she got worse after she read the latest on the plans to re-develop our place…. And now, now she's gone.'

With that, her head hung down further and she sobbed like a baby. I put my arm around her, doing my best to console this genuine, lovely lady.

At the very same time, I resolved to do whatever I could to save our building.

10

Goodnight, God Bless...

The sad and tragic death of Margie, affected the residents of Benhill very badly. In the short time I had lived here, I had grown really fond of the Cotter sisters.

I liked the fact that they didn't give me an easy ride. They made me work for their friendship, well at least Dot did, but old Margie would listen to her elder sister and then put the barriers up. They were a formidable partnership.

I really admired that Dot had stood up for her principles and wouldn't break them when I told them about my plan to dig up the grave to get to the gems. She wasn't having any of it and told me so, no matter as to the reason behind why I was doing it. I could only admire that. She wouldn't change her mind, even if she felt any peer pressure from the rest.

I also truly admired the way she looked after her sister when it was obvious to all that it was becoming a thankless task. It could be said that Margie would have been perhaps better off in a proper care home, but as long as she wanted to stay with Dot, Margie wasn't going anywhere.

And now, today, we are gathering to bury her.

It was a really horrible day for this little tight knit community of elderly people.

Over the past few months, I had observed the way that they looked out for each other.

This was the result I think, of the realisation that their close neighbours were really all most of them had, as a constant in their life. Sure, some of them had sons, daughters, grandkids, nieces and nephews, but the blunt truth was that the majority of these good people in here rarely saw any of their immediate family.

I would often hear excuses like – "my son is so busy he has cancelled his visit again. I told him, don't worry, it's not important" - when I really knew, it was important, and it hurt the let down person more, much more, than the absentee visitor could ever know. This inaction often left people isolated, feeling unwanted, undervalued even.

There is no doubt to my mind, that the outside world our kid's live in is getting faster and faster, what with mobile phones, lap tops and computers all eating into their time.

This has had the effect that the younger generation now react faster to things that are thrown their way, they do things instantly now, because they now can.

Like paying a bill on their phone, shopping on-line, or just wasting time on bloody Facebook or that Twitter thing.

They simply do more 'stuff' during their working day, filling it up, because they are forever plugged into something. You see them on buses. They have wires coming out of their ears listening to music, whilst texting or playing stupid games on their devices, all at the same time.

I sit there thinking as I look at them, so, you can find time for all that, but you can't find time at the end of your day for things outside this mobile world.

It appears to me, that unless it's wired up and plugged in, they look like they are struggling to deal with it.

Perhaps once in a while, you could put the kit away and go and visit an elderly relative. Wouldn't that make a nice change? In a lot of cases, our sons and daughters are failing to attend to their responsibilities.

And it is their responsibility.

Some of the antics I see and hear about with so-called family, in respect of these old people borders on neglect.

Strong word I know, but never truer in a lot of cases.

We have plenty of old girls in here, many in their nineties, that I see bent double with age, somehow pushing, or in most cases just about hanging onto, a shopping trolley, as they go out for their daily shop.

I look at them often and think surely, your son or daughter with their flash motor could pick you up a bit of shopping whilst they are buying theirs? I'm sure some do, but not many or enough.

Of course nowadays these poor, vulnerable people are left exposed to villainy out on the streets, as demonstrated with poor Vera and her vanishing pension the other week.

When I first moved in, I was forever walking to the shops with the old un's and pushing a full trolley back home for them. I just sort of fell into the Good Samaritan routine.

However, Pauline soon put me right.

'If you don't harden up Vin, you'll be doing that all day every day. Sorry to sound so hard,' she said 'but not down to you is it? I mean, fair play for helping out and that, but you'll lose out in the long run, I'm tellin' ya'

And she was right. I soon found out, that all I was doing all day was stuff for other people and getting no time to myself as a result. So, I reluctantly knocked it on the head.

Thankfully, and luckily for me, it is different with my boy Matthew. We started off with that big gap in our relationship, which was all down to me of course. Somehow though, that got mended and we are great together now. I especially love having his Trudy and their two girls as part of my life.

At the same time, if I'm being honest, I also love having my own space. In here I can be distant when I want to and those closest to me respect that. If I want to shut the world out sometimes, I can. I truly value that.

Having just said that however, I have also thought of asking Pauline out for a meal or to go to the pictures with me.

There I've said it...

I had thought of doing this, from the first minute I saw her in here. She's a lovely lady and I think we could be good together. We're similar ages, come from the same background and get on really well, so I can't deny the thought has crossed my mind.

Sometimes I could do with a good old cuddle. Maybe a kiss or two, and ...hang on, hang on...this is Pauline I'm talking about, behave yourself Vinny.

The truth is, what stops me acting on those thoughts, is that I really don't think she's over the death of her Bill. I really don't think she will ever get over something like that. They went too far back, had too much love for each other. They were devoted and Bill's death had only strengthened that devotion.

On top of that, it was obvious her two boys are very, very protective of her. I see that by the amount of times they come to visit her each week. One or the other is in to see her most evenings after they've finished work.

If I asked and she said yes and then it didn't work out or I upset her in some way, I know for certain, I would get a visit from her Chrissy and Terry! And I'm in no rush for some of that, I can assure you.

I keep asking myself, am I too old for that kind of commitment if it went ok though?

Maybe the truth is that I'm just looking for a bit of nice, female company sometimes?

Occasionally I have every intention to go and ask her out for a date and then I get tongue tied.

Yeah me! - Tounge tied, who'd have believed it.

Sadly, losing Margie like this though, has been a sharp reminder that life is so short. One minute, you're part of the furniture and then...boomf! Gone!

Us at the sharp end are of course facing our own mortality on a daily basis. After a really bad night, when all my old demons come back and disturb me, I sometimes open my eyes not sure if I am still alive or have passed on. I'm serious. It takes me a minute or two and then I think, ok, right I'm still here. Let another day begin!

As for Pauline. Well, I'm still debating whether to ask her out.

Flaming hell, I really am a right old plum sometimes…

Back to today, back to reality. I picked up my black suit from the cleaners yesterday and bought a new white shirt from Marks' on the way home. Sadly, I have been to so many funerals lately, I could with a fresh one.

I get plenty of calls from relatives of old mates from the 60s, or from the families of those I spent time with in the shovel, telling me so and so has left us. Add those to the old work colleagues who have died and I've got a season ticket up at the crem.

I try to go to as many as I can, but I always feel like I leave a little bit of me behind at each one. Tough days they are. Tiring. Hard to get through.

Invariably at the piss ups after, those of us that are left all say, we really should start meeting up at occasions where a death isn't central to it, but we rarely do. Strange that really.

Speaking of which, time to get ready for another one; the funeral cars will be here soon.

In the middle of polishing my right shoe, my doorbell goes. I open up to find old Tubbs standing there. He always looks well turned out on a daily basis and today is no exception, with his clothes clean and pressed. Though lately it has to be said, I have noticed some of the garments have seen better days.

Take today for instance, he has done his best bless him, but the old suit he is now standing in front of me in, has been around the track, more times that Usain Bolt. The thing has been cleaned and pressed to within an inch of its life and it looks like it badly want's to retire.

He catches me looking at the slightly fraying cuffs and trouser bottoms.

'I know man, I know, I can see you looking, but I don't want to buy a new one, little point unless they want to bury me in it.

My Carla is always on at me, saying "come on dad, spend a few pounds on some fresh clothes", but I tell her I aint got long left and the money I would spend on those things, will be going to her and the boys instead.'

'Oh leave me out,' I chuckle 'you'll see us all out you will. You'll be at mine before I'm at yours son.'

'I hope you're right, but I don't think so Vin, not the way I feel some days. Some days I just want to shut my eyes and drift away.

Phew, this is going to be a hard day today.'

I just nodded and reflected on what he had just said, as I tied on my newly polished right shoe. I didn't know he felt like that.

'Thought your Carla or one of the boys might be about today, go with you like?'

Tubbs looked reflective 'Well, I did mention it, but they were all working, so...'

I just nodded, busy lives as I said earlier.

'How long we got?' I asked Tubbs, changing the subject, as I slipped on my jacket, and straightened my tie.

'About ten minutes, why?' he replied.

'Good,' I said. 'just long enough for you to help me with

this last crossword clue I've got. Get this and I've finished it'

'Ok, fire away' said Tubbs looking all studious.

'The clue is, another word for a postman?'

'How many letters?' asked Tubbs.

'A bloody great sack full!' I replied and smiled a "gotcha" smile at my old mate.

'Sweet Jesus, today of all days… really man?'

Tubbs tried to look like he had the hump, but a little smile played on his lips, with him trying as hard as he could to suppress it.

'Sorry mate, couldn't resist it. You sounded like you needed cheering up son. Anyway, Margie has gone, and some would say to a better place. I know she wouldn't mind us having a little laugh.'

'Yeah, you're right. You are still a damn fool though.' Tubbs said, now smiling.

'Right,' I said smiling back at him, 'it must be nearly time we were off.'

'Yep, nearly. As I understand it Pauline is going in the car with Dot. You and me are in with Wendy and a cousin of Dot and Margie's, didn't catch her name. She has got her fourteen year old daughter with her. Sounds like no other family will be coming.'

'Shame. Oh well, what can you do? Come on then old son,' I said feeling jittery 'lets get it it over with.'

We walked out to the front of the block and found the highly polished hearse and two other long black motors already in position, surrounded by the funeral directors in their smart sombre black suits.

Margie's wood and brass coffin was in the hearse already and the funeral fella's had put a few wreaths in there with it. Me, Pauline and Tubbs had chipped in and got a nice one between us. We let Pauline pick it out and I noticed she was now carrying that in her left hand, with her right holding the hand of Dot as they now walked past us and towards the lead car that would directly follow the hearse and the coffin.

Once they and Dot's cousin and her kid were settled in, Tubbs, Wendy and me climbed into the second vehicle. There was a clean, fresh smell in the car and it hummed as it glided towards its destination.

It was a quiet, slow, twenty-minute ride up to the cemetery at the top of Peckham. Shoppers and passers by, stopped and peered into the cars, to see if they recognised anyone and some made the sign of the cross as the cars cruised past.

It's funny the things you think of in that silence that envelopes you on the way to say a permanent goodbye to a loved one.

For me, it was Maurice Samuels. He was never far from my thoughts these days I found.

On arrival at the rag stone chapel, we slowly followed the coffin, Dot and the rest in and settled down on the wooden pews, a couple of rows from the front, picking up the order of service sheet that rested upon it.

I noticed a couple of faces I didn't recognise among the twenty or so people gathered together. Not many really when you think of it.

The service that followed was the usual affair really, a couple of hymns and a prayer or two. If I'm honest, I kept looking round the church, wasn't really concentrating. I looked at it's brick pillars, it's uplifting, colourful stained glass windows, the scoreboard on which were indicated the numbers of the hymns being sung today. In fact, I looked at anything and everything, except at the coffin. I would be glad when this was all over.

The vicar said a few nice words about Margie and her years as a nurse and a few of the connaught's among us nodded and smiled. It was then that I realised that they were ex colleagues.

Dot declined to say anything in the church - don't think she could handle it - and her cousin with no name, turned out to hardly know Margie. Her flaming kid had already given me the right hump half way through the service, when she had taken her mobile phone from her coat pocket and seemed to checking for messages.

Choice that. Real classy.

As the service neared its end, there was a lot of quiet, reserved sobbing and weeping at the front. Dot had walked up to the coffin and put hear head against and very quietly said 'I will love you always.'

This had left Pauline in bits. Me and Tubbs were just one row back with Wendy, Ethel and Vera, and we did our best to comfort her.

Those two elderly ladies had got a flounder to be here today, bless their hearts.

The coffin was lowered from it's resting place during the last hymn, 'Praise My Soul, The King of Heaven'. As the hymn finished, Tubbs was sobbing into a fresh, white handkerchief and I must admit, I had a lump in my throat too.

I noticed that old Vera was the colour of milk and wobbling a bit on the pew. Aged ninety four I thought for one minute she was thinking of going to join Margie for a "buy one, get one free" funeral job, but thankfully she steadied herself, the poor cow.

After it was all over, I made my way outside, breathed deep and sparked up. That fag felt good I'll tell ya.

After the snout and giving Dot a quick cuddle, I walked round to check that everyone had a lift back to Benhill if they wanted to come back for a cup of tea, or maybe something a little stronger.

Once back in Camberwell, we all made our way up to Dots flat for the do. From the spread on offer, it looked like she had been throwing money about like a sailor on shore leave.

There were rows and rows of bottles of wine, spirits and beer, as well as trays of sandwiches and a nice bit of cake. Pity there was so few of us to get through it all, though the pie and liquor made a decent dent in the vino rouge and the Sexton Blake within minutes of arriving. The men of the cloth never hold back at a funeral do, I notice.

I made my way over to speak to the Cotter's cousin.

'Hello love,' I said smiling 'sorry, I didn't catch your name?'

'That's cos I didnae drop it pal.' She replied in a Scottish accent as thick as a boarding house sandwich. Her mobile infatuated child stared at me with a look on her face, as if she would have killed me there and then, given half a chance.

'Right. Nice to meet you two, too! Please excuse me ladies' I said quickly, as I turned back towards Tubbs with a 'help me' look on my face.

Tubbs looked at me puzzled 'What gives?' he asked concerned.

'How does that song go?, 'We'll Keep A Welcome In The Hillside'. Don't think those two over there know that one.'

Kindly, Dot had seen the bite I nearly got off her cousin and she appeared by our side, with a bottle of ten-year-old malt whiskey for him and me, knowing it was our favourite.

'There you go boys,' she said smiling as she handed us two crystal cut glasses 'you cant be optimistic, with a misty optic.'

I smiled and thanked her as we poured a small amount of malt in each glass each and raised a toast to the recently departed and her lovely sister.

'Absent friends.' Said Tubbs and we knocked back that lovely drop.

Dot then cleared her throat, as she prepared to give a little speech.

'Cough...'

The room slowly became silent.

'Thank you, thank you.' Dot was visibly suffering.

'I would just like to say thank you all so much for coming today. Obviously it is a sad occasion. But if I'm honest, it was really a release for ma sister Marjorie. Her last year or so had been one of confusion. She tried hard to make sense of it all, but the frustration in her efforts was plain to see. She was a fighter though and never really gave up.

As most of you know she hadn't been too well recently and it had been a struggle to keep an eye on her in so many ways. I did my best to keep her as comfortable as I could and I had some great help from many of you in this room today.

I would like to say thanks to Wendy and the staff at Benhill who have been lovely to me and Marjorie, especially in the last few months and particularly today.

I would also like to express a few special words to Vincent, Pauline and Grenville who have been true friends to Marjorie and me in the last year or so.

All of us found ourselves here at Benhill after various circumstances conspired for that to happen and even though at first we were slow to open up to each other, we finally ended up as the best of pals. That meant a lot to us Cotter sisters, I can assure you of that. We also went through a tough time here, before Wendy arrived, and many of you will know well the part Vincent played in sorting out the unfortunate Maureen woman.'

Me, Tubbs and Pauline grimaced at the name and memory of Maureen.

'Actually, Vincent. I owe you a sincere apology.'

She had caught me unawares here. I looked at her, with my malt at my lips. What does she need to apologise to me for?

Dot looked at the puzzled faces in front of her.

'Let me explain' she said. 'Vinny came to us all recently

with the story of his own past. He opened up to us, which must have been hard for him to do.

My word, such a tale it was. He asked for some help, and I'm afraid I said no. I was so weighed down by looking after Margie that I just wasn't thinking straight. Well, since what has happened, I have thought of little else.

I now realise he was only trying to help us, all of us, and I would like him to know, if I had that time again, I'd say yes next time. I really would.'

I gave my glass to Tubbs and walked over to her and gave her a big hug.

'Bless you Dot,' I whispered 'bless you...and you know what? I aint finished yet.'

I let her go and she smiled at me. I knew then, I had to get the old me back into action as best I could.

So,' continued Dot 'please charge your glasses.' She then raised the glass in her hand.

'To my sister I say - Margie - Goodnight and God Bless.'

The little gathering went on for a further hour or so and then everyone, began to drift away, including me. I found my mind was back on Maurice. Something would have been done about that.

Over the next weeks I decided to get a bit fitter. I had let myself go a bit, too much to drink and too many fags had become a daily habit. Time to slow that down and get a bit of shape back.

I joined the local gym down the Walworth Road, which is above a row of shops below. I had noticed it a few times, when going by on a bus. All it's windows were constantly steamed up. I found a leaflet at the town hall, when I was up there paying my rent and discovered they did sessions on certain mornings for the over fifty fives. Got to be honest, I felt a bit of a plum at first, as I changed into my old tracksuit in the changing room, but nobody there took much notice of me after a couple of minutes of being the new boy, and after that I just blended in.

There was a right old mixture of shapes and sizes in our group. The majority had been sent here by their GP, and bless most of them, they were trying to do their best.

The equipment at the gym was pretty good and before long I was doing a bit of light jogging on the running machine. I also lifted a few weights and did a lot of stretching exercises.

Within a fortnight of this, I noticed I had lost a bit of weight and I felt better in myself and I was certainly sleeping better at night.

I had made my mind up, and all this, was a way of making a statement to myself. If I was going over the top, one last time, I knew I wouldn't be able to get back to the old caper without a bit of effort. I needed to be fitter if I was going up a drainpipe for old times sake!

Over the course of the next few days, I also began to hang around Hatton Garden, getting to know the comings and goings of Maury's shop.

I needed to know who arrived when and at what time did they leave? I arrived very early one morning and looked all over the building from the outside when there was no one about. I made myself comfortable, sat in a cafe opposite, just keeping an eye on things, jotting down a few notes.

I studied this information religiously when I got back home. I had also decided to pack up the booze and fags for the duration of what was to come. Blimey, that was tough at first, real cold turkey stuff, but gradually I got used to it. So, as I made do with a cup of lemon and ginger tea, I pored over the paperwork.

"Shop opens to the public at 10am. A member of staff in there from a quarter to, turning lights on etc. Shop not shut for lunch. All off the premises by 6pm. Four staff in total."

If my old legs could get me up and into the building I would have plenty of time to do the business. With Elizabeth's 'tom' already sold, my plan now was to aim at getting as much gold and other trinkets as possible out of the shop.

That precious yellow metal was now fetching silly prices at the minute and I knew of at least six places or so on the Walworth Road who would take it off me, without too many questions being asked as to it's source of origin.

Unlike previously, this time I had decided to keep schtum and not tell a soul about what I was up to. It was best they were all left out of it. As I saw it, I would get the gold, sell it on and hand the dough over to Pauline's boys.

No doubt, Maury would suss it was me who had got in and robbed them and he would then set the law onto me, and if they could make the charges stick, well so be it. Hopefully, I would have time to set the next part of the plan in action and it wouldn't interfere with what I had lined up.

I would tell Terry and Chrissy to wait a couple of months to let the dust settle and then hand over the dough raised from the sale of the newly pinched 'tom' to the council, instructing them to say the money they were handing over, was a private donation to help keep Benhill open.

Even now, a week before I planned to do the job, I was resigned to going back inside to tell you the truth. What was that old saying - 'if you can't do the time, don't do the crime'.

Spot on that.

I knew it would have killed Tubbs and Pauline stone dead, if they got nicked anywhere near all this, and there was no need for that. No, this one was down to me, besides I had made my mind up, and I am one stubborn sod when I've done that.

I circled the date of the proposed blag in my pocket diary and doing that raised an ironic smile. It was the 22nd of September. Fifty years to the day of the Elizabeth Taylor robbery.

I took that as a sign. Meant to be old son, just meant to be.

Having cased the outside of the shop already, I now needed to get someone inside to find out what alarms they had in there.

I thought back to what Dot had said after the funeral, of how if she had her time again, she would help me. Well, now was the time to find out how serious she was.

I found her in the laundry room, muttering away to herself.

'Aye, fold that one there…and that one…'

I guessed she was thinking she was speaking to Margie. They had been so close for so many years, when Margie went, it must have been like losing a limb.

I slowly walked up behind her, trying my hardest not to startle her, as it was obvious she was unaware I was there.

'Er…Dot…'

Of course, as soon as I spoke, she jumped three foot in the air!

'EASY Dot, easy,' I said trying to calm here down, 'it's only me.'

'Sweet holy Mother , you scared the bejesus out of me there Vinny. Och, my word. What you doing creeping about ya little tinker?'

I laughed. 'Honestly Dot, I tried my best to let you know I was there, but you seemed lost in another world mate.'

She looked reflective, rewinding her thoughts back a few seconds.

'You're absolutely right Vin, I was miles away – I was actually thinking of my dear sister. We always did the washing together….'

As she said that sadness covered her face and for a moment, it was creasing up as if to cry. But she stiffened her resolve, bless her.

'Listen Dot, got something to ask you. Bit awkward to tell you the truth, but you mentioned the other day, that you would be willing to help me, you know...' I looked around, making sure no one was ear wigging our conversation. 'With that bit of business.' I winked at her as I finished talking.

'Oh aye, aye I will. But I don't really know what I ...'

'Listen, listen,' I said quickly, trying to reassure her 'I wouldn't ask you if I didn't need to, but Pauline and Tubbs have done their bit and now I need a fresh face.' I smiled directly at her.

'What...what do I need to do?' she asked blushing.

'Really, it's nothing to be scared of, honestly. Believe me, I wouldn't ask if it was too dodgy.'

I walked to the doorway of the launderette and made sure there was no one in earshot.

I walked back to Dot, smiling as I did so.

'Ok. I'm going to give you the address of a jeweller in Hatton Garden. I want you to go in there on the pretence of having a look round for a pocket watch for your husband, but....'

I noticed a little bead of sweat had formed on Dot's top lip. She looked a little nervous.

'Listen Dot. Maybe...you really don't have to do this you know.'

'NO, no. Please carry on. I really want to help Vincent. Go on. Please.'

I smiled. I could only admire her spirit.

'Ok if you are sure. Whilst you are in the shop, I want you to have a look to see if there are any alarm boxes on view. If you notice any, make a mental note of the make and size and then count how many you can see. And that my sweet Dot is that, that is all I need.'

Dot looked pleasantly surprised.

'That's it Vin? Are you sure?'

'Yes my love. That is all I need. I know I can trust you to do that. But listen. One last thing. Not a word to Tubbs or Pauline about this, or anyone else for that matter, you hear me? If either of them find out, the whole thing will be called off.'

'You can trust me Vinny. You can. I meant what I said the other day.

Besides what can go wrong? I'll have my Margie with me to make sure I don't mess up.'

I smiled. 'Cheers Dot, you're a trooper.'

I planted a kiss on her forehead and let her and her sister get back to their washing.

11

Like Putty In My Hands

My body gradually got used to the amount of exercise I was now doing. I felt fitter, stronger.

However, my old nemesis, sleep, began to elude me once again. Once I closed my eyes, all I could think about was the date I was due to go into the jewellers.

I was, in effect, now turning my back on years of going straight and also going against all the principles I had lived by for the past forty odd years.

Not an easy thing to do as I was now discovering, as night after night I just lay awake and worked out how I was going to pull this job off.

The doubts about it all were creeping up on me all the time, and even disturbing my waking hours, when my mind drifted on to the subject.

At night, I could hear voices telling me that I was a stupid old man, that I was bound to fuck it up, and that I would spend the remainder of my life behind bars.

I just couldn't shut out the negative thoughts, even my old favourite from my prison days, of counting down from a hundred, failed.

I must have also counted fifty thousand sheep in a couple of nights of just laying there. As a result, I'd even gone right off Lamb dinners.

I had thought about starting the drinking again, hoping enough malt would knock me out, but I had the feeling it would only have the effect of me being pissed and laying there counting drunk sheep!

The oddest sensation I had when I closed my eyes was spinning round and around and around. I physically had to lie on my back and place my arms either side of me, palms against the bed to steady myself.

In truth, I felt like I was slowly going mad.

I now only had five days to go to T-Day – 'Tom Day.' The planning of how to get into the shop and then to neutralise the alarms was the one thing I hadn't really solved. I was going over all the permutations in my swede.

Each time I visualised it, I always managed to get in to the shop in my minds eye, but I was forever getting stuck on the killing of the alarm and then opening the safe.

I was no peter man, but I once knew plenty who were. I had actually toyed with the idea of bringing someone in, another pair of hands so to speak. It would share the planning load, but it would also mean I would have to share any ill gotten gain we got our sticky fingers on, and I wasn't sure how much of that I would get in the first place.

Besides, any decent, professional blagger would only take a job on once they had weighed up the amount of dough expected to come their way against how much bird they would stand for if all went tits up and they ended up doing stir.

And before I actually got to that point, who exactly did I know now? It had been years since I was active. I mean, it weren't like I could put a small ad for an accomplice in Villains Weekly was it?

Going from the memory of the layout of the shop, from that time I popped in to find Maury, I recalled there was a lot of good quality gear laying about in various cabinets, cupboards and display cases.

Granted they would be locked, bolted and most of the good stuff in the safe, but I had already decided that if I couldn't get the bloody thing open, I'd nick anything I could gain access to and that would have to do. All a bit desperate really, but that was exactly what I had become. Bleeding desperate!

Was this a professional job? You must be kidding. This was strictly amateur hour stuff.

In my heart of hearts I knew this was basically a doddery silly old sod having once last tilt at the world. If I got away with it and got my hands on a few bob, well lovely. If I naused it up and the old bill pinched me there and then, well it was hands up, come and get me sheriff.

The only person I would find it hard to look in the face if that happened would be my Matt. I would just hope he'd understand why I did it. It would be difficult to square it all with him, but I think I knew him well enough now to think he'd understand.

'Oh, fuck this, this is bloody pointless.'

Yes, I said this out loud and to no one in particular. Something else I had been doing lately was talking to myself on a regular basis. As I said, I was slowly going potty under the stress of it all.

I got up and put the kettle on. I poured myself a hot chocolate, walked in to my front room and stuck the telly on. The kitchen clock was chiming one bell. Bloody one in the morning, flaming hell.

I picked up the remote and flicked through a few channels, swerving the stupid American 'I Married My Sister' shows and endless 'Doing Up Your Motor' car programmes.

I was looking for a film to watch. Anything that would take my mind off Maury. There just had to be one on there.

Flick.

Flick.

Flick.

I had ended up on the Film Four channel, currently showing an old black and white film, which going by the accents was in French. I hate subtitles, but needs must tonight, so I decided to stick with it. Thankfully, before long I didn't need them. There wasn't that much talking anyway.

From the looks of it, a gang of geezers were up to a caper, and it looked like the early stages of a robbery being planned. I looked at the time and it was now twenty past one. I picked up the free TV guide from last Sunday papers and scanned down the listings.

Found it. Turned out I was watching a film called "Rififfi" from 1955. I noticed I had missed half hour or so of it, but I had found myself being drawn in on the action, so that didn't really matter.

Back to this gang, who were down in what looked like a basement, trying to find a way of stopping an alarm going off.

'I know how you feel mate.' I heard myself mutter.

A very sweaty bloke, snout dangling from his mouth, which I took to be the leader of the gang, had purposely tripped the alarm, which set the bells off ringing. As quick as a flash, he simply squirted foam from a fire extinguisher into the metal casing and grill of the alarm, filling it up to overflowing.

The noise coming from the box instantly quieted down to a very dull rattling noise. Our smoking hero then jemmied open the outer lid of the metal box and cut some wires. A little light came on indicating that a relief battery had come into play, but he simply squirted the rest of the foam inside of the box, the result of which meant you hardly hear a sound.

The rest of the gang stood around their leader and smiled. Looks like they had it sorted.

I sat there smiling too. Whoever or whatever was keeping me awake tonight and had guided me to this film had done me a right favour.

I sat through the rest of their actual robbery and it went ok for them as they turned over a large Mappin and Webb. There was even a sequence in the film, where I don't think anyone actually spoke for twenty minutes and it was that time they did the blag.

There was a real tension watching it and such a relief, for me anyway, when they finally made their escape from the premises.

What happened in the end I hear you ask?

Go and buy the bloody DVD!

Once the film had ended, I turned the telly off, remained in the armchair and managed to grab a couple of hours of shuteye.

Once awake though, I decided to find Dot in an hour or two and get her on the shake.

Today was the day I had asked her to visit the Hatton Garden shop and get the info. I was now looking for, couldn't come quick enough for me.

She looked tense and nervous, when I found her sitting in our lounge, but she told me she was determined to go through with it and that was that.

Well, she played a blinder. That very same afternoon she came to my flat and gave me a neatly written out detailed list of where the alarms were and how many extinguishers they had.

'Did I do alright Vinny? Is everything you need there?'

I smiled as I read her paperwork.

'Its perfect Dot, honestly. I couldn't have asked for more. Cheers love.'

'Oh good gracious, that's good to hear. I wasn't half nervous.'

She sounded very relieved.

'Any dramas? Anyone notice you?' I asked this as

nonchantly as I could.

'Don't think so, at least, no one said anything. I told them I was just browsing. I had a good look around, memorised the number of extinguishers and made my excuses and left. My hand was shaking as I wrote the information down outside. I'm just pleased it's what you wanted.'

Once again I smiled at her. What a good 'un she was.

Well, that was it. I now had all the information I needed. Now, it was all down to me.

The 22nd fell on a Saturday night. My theory behind the choice of that day being the shop would be shut on the Sunday, so I might have a few more hours to do the dirty deed without being disturbed.

This now being Thursday afternoon, I had just two days to wait.

I mulled it over and thought it best to ring my Matthew. I knew I couldn't say anything about what I was up to, because I knew if he got wind of it, he would try and talk me out of it and stop me somehow.

But I still wanted to call him, just to have a chat, well, you know, in case it all went bandy my end on the Saturday and it was the last time I spoke to him as a free man.

As ever it was lovely to hear his voice say 'Hello dad' and we chatted for half hour, all over the place we went without actually saying anything of any importance. My mission had been accomplished, so I began to say my goodbyes.

'How are the girls son?'

'Yeh good dad, both cracking on.'

'You'll notice that mate, time just flashes past in a blink of an eye.'

'Tell me about it, look at the age of me. Haha.'

'Turn it up boy, how d'ya think that makes me feel. Having a son over fifty. Dear me ...'

And I too started laughing.

'Listen, I got to go, just wanted to say...er...'

'What? Dad, what's up mate?'

'There's nothing up, really...just wanted to say I send my love to you all and give Trudy, Bella and Evie a kiss from me.'

'Course, yeah no worries on that score mate. You take care, hear me? Love ya dad.'

'And you Matt. Bye mate. Bye son...'

I put the phone down and sat in silence for quite a while, whilst I thought of the amount of the early years I missed with young Matt, and here I was now dicing with missing the later part of his life as well.

Over the past couple of weeks I had been thinking about my first year inside. As that old blues song goes, 'I was so down, I had to reach up to touch bottom.'

In that first year, I had lost faith in ever being a good citizen again. As a result of that overwhelming feeling, I thought it wise to get myself an education in the secrets of the street.

They say prison back then, was like college for the criminal classes. Whatever crime you were thinking of taking part in once back out on the street, the technique to bring that off could be learnt inside.

You name it. Fraud, forgery, bank robbing, safe cracking, the long firm game...the list went on and on.

One fella I met over lunch one day, claimed he had turned the taxman over so regularly in years gone by, that the Inland Revenue now sent him Christmas Cards.

I'll be honest and say in my first year I dabbled in all of the above, and learnt as much as I could from the other cons, all of whom were willing to lay down their secrets for half ounce of bacca or a couple of tins of peaches.

I learnt the ways of the peter off old 'College Albert, Albert Morris to give him his proper name. What he didn't know about getting into a safe wasn't worth knowing. Hence the nickname. It was an education being around him.

Hard man though Albert, tough as teak he was.

That first year inside, I made the mistake of telling him I was having trouble at home with Brenda and he bluntly said I'd be better off without her.

'Loads of geezer's in here doing a five stretch cos mum has dobbed them in, tellin' ya. If the old woman gets the hump with ya and you 'appen to be "at it", bang! One word to the law, and she's got a clear path with you out of the way.'

Tried to argue with him, that my Bren and me weren't like that, but he weren't listening.

'You mob today are like a bunch of bleedin ballerinas, gorn soft you have. In my day, if the missus played up, well, a wallop on the chops straightened them out.'

Hard man, as I say.

Over the course of the next few weeks, for some reason he started to take a shine to me however. Think it was because he was also out of South East London.

'You know the Barclays at New Cross? He said one day. 'Done that one.'

'What over the counter?' I stupidly asked.

'Nah, as a painter and decorator! What d'ya think son! Course, we went over the top. Grabbed a plum from that we did.'

When it came to safe breaking, there was none of the dynamite or jelly for old Albert. No, he did it all on the combination. He had the fingers of a concert pianist and he taught me a few twists and turns of a dial. Fascinating to listen to, well at first.

But coming up to the end of that first year in the booby, I knew this life wasn't for me. I began to feel strongly, the error of my ways. Funnily enough, I was embarrassed to admit this to Albert, thought he would look down on me. But actually, the reverse happened. He was proud that I had decided to leave that way of life.

'If it aint for you, then you shouldn't be doing it. It aint for everyone. One thing though,' he said 'promise me, you'll get an education while you're in here. Do you the world of good that will.'

And that's what I did. I took up reading books, any book I could find. Fiction, autobiographies, history, just about anything. I even passed a couple of exams that I didn't go near when at school. English and History, something to be proud of.

In the intervening years, I had forgotten all about 'College Albert' and his lessons all those years ago. Of course, being inside I never had the chance to try out the techniques, so I never truly knew if they worked or he was filling my head with rubbish.

Well, I guess I was about to find out...

On the day of the appointed Saturday I decided on radio silence. I wouldn't talk to anyone today, trying to keep my mind solely on the job in front of me, no distractions. I also wanted to preserve as much energy as possible

There were a couple of rings on my doorbell and my phone rung a few times but I blanked them, all day. I remained in my dressing gown and I made myself some lunch and sat in peace and quiet all day.

I ran my plan over and over in my head all day until I felt I was prepared and ready. Then I tried to relax, to unwind.

At around five, just as the sky had started to become dark and gloomy, I had a quick shower and I began to dress. Within ten minutes, I was wearing some clothes I had recently bought at the Army Surplus store on the Walworth Road. Black army style trousers, black pumps and socks, topped off with a black roll neck and my thick old donkey jacket.

I had my black leather gloves and balaclava in my pocket and I packed an old canvas rucksack, with a couple of sandwiches in tin foil, some tools – pliers, a small hammer and a couple of screwdrivers – plus a small torch, my hip flask and a rolled up, thick old rough hessian doormat that I had got from East Lane market a week earlier

I left the flat at just before six and thankfully I didn't bump into anyone as I left by the back door. I was now in no mood for chit chat, I just wanted to get weaving.

On the bus down towards Blackfriars, I looked out of the window on the top deck and into the flats of the people residing along the route. They all looked cosy, comfortable and safe in their homes and I envied them that at that precise moment.

Would I be going back to any of that after tonight?

At about a quarter to seven, and three stops past Blackfriars Bridge, I pressed the bell and then left the bus.

I slowly walked up a couple of streets towards Maury shop. As I got near it, I stopped and looked up noticing the sky was now pitch black, as black as Newgates Knocker as my old mum used to say.

That memory provoked a small smile.

By this time of the evening, it was dead quiet all around me, with only a few people milling about. Just how I liked it.

I was now opposite the shop. I stood across from it, in the shadow from a tall office block to my right and just looked for any sign of life. From what I could tell, it was closed, empty and shut up for the weekend.

I suddenly felt some pangs of hunger, so now seemed as good a time to eat as any, so out came the ham and mustard pickle sarnies I had prepared earlier, and I munched those as I continued to keep dog eye.

After ten minutes or so, all the food was eaten and I had

still seen no sign of anyone on the premises.

I had a quick scout round about me. I couldn't see or hear anyone, so I walked up to the front door of the shop and banged on it with my fist as hard as I could and then stepped back slightly, raising my head, listening as keenly as I could for a sound.

As I was hoping and praying no light came on from inside, I didn't hear any raised voices and no nosy neighbours popped their heads out any windows either.

Finally satisfied the field was clear, I reached into the deep pockets of my donkey jacket and removed the balaclava and gloves and put them on. I took the rolled up door mat from inside my rucksack and stuffed this partly down my waistband.

I walked off to my immediate left and up a little alleyway I had discovered on my recces. Directly now in front of me, was a brick wall about nine foot in height. All along it's top edge, it had sharp, jagged pieces of different coloured glass protruding from it.

My guess was that once past this wall, I would be into the yard that backed onto the shop.

A wooden doorway was built into the wall. I jiggled the handle of an old battered door, but this was, unsurprisingly, locked. I thought for a second about jemmying it open, but then considered that this might make too much noise. No, there was nothing else for it, I'd have to go over the wall.

I stepped to the right of the door, and reached up both my hands and managed to get a decent grip on the small cracks between the bricks. I then put my right foot into another gap lower down and then straightened that leg, keeping the weight on it.

This motion propelled the rest of my body upwards and I then reached higher with my left hand, trying frantically to get a decent hold, only my right hand fingers weakened and I lost contact with the wall and slipped back down.

I slumped to the ground, shaking my now stinging hand.

Fuck it. This is ridiculous, five minutes in and I'm already puffing and struggling.

It was like my mind was in some sort of denial I think, trying to shut all this down, or so it seemed.

It was like it was saying 'oh no, not this game again.'

I forced myself to concentrate. 'Come on', I whispered, 'you can do this, you old tart.'

I steadied myself and once again, I reached up and got a nice grip with my left hand. I repeated the right leg movement and this time I remained in contact with the wall. My right knee was now aching, with a strong pain growing steadily. I tried to ignore the distress signals this was sending up into my brain, as my right hand reached up to the top of the wall.

I was now conscious of the glass I could feel above me. I reached down and pulled the doormat from my waistband and placed it over the shards, hoping it would afford me some sort of protection.

I gripped the wall just beneath its top and inched up both of my feet higher, gaining two decent toeholds. Again, I straightened my right leg and after another couple of movements, I now had both of my gloved hands on top of the mat. I again inched myself up, and rested both of my elbows, where my hands had just been. I could feel the points of some of the glass edges poking into my left elbow, going straight through my jacket, but I knew I couldn't turn back now.

I was rapidly running out of breath and sweat was running down my face and back. My body was shaking slightly at the effort I was exerting; and began to put my aged limbs into a sort of shock.

I resolved to give it one last push and managed to get my belly on top of the wall. I could once again feel sharp edges biting into me, but I did my best to ignore them.

I couldn't lie there for more than a few seconds, before the pain became too much however.

I swung my legs over to the shop side of the drop and slowly tried to lower myself down the wall.

Only I found my grip was weak, much weaker than I anticipated and my right knee was now screaming at me to pack this all in.

I managed to lower myself for a few seconds, but then my grip gave way and I fell quite heavily to the ground.

I landed with quite a thump, which did my knee no favours.

I sat still in the shadows for a minute or two, my chest heaving at the effort I was putting in. I remained motionless as I scanned round to see if the racket I was now making had roused anyone.

Plumes of cold air came from my nose and mouth as I sat there as silently as I could. Once again, thankfully, no one was disturbed.

After recovering as much as I could, I edged over to the back of the building. More in hope, than anticipation, I tried the handle of the back door, the continual turning of which failed to open it.

I looked to my right and saw a wooden framed window about four feet from the ground. That would have to be my way in.

I managed to shimmy up the black metal drainpipe that ran parallel with it and then stood on its window ledge.

I ran my gloved hands all round the edge of the windowpane and noticed the putty around it was in a bad state of repair. Instead of breaking the glass to gain entry as I first planned to do, I now reckoned I could loosen the pane of glass out of the frame, by dislodging the old dried out putty.

I reached into my left hand pocket and removed the small

pliers I had brought along and began scraping around the edges for all I was worth. Sadly, the tool was too small to have any real effect; I needed something larger and sharper.

I jumped down again from the ledge, and rubbed my right knee as I landed. I didn't know what I had done to it, but I knew it would be playing me up in the morning.

I tried my best to focus my eyes on the ground in front of me, hunting round for something which would help me chip away at the painted putty flakes that were just about holding that glass in place.

After a bit of rummaging I found a decent sized piece of sharp edged slate roofing tile.

Perfect!

I made my way back up onto the window ledge again and began to drag the slate down one side of the window. I then went along it's top, down the other side and finally the bottom. I rocked the pane with my hand and it was wobbling nicely. I then concentrated on the bottom edge, managing to get a couple of fingers under the glass.

After a bit more scraping and a bit of to-ing and fro-ing, on both sides, I gradually managed to slide the pane out of its surroundings.

I puffed out my cheeks as I held it in my hands. Phew!

I peered inside through the now empty window frame and made out the top of a draining board in front of me. Of course, I now remembered. I was looking into the kitchen, in which I had sat down with Maury, a couple of weeks back.

I placed the pane to one side and then climbed in the gap, there beig just enough room for me.

I then carefully replaced the loose pane of glass back into the frame of the window, and put a kettle up against it, which held it in place nicely.

As a result of my previous visit; I knew where I was in

relation to the front of the shop. I felt my way in the darkness as I walked through the connecting hallway from the kitchen towards the shop itself.

All that stopped me from getting into the shop properly was a closed door at the end of this passage. I tried its handle but it wouldn't budge. In the dark gloom, I reached up and found a bolt at it's top which I pulled back. I tried the door again. A little more movement was noticeable, but still it wouldn't open. I now felt down towards the bottom and again found another bolt. I again pulled this one back and tried the door. This time, although still stiff, it slowly opened.

I was in. I made my way slowly into the front of the shop proper.

I crouched down and got my bearings of everything that was now in front of me.

It was all lit up by the streetlights directly outside it's main window.

I immediately reached down to my left by the back entrance and felt the top of a fire extinguisher, exactly where Dot said it would be. Good old Dorothy.

I freed it from its wall bracket and carried it as I searched around for the main alarm on the wall. Thankfully, nothing had gone off yet, so I guessed that it was only wired up to the main door and the shop window.

I eventually spied a grey metal alarm box about six feet up on the wall behind the main counter.

I released the nozzle on the bright red extinguisher and aimed it into the front grill on the outer casing. Slowly at first, the white foam oozed out. It quickly did its job of filling all the space around the alarm mechanism. Soon, the excess was running out of the front of the grill.

So far, so no noise.

I flipped open the front of the box, exposing it's inner

workings. As the alarm door opened, it's metal clapper started to vibrate and the whole thing began a dull rattling noise.

I quickly and carefully located, and then cut, the internal wires with my small pliers.

Thankfully, the initial noise stopped. Then the reserve power from a battery kicked in, but once again the foam dampened the noise this generated. Merci Riffifi!

Phew. By this stage, my old pump was going three hundred to the dozen, but somehow, I was still in the game.

With the alarm now out of action, I put my small torch between my teeth and ventured round to see what I could find.

I started to jemmy a few drawers open with my short handled screwdriver and subsequently found a few small bits of tom. A quick look revealed the contents to be watch chains, a tray of old wedding rings, and some old war medals.

Nice gear, but worth a couple of thousand at best. I hadn't done all this for a few poxy grand. I needed more.

I had to find the safe.

I scouted around for a further minute or two and then located it behind the large wooden desk I had seen the younger bloke sitting at, when I visited the shop.

The safe was a huge. A big black beast of a thing. I shone the torch on it and it's light picked out the embossed words upon it - Stanhope and Sons – Safe Makers, London est. 1905'.

I foolishly found myself admiring its beauty, before sharply reminding myself that I had a job of work to do here.

I took both gloves off and removed my sweat sodden balaclava. I wiped my brow and eyes with it and then took a deep breath, before replacing the glove on my right hand.

I got myself comfortable and set about twisting the dial on its front, trying to raid my memory bank for the technique of old 'College Albert'. I spun the dial around and around and around, looking for that elusive noise that I had heard so much about. He had mentioned that nearly all old fashioned combination safes had a group of two locks and they had to be locked a certain way. If this wasn't done properly, an experienced peter man could manipulate the dial and it was 'open sesame'.

Sadly, there was no sign of that here, as I battled on, man versus the safe. As I took a breather and let go of the dial, I glanced at a couple of nice wall mounted clocks both telling me it was now just after 8.30pm. By my calculations, I had been on this job for an hour and half, and that half, had been playing silly beggars with this safe.

The truth was, I was getting nowhere with it. I felt miles away from the world of Albert. As I sat there, slowly turning the dial, the realisation of what I was doing was slowly dawning on me.

'Who are you kidding Vinny eh,?' I muttered to myself. 'Fuck me. You must have been mad mate to even think you could sort this.

You silly old sod, if brains were made of chocolate, you wouldn't have enough to fill a Smartie son.'

CLICK!

That sound made me shut up. That sound made me lean back, amazed at what I had just heard. It was the elusive sound Albert had described. It was the sound of a retracting bolt.

A smile crossed my now weary face.

My inner voice was screaming at me.

THE BLOODY SAFE IS OPENING!

The smile was now fixed on my boat. I tried to compose myself and carried on.

I spun backwards, one, two, three, and four past the

previous number. Slowly, very slowly I twisted the dial one more turn, creeping up slowly on the little crows foot marking carved in the metal above the dial.

CLICK!

My palms were now very sweaty and I wiped them on my strides. Old Albert's theory was coming into sharp view now. It was all coming back to me. I could hear him in my head.

'The majority of people who set the combination, go for either four right, or four left. Don't know why, but it always seems to be the case. The rest of it, well, its up to you. Just turn slowly between the two, to find that elusive, beautiful, clicking noise.'

After cracking the amount of peter's he had in his lifetime, Albert must have surely known the coup. On the evidence so far, he was speaking the truth, not a load of pony, as I might have feared.

I went forwards again. 3…2…1…and…

CLICK!

The sweat drips from my forehead, were exploding onto the highly polished wooden parquet floor of the shop.

Albert came by again…

'One thing I have noticed over the years, is that people rarely have more than four numbers in their combo. My guess is that they can easily remember four. Anymore and they could nause it. Scientific, see.'

'I hope you are right Albert mate.' I whispered as I turned the dial clockwise. 8…9…10.

No CLICK! This time though, more of a CLUNK!

It made a noise that sounded like a lead weight had been dropped on to the floor of the safe.

'Eventually, you'll hear a louder wallop. If you do, the last piece of the jigsaw is in place. You're in then boy. Open Sesame son.'

Thank you Albert I mouthed. I reckon what I had just heard, was the noise of the final bolt retracting. In theory, if I pulled on the dial, the door should swing open.

Again, I leaned back. I wiped my brow on to my right hand and steadied myself. I placed my fingers around the dial and...

CHIME! CHIME! CHIME!

Jesus! Those flaming wall clocks nearly put me in my box as they reached the hour of nine and chimed their collective heads off.

I puffed out my cheeks and breathed deep, trying to stop my ticker racing.

Come on son, come on. This time. I put my left glove back on and grabbed the dial with both hands and pulled it slowly towards me.

My fingers were so sweaty, I couldn't get a decent grip. Nothing moved. Gloves off again and I re-wiped my hands and fingers on my black army trousers, leaving a damp trail along my thighs.

Gloves back in place, I gripped at the dial, as tight as I could and pulled. This time, I felt a little movement in my hand, I pulled again, slowly the safe door opened towards me.

I WAS IN!

I pulled the door back as far as I could and then shone my torch inside. I could see bundles of manila folders stuffed with papers, but little else. I took out the paperwork, had a quick look at it, but pages and pages of invoices were no good to me. I put them on the floor beside me.

Once again, I shone the torch towards the back of the dark inner, of the cavernous safe.

Something there had caught my eye. But what was it?

I looked again and spied a black mass with a glint of gold coming off it.

Nothing else for it. I reached in and grabbed the object I

could see with my left hand.

It looked like a velvet bag.

I pulled it out towards me. Yeah, definitely velvet. I could see it now, luscious, black velvet.

Then, fifty years of my life suddenly flashed in front of me.

It couldn't be...It can't be...

I shone my torch again towards what I was holding and it's light illuminated the gold stitching of the word.

'Elizabeth'

12

Call My Bluff

My knee was now giving me right gip as I sat in the sherbert on the way back to SE5. I just wanted to get indoors as soon as possible.

I looked at the black velvet bag, which I was now cradling in my lap. I couldn't resist yet another look inside though and I loosened the string and took yet another quick peek at the contents.

As I looked up, a smile breaking my face in two, I caught the cabbie looking at me in his rear view mirror.

'Alright mate?' I said to him, fronting him up with a flash of the eyes.

He straightened up and got his minces off the mirror and onto the road in front of him. I would guess he was in his late fifties, and he had a dog-eyed weariness about him. Reckon he'd done nights for too many years going by the state of him. He had a black and white dog-toothed baker boy style cap perched on top of his head.

'Eh? Er yeah…down the Walworth alright for you guv, road works up Camberwell New Road that'll put a fiver on your bill.'

He acted like he hadn't seen anything, but I knew he had.

'Yeah, that'll do, How's the game. Busy?' I was trying to take his mind off what I was holding.

'Kipper mate. Glory days are gone. I only do nights, all I know. It's all mini cab pirates and Buttaboys out there now.

'Who?' I replied.

'Buttaboys. As in. 'He's new in the game, nothing buttaboy. Geddit?'

Smiles all round.

'Bet you've made a packet of fags out of this over the years though haven't you?'

I was rarely in the mood to chat with a cabbie, but willing to make an exception tonight as I wanted to get his mind off what I was holding and back on his trade.

'Can't lie, made a decent drink years back, but the punters aint there no more. Too much competition out there now and all chasing fewer and fewer Normans.'

This chat had had the desired effect. Thankfully, it seemed to take his mind, and more importantly his eyes, off the black velvet bag.

We arrived at Benhill at just after 10.30 pm.

Result. I had been out, done the business and was back in time for the second half of Match of The Day.

'Ere'll do ya mate?' I said as he pulled into the little area in front of the block. I gave the cabbie an apple for a fair of £17.50

'Keep it fella,' I said as he leant over to hand me the change ' I've had a decent night.'

'Ta captain. Thought you had. You kept breaking out into a big smile. Be lucky.'

He winked as he pulled his cab away from the front gate.

Saucy bark, I thought smiling.

I made my way to my flat, clutching the bag tightly in my mitts. Thankfully, once again I managed to get to my front door, without bumping into anyone.

Once I was in, I immediately fell off the wagon I had been sitting on for the past few weeks, and pulled myself a double Scotch and added some ice. I sat down and held the glass to my lips. I could hear the faint tinkling of the ice hitting against each other as my hand shook. I was still full of adrenalin.

Phew…what a night.

I placed the drink down on the coffee table in front of me and got up to Chubb lock my front door and closed the curtains.

I wanted to make sure no one disturbed me for the next ten minutes or so.

I picked up the black velvet bag and loosened the black cord around its neck once again.

I gently shook the contents of the bag onto my coffee table. The clunk of its contents hit the wooden surface with a dull thud.

The glare of the colourful stones now in front me gave off a show like a small firework display. They were beautiful and what's more I was sure they were the tom I nicked in 1962. I had only really seen them at Maurices mums place all those years ago, but I never forget a face…

'Hello boys' I said smiling at them 'well, I didn't ever expect to see you again.'

I poured them all back into bag. I walked into my bedroom and put them under my pillow.

I then went in the bathroom and undressed. I wanted to see the damage that that glass had done. I had quite a few cuts and grazes on both legs and arms. Nothing life threatening though. I just applied plenty of TCP to them which stung like hell and then got into my pyjamas.

I was soon in bed and turning my clock face down. After checking the black bag was in place under my head, I lay back, relaxed and shut my eyes.

I was soon dead to the world, sucked into a comforting blackness that just enveloped me. I felt light as a feather on the bed, hardly touching the surface. Can't remember any dreams, just a deep, deep sleep.

When I finally woke up and put on the bedside lamp I had no idea what the time was. I had to look twice at my now upright bedside clock as it stated it was now nearly mid-day.

As I lay there, I slowly gathered my thoughts together, piece-by-piece, the previous nights exploits came back to me and that smile returned to my face again.

I immediately felt hungry, so I pulled on my blue toweling bathrobe, slipped into my slippers and was soon in the kitchen rustling up a full English.

Soon the bacon and sausages were sizzling away. As I stood waiting to turn the bacon over and for my kettle to boil, I noticed the answer phone light was flashing. I guess I had slept through my telephone ringing.

I pressed the play button and after a few clicks and a bleep, a well-spoken automated voice was telling me I had one message from '09.30 today'. I pressed 'one' to hear a voice I instantly recognised.

'Vincent – Maurice here. I do hope you are well. I got your number from our mutual friend Spencer. He wasn't best pleased to be disturbed at what he called an un-godly hour on a Sunday, but I told him it was urgent that I spoke to you, so he kindly obliged. Don't be upset with him will you.

I popped into the shop today, to pick up some paperwork for a job I have got on tomorrow, only to find we had a visitor overnight. Of course, it could mice...but I thought I'd speak to you before I called Rentokil. Please call me on the following number, I think we need to talk.'

He then rattled off a mobile phone number. A wry smile crossed my lips. Well, it didn't take him long to find me. I smiled at the thought of Maurice discovering the missing items.

I replayed the message and quickly scribbled down the number on the back of Fridays South London Press.

'Beep. End of message. You have no new messages.'

'You can wait Maury my son, just like I had to' I muttered.

My smile continued as I carried on turning the bacon.

After devouring the lovely breakfast and having a quick shower, I was dressed and ready to leave the flat. I took the velvet bag from under my pillow and wrapped it among my dirty washing in my laundry bag.

Within minutes, I was on a 36 bus on the way to Victoria station. Once there, I called my son Matt on his mobile, I told him I was on the way down to him on a flying visit, nothing to worry about, just wanted to pick his brains. Told him to meet me at the café at the station, no need to go to his place.

Matt sounded a bit confused by the call. Couldn't blame him I suppose. As for me, I was finally now ready to let a few people in on what I had been up to in the last couple of weeks. And Matt was at the top of that list.

I was down at Whitstable station about two hours after calling the boy and I found him already seated at a table with a coffee on the go, by the time I got there.

'Aright son.' I said as I got near him . He immediately stood up and we hugged. That felt good I can tell you. I shouted up a cappuccino from the pretty little waitress, and I then sat next to Matthew. After a few pleasantries about his darling family, I cut to the chase.

'Listen Matt, I need your help in finding out a bit of info. but want you to remember that whatever happens, I will take sole responsibility if anything comes on top.'

'Dad, what the flaming hell have you done mate? I know something's going on. What with that call the other night and now this...'

Matt looked like he had the right hump.

'Nothing for you to worry about, believe me.' I said, trying to calm him down.

'Dad, come on. It sounded like you wanted to say something, but you just couldn't say it, whatever it was. I guessed something was up.'

'Listen son,' I said 'nothings up mate. I just need a bit of info. is all.'

'So why all the talk of "if things come on top". That doesn't sound particularly like nothings up to me mate.'

He was right. He wasn't a silly bloke and here I was treating him like one. The time to front it, was now here.

I stirred my cappuccino over and over as I slowly began relating the tale of the previous evenings outing and slowly he looked more and more amazed as I spoke.

'You did what!' He said little too loudly.

I sat smiling at him. 'That's it, that's all I'm short of. You creating a bleedin' scene, so all these nice middle class suburban people here, begin looking at us.'

Thankfully he dropped his voice a few decibels as he spoke again.

'Well, what the hell am I supposed to say when you land a story like that on me?'

I looked him straight in the eyes.

'Look, I know it sounds crazy, but it was something I had to do. It wouldn't go away. No matter how hard I tried, and believe me I tried bloody hard, it just wouldn't go away, I owed Maury one and now it's done. Besides, I'm already planning the next step.'

'But dad, Christ, won't this fella, Maury or whatever his name is, come looking for the goods and more worryingly, for you?'

'Yeah, that's an outside bet to happen, but he doesn't know

where I live and you know what, I aint too worried about him to be honest. We've got history and I like to think I've settled an old score.'

'Fuck me.' He sighed. I thought to myself, this must be bad, because that's the first time I've heard my son swear.

'Ok, so,' he continued 'what do you need me for then?'

I smiled 'Thought you'd never ask. I need you to look up the Elizabeth Taylor Estate for me and send an email based on this.'

I handed him a piece of scrap paper, on which were the words I had written whilst on the train down here and which I now wanted him to send over.

'Copy that word for word and ping it, or whatever you do with emails, off for me.'

Matt picked up the scrap of paper and began to read it. After a couple of a minutes, he spoke.

'Oh come on, you aint seriously thinking they are going to run with this are you?'

'Yeah why not,' I said 'they end up looking like a bunch of good guys with that ending.'

Matt just shook his head.

'I can only wish you luck dad. And after what I have I heard in the last half hour, I need a lie down. Look, why don't you spend the afternoon with us? Trudie has got roast chicken for dinner, plenty of room for one more.'

As tempting as that offer was I told him, I had to get back. I had plenty of business to attend to.

We finished our coffees, we hugged and shook hands and he promised me he would call me if or when he got a reply.

I got on the next rattler back to London and on arrival at London Bridge, I took the scrap of paper on which I had written Maury's number on, and phoned him from a phone box on the concourse.

Obviously, he had my home number, but not my mobile and that suited me fine.

He told me, he was pleased to hear my voice. He also told me he had managed to hold off the owners of the shop from calling the OB, as they couldn't find anything actually missing from their own stock. He told them the only loss that had occurred, was down to him and that he would sort that out himself. They reluctantly agreed, for now anyway, the result of which bought us both a bit of time.

I told him I couldn't make a meet today, cos I was on family business, but I arranged to meet him the next day over at 'The King Louis Of Camberwell'.

He didn't sound too keen on having to come over to my patch, but as I now held all the aces, he had little choice in reality. Besides, I wanted to have my manor at my back in case he started anything silly. He huffed and puffed, but we finally agreed on a Monday lunchtime meet.

That evening I took Pauline, Tubbs and Dot for a nice Italian meal at Caravaggios on Camberwell High Street. I ordered up a couple of nice bottles of 'over a tenner' wines and we settled down for a good evening.

My companions were all delighted to be asked out, although I could see they were a little curious as to why?

'Well,' said Pauline with a smile in her voice, as I poured her a glass of chilled Vino Blanc 'where you been for the last few days? No one's seen you.'

'Had a bit of business on didn't I.' I said smiling.

'Business? What kinda business? 'Asked Tubbs.

'Never you mind mate.' I said 'all will be revealed in the fullness of time. Now what you eating, they do a nice drop of Fruits of The Sea in here'

'Wassat?' asked Pauline.

Scallops to you girl!' I said laughing.

'Vinny' laughed Tubbs 'you're up to something peculiar you are. I know you.'

'Don't you concern yourself about Vinny,' said Dot 'he knows what he's doing, eh Vincent?'

I just smiled at her. 'That's right mate. Now, raise your glasses please. Cheers to you all and may you get all you wish yourself in life.

There's no need to be alarmed eh Dorothy?'

And at that both me and Dot laughed out loud.

'Flaming mad the pair of 'em' said Pauline nipping at the vino.

It turned into a lovely evening, hearing stories of their respective long lost partners and family. I spoke at length about my Brenda. Of how I had messed that up and also the mistakes I made with my Matty. The wine flowed as did more tales and by the end of our meals we were coming to the end of the second bottle.

We all stumbled the few hundred yards back to our sheltered homes and after checking my special laundry was still in place, I then began to think about Maury and tomorrow.

I was up bright and early the next day, as was the day itself. It certainly felt like the sun was shining down on the righteous today.

I had a wet shave, and got out my best suit for the occasion. Freshly ironed crisp white shirt on, best cufflinks in and shoes, highly polished.

At just after the appointed time of mid-day I arrived at 'The Louis'.

As I walked in, I noticed Maury and two other younger gentlemen sitting at an adjoining table about ten feet away.

Maury nodded towards me and one of the other two stood up as he did so, but Maury put out an hand on the fellas arm and made a gesture of sit back down to him.

I noticed they all had full glasses of what looked like water in front of them. I nodded to young Neville behind the ramp and ordered up my usual vodka and slim-line.

'Nev' I whispered, 'do me a favour son. If those three over there get lively, watch me back, eh?'

'Of course Vin, goes without saying. Think you'll be alright though from looking at them. Look a right load of nebbishes to me. Only drinking Chateau du Tap.'

I winked at him, as I picked up my drink and then turned and walked over to their table.

'Hello Gents' I said 'lovely day for it. Mind if I join you?'

'Ever the joker Vincent, always admired that about you.' Maury was smiling, but he didn't sound too happy.

I sat down and made a point of looking at the two lumps either side of him and then back at Maury.

'Oh, how terribly rude of me. May I introduce my two sons, Lawrence,' and he nodded to his right, 'and Sam here, his younger brother.'

That makes you Samuel Samuels then son, I thought. Nice of the old man to do that to you.

They were both dressed in decent suits. I knew from memory that Lawrence was roughly the same age as my Matt and Sam looked a few years younger. He, of the two, looked the more agitated to be sitting there.

I looked at them both, square on.

'Nice to meet you boys. Me and your dad go way back.'

Sam spoke next, in an educated acent. 'Oh we've heard all about you sir.'

'Oh, sir is it sunshine? Like it. Brought the boys up well then Maurice? Good schools and all that, eh? Not like our day mate, not like that for you and me was it eh? Leaving school at fourteen to find our way in the world.'

Maury smiled. 'Different days now Vinny. The least you can do is leave your children in a better place, when you yourself shuffle off to meet the God of your choice.'

'Wise words.' I said 'Wise words indeed.'

But Maury hadn't finished. 'Which of course brings us here today. A certain, er, parcel has gone missing and I...we...want it back.'

Maurice was obviously in a rush to get things sorted. He was off and running.

'We'll get to that Maury, believe me. But I just want to establish something. Do these fine, well-brought up young gentleman, know the full extent of your past? I mean, before the time you started hitting the glittering pavements of Hatton Garden?'

'They do indeed Vincent. I have told them everything of how we met and how our paths separated before re-joining again very recently.'

'So,' I said suddenly changing the jovial nature of the banter 'they know how I came to you and you tucked me up then?'

'Tut, tut, tut, come now Vincent– such emotive words.' Maury was now smiling.

The eldest, Lawrence, decided to pipe up. 'The way we see it, is that you, er "tucked yourself up". My father held onto those certain items for a long time. Longer than, perhaps, he should have done. Then due to you not reclaiming them after a decent length of time, they simply became his property.'

'You might sound refined son, but you are talking absolute bollocks.' I replied.

'I beg your pardon?' said Sam.

'You heard, you pair of stuck up pillocks. You can't really know anything of my first meeting with your dad. If you were given the truth, you would know you are talking absolute nonsense.'

I slowly raised my Vodka to my lips, as I fired off that last sentence.

'Do we have to listen to this, this, piece of rubbish father.' said the younger boy.

I looked pityingly at the kid.

'Don't know why you brought them here today Samuels? Really, I don't. It can't be that they are supposed to frighten me, surely? Mouth full of toecaps planned for me later is there? Eh Maury? From these two?'

With that Sam jumped up and made a move over the table towards me. Once again his old dad pulled him back.

'Down boy.' I said as he glowered towards me.

Maury raised him his right hand, which had the effect of setting his son back in his seat.

'Frighteners Vincent, these two? No, you've got it all wrong my friend. These two are my business partners. They joined me a few years ago now. So you see they have a vested interest in getting back what they and I must say, I, now feel is mine.'

'OK, so if that is the case, I take it you've finally called the old bill about the supposed robbery you mentioned on the phone earlier then?'

'Nothing supposed about that robbery sir' said Lawrence. 'We have all witnessed the safe door open and the parcel missing from inside.'

'So, you've got outdated security. Is that really my problem? Is it my fault that someone is too tight to upgrade the er, defences.'

I then repeated my original question.

'So, what did lily law have to say for herself when you finally got through?'

Maury leant forward towards me as he spoke. 'As I mentioned earlier, we have managed to keep them out of it, for now. Thought we would be able to sort it face to face.'

'Call this face-to-face do you Maury. Looks like three faces to one, as I sit here. Mind you, I shouldn't really be surprised. You did always like the odds stacked in you favour.'

Maury smiled.

'Ok, perhaps, I should have come alone,' he said 'but I didn't know what I was walking into. A back street boozer over on your manor, anything could have been waiting for me.'

'You've been watching too many gangster films mate.' I said sarcastically.

'Perhaps you're right, perhaps I misjudged you Vincent.'

'Oh, you have my son. You have all along, right from our first meeting all those years ago. But it's all a bit late now isn't it? One thing about me Maury that you perhaps should have learnt by now, is that I hate injustice and being wronged. If I feel that has happened to me, well, I never give up. I'm a stubborn bastard I am. I remain in the game. I stay longer than the mother in law, know what I mean?'

Maury broke into a smile 'I'm beginning to realise that.'

I smiled back at him.

'Before we go any further. One question for you. One that has been bugging me since discovering that MY goods weren't in with the departed Myra, but intact, in a safe in Hatton Garden.

Why didn't you fence them, as my grand daughters are fond of saying, "back in the day", as you said you were going to?'

Maury smiled again.

'When it came to it, I just couldn't do it. I knew you were keen to sell, but I knew that I wouldn't see the likes of those gems ever again. They were the ultimate in our profession, such as it was. It was like me winning the World Cup, them landing in my lap like that. So, I didn't want to let go.

With the sudden of death of dear mother, I saw an opportunity that I just couldn't resist. I just knew you would be at nicked at some point, you just had that look about you. So I hung onto them and waited.

Once you went away, from then on, I referred to them as my pension plan.

When it is time to retire they will come in very handy.'

'They would have come in handy,' I said. 'Notice the past tense there Maury. Learnt all that studying in the nick.'

'Listen Mr. Hawkins. I've had enough now. Give my father his property back, or we will call the police right here and now.'

Sam had obviously had enough of me and his dad going down memory lane. He was now very jittery. No patience these kids.

'Really?' I said 'is that what you want to do son? Is it? Really?

Well, I aint stopping you. Go on, do it son.'

It was my turn to adopt an angry tone in my voice.

'Crack on Samuel Samuels, don't let me stop ya son.'

Sam looked at his father. He was looking very flustered. This wasn't going to their carefully laid plan.

I took out my mobile phone and placed it on the table between us.

'Oh, silly me, how embarrasing!' I said as I did so 'I know what you're now thinking now. You're thinking that this is a really old model. Looks like a fucking house brick, compared with the ones that people have got now.

I know, I know. But you know what? It gets a great signal in here, in this boozer. Never lets me down. In fact, why don't I call the old bill for ya? Save your money son. Think of it as my treat, eh? Shall I?'

Maury and his eldest son Lawrence were silent, but young Sam was rising to the bait.

'Ok then, please do that. Would love to hear you talk yourself out of this mess you've got yourself in.'

I smiled at him.

'Mess I'm in? Are you sure? The mess I'm in? Ask your dad why he really hasn't rung and reported the robbery in Hatton Garden.

GO ON SON... ASK HIM!'

I shouted the last five words as loud as I could.

The lunchtime trade in 'The Louis' all spun round and looked at our table.

Maury was going redder and redder by the second. His blood pressure must have been at boiling point. His youngest son Sam looked at him and then at his older brother and they returned his gaze and then shook their heads.

'That's right my sharp lad.... Your dad can't can he? He's in Schtuk son. Right up to his Jermyn Street shirt collar.

He can't bring up what was in that safe, with either the police or the owners of the shop, cos if he did, he'd get at least an 'handful' for perverting the course of justice. He knew back when we first met, what he was holding, he knew fine well. And believe you me young man, your dad going inside at his age would kill him. Stone, flaming, dead.'

Maury looked to the floor of the pub.

'I know that for certain see. I've done time, proper time. Too much time really, lost a lot whilst I was in there. My marriage, my son, most of my friends. But you know the one thing I didn't lose in there? I didn't lose my own twisted logic of right and wrong. There might not be too much honour among some thieves, but there is a code, and your old man, he broke that.

So my conscious is sort of clear now. I'm guessing old Liz

Taylor would have called in the insurance on that parcel years back and no doubt bought another load of sparklers with the money they gave her.

No son, the best you would get is your word against mine and I'm more than happy to take my chances.'

With that Maury just stood up and started walking toward the door. Lawrence knew the coup too and just folded. Silly Sam however, was still a bit lost.

'Where are you going father? Is this it? Is that it all over? Dad!'

He then followed his retreating father out of the saloon door. Maurice didn't even look back. He knew it was over. He'd chosen a few more years of freedom, over a couple in stir. He knew I was right. If he went in there at his age, it would have killed him. He just knew that.

'A long life to you Maury, a long life.' I said to his disappearing back, as I drained the last of my vodka.

I sat and watched them all leave and then reflected for a minute or so on the last forty eight hours and I then ordered up another vodka from young Neville.

'That all seemed to go ok there. I take it you won't be needing me then Vin?' He asked as he held up a glass to the optic.

'False alarm Neville mate...false alarm.'

And I smiled as I thought of a black and white French film and an elderly Scottish lady.

On the way home from the 'King Louis', my Matt called.

He started off by asking me if I was alright and I explained that the little dispute about ownership appeared to have been settled in my favour.

I could hear the smile in his voice as he told me he had heard straight back from the people at Elizabeth Taylor's Estate. They were going to check out the matter with their legal team, because it all sounded 'highly irregular' and they would return to him as soon as possible.

Good way of describing all this I thought. Highly irregular.

For the next couple of days, I kept myself to myself and if I did venture out to the bookies or the paper shop, I was forever looking round corners for the brothers Samuels to jump out and give me a good kicking.

But it didn't happen. No sign of them.

It appeared that after all this time, old Maurice had just wiped his mouth and walked away. He'd swallowed it. He knew I was prepared to tell the whole story to the police even if it meant me going down for a stretch too, and that frightened the fucking life out of him.

On the following Saturday morning, my external intercom rung.

'Dad, it's me. Got some news for you. Buzz me in.'

I did just that and within thirty seconds, my Matt was on my doorstep with a letter in his hand.

'Well, here it is. The final say from the Elizabeth Taylor Estate, they have spoken.'

'Cuppa?' I said, trying to style it out and play it cool.

'Yeah,' he said, sounding surprised. 'Go on then. I'll read you this while the kettle's boiling eh?'

He took a bread knife from the worktop and sliced open the envelope.

'Ok, here we go' and Matt began to read.

'To whom it may concern.

The Estate of Elizabeth Taylor would like to put on record that it is prepared to do as instructed by Mr. Vincent Hawkins of London, England.

As a result of this, the Estate request that the said items (Jewellery) are returned forthwith and acknowledged as property of the Estate, without further recourse.

The Estate recognises and acknowledges that the value of the said items has now risen by an estimated twenty five times their original valuation, since the original and unexplained loss in the year of 1962.

The Estate now concurs to file a report that though thought stolen from The Barbury Hotel, London, England in the said year, they were in fact discovered in a recent property move, after the sad demise of their owner in March 2011.

The Estate agrees to sell the jewels at a forthcoming New York auction house with other pieces from the owner, which will be catalogued and known as 'The Elizabeth Taylor - London Collection.'

The Estate agree to re-pay the insurers their costs from 1962 and then fifty percent of their current value will be donated to Southwark Council of London on the understanding that the monies will go to the upkeep of the housing complex where Mr. Vincent Hawkins and his fellow residents now reside.

This will remain open for business and be respectfully maintained for a further guaranteed twenty-five years.

It is with delight, that the Estate agrees to the suggestion, from Mr Hawkins, that the The Benhill Care Home be re-named 'The Elizabeth Taylor Court.'

Signed

B. Sprinkle (on behalf)

The Elizabeth Taylor Estate

Matty folded the piece of paper in four, put it in his pocket and then took off his glasses. He held out his hand and shook mine, before giving me a big cuddle.

'Blimey dad. Not sure how you did that, but one thing is for certain.

You truly are, one diamond geezer.'

The End

A GLOSSARY FOR THOSE AMONG YOU WHO DON'T KNOW YOUR 'OB' FROM YOUR 'OP's'...

APPLE = Twenty. £20.00 in money slang. From Apple Core – Score. As in three score and ten.

BACCA = Shortened slang for rolling tobacco.

BATTLE CRUISER = Public house. From Battle Cruiser – Boozer. A place where booze -colloquial term for alcohol - is served.

BED AND BREAKFAST = Prison slang for short jail term.

BEJESUS = An exclamation of shock or surprise. Derived from 'By Jesus'.

BENGHAZI = Toilet. Benghazi (City in Libya) – Khazi – Said to derive from Casi Di Tolleranza (House of Tolerance – Bordello/Brothel).

BERK = Polite way of saying C**t. Slang derived from The Berkely Hunt , a pack of fox hounds dating back to the 12th century.

BERTIE SMALLS = A bank robber who became the first 'Supergrass'.

BLAGGER = A rogue. Derived from 'Blackguard' – someone who acts in a dishonourable way.

BOATS = Faces. From Boat Race.

BOOBY = Cell. Originally at a police station house. From 'Booby Hatch' with a booby being an idiot or thick person put into a secure place.

BRAHMER = The Best. Top notch. Derived from Joseph Bramah, who designed superior 'water closets', some of which are still in use in The House of Commons and Osbourne

House, Queen Victoria's residence on the Isle of Wight.

BRAHMS (and LISZT) = Pissed. Derived from composers Johannes Brahms and Franz Liszt.

BRASS = Prostitute. From Brass Nail – Tail. 'Nice bit of tail'.

BROWN = Dead. As in Brown Bread.

CASEYS COURT = Chaotic. Derives from the Victorian comedy music hall act by the same name, of which Charlie Chaplin was once a member.

CHARGE = To fill/Level . Derived from French.

CONNAUGHTS = Strangers. From Connaught Rangers, an Irish regiment of the British Army, which began in 1793.

COUP = To know about a certain situation, action or move. 'He knows the coup'. French origin

COVENTRY = (Be sent to) – Said to derive from English Civil War, when prisoners were sent to Coventry , where they did not receive a warm welcome and were thus shunned by the local towns people.

DOG EYE = Look Out/Scrutinise. ' Keep dog for me'

DOODLE BUG = Drug. A doodlebug was the nickname for the 'June bug' in the fields of the Southern Counties and for the German V-1 'flying bomb' from World War II.

DRUM = Home/House. From Drum Roll – Hole. A basic dwelling.

DWELL THE BOX = To stay put/where you are. Remain/reside

FACTORY = A police station.

FILCHED = Steal/Pilfer.

FLOUNDER AND DAB = Cab/Taxi. Flounder and Dab are

two types of fish.

FLY BLOW = Derived from Fly Blown. Dirty, squalid and run down.

FOLDING = Money. Folded cash. 'He's holding folding'.

GANGER = Head Labourer. Lead man in a gang.

GELT = Money. Yiddish, from Old High German.

GRASS = Informant. From 1893 dictionary -Grasshopper – Copper. To work for the police. Become a surrogate policeman.

GYPSYS KISS = Piss/Urinate. From 'just going for a gypsys'.

HANDFUL= Five. Hand full of fingers.

HANK MARVIN = Starving. Hungry.

JACK and JILL – Slang for the bill of sale or for services rendered.

JELLY = Gelignite. Explosive material.

JEMMY = A short steel crow bar used by the criminal classes to prise open wooden boxes/crates.

JIB = Swerve. To move suddenly. Been corrupted to mean, to move without paying/ 'I jibbed the train'.

KETTLE = Watch. A couple of explanations for this one. Kettle and Hob – Fob. As in fob watch. Also - Kettle of Scotch - the alcoholic beverage was stored in something called a Kettle, before glass bottles came into common use. I guess you pay your money and take your personal choice.

KIPPER = Flat. As in 'it's the kipper season, flat, nothing happening'.

LINEN DRAPER = (News) Paper. A draper (merchant) who sold linen and other goods.

LONG FIRM = Fraud.

LUNCH = Reference to the large breasts of a woman.

MINCES = Eyes. From Mince Pies.

MONIKER = Name. Also a 'mark' left on property by a tramp/vagrant to indicate they had been present there.

MORT = A woman. Dublin slang.

MUM= Prison/Police speak for wife.

MUTTON = Deaf. Derived from Mutt and Jeff, American cartoon from early 1920s. 'He was stone mutton the geezer'.

NEBBISH = A nothing/weakling. Derived from Yiddish.

NEWGATES KNOCKER = Black. The term refers to the iron door knocker from the prison at Newgate.

NORMANS= Punters/Customers. From Norman Hunter, former footballer for Leeds United and England.

OP's = Other Peoples.

OB = Old Bill. Police constables from the time of King William IV.

PAT MALONE = Alone. Australian slang for being on your own. 'You drinking with Pat Malone mate?'.

PECKHAM = Tie. From slang Peckham Rye – an area of South East London.

PEEPERS = Eyes. To peep/ be a voyeur.

PETER = Metal Safe and/or Prison Cell. Said to have biblical connotations. Essentially a safe place.

PICKNEY = Child. From Jamaican patois and slang.

'Whoofa pickney dis?'

PIE AND LIQUOR = Vicar. Man of the cloth. Pie, mash and liquor was the original 'fast food' for the working classes.

PLOD = Police. PC Plod being a slang term for a particular dim witted one.

PLUM = £100,000.00 in money slang.

POMP = A show/parade of power/magnificence 'In his pomp'

PONY = Crap. Pony and Trap – Crap. Derived from the old French word Crappe meaning waste or rejected matter.

PORKIES = Lies. From Pork Pies.

RAMP = Pub/Bar counter.

RATTLER = Train. From rattling noise a train makes when travelling.

RECCE = Military term, derived from Reconnoitre, the verb of Reconnaissance. To explore.

ROCKING HORSE = Sauce. A condiment, brown or tomato. 'Pass the rocking horse chief'.

SCENIC RAILWAY = Scarring from a stab wound or from being sliced with a knife. 'His scar looked like a scenic railway'.

SCHNOZZLE – Nose. Possibly derived from Yiddish 'snoyts' and German Schnauze 'Snout (animal)'.

SCHTUK = Trouble. Thought to be from Yiddish/Cockney German combination. "I'm in dead schtuk mate'.

SCHTUM = Quiet. Derived from Yiddish/German.

SEXTON BLAKE = Cake. Blake was a fictional detective in stories from the late 1890s.

SHERBERT = Taxi/Beer – From Sherbert Dab (confectionary) – Cab/Taxi and fizzy drink drink usually lager.

SHOVEL = Prison station/cell. From Shovel and Pick – Nick. As in you're nicked/arrested).

SHRAPNEL = Pieces of metal from artillery shell/Loose change. 'Got a pocket full of shrapnel'

SKIN AND BLISTER = Sister - 'She's my skin, what can I do?'.

SNOUT = Cigarette. 'In and Out'.

SPIELER = A long rambling speech/A gambling den. Derived from German word for gambler/player.

SPANISHED = Got rid of. From Spanish Archer – El Bow. 'Elbowed it didn't I?'

STIR = Prison. From Romany word 'staripen' meaning 'a prison'.

STRIPE = One Pound. 'Want one? Only a stripe'.

SWEDE = Head. A popular put down. To have a vegetable shaped head. "Look at the swede on him'.

TEA LEAF = Thief.

TIMBER = Heavy. 'Put a bit of timber on'.

TOM FOOLERY = Jewellery. Often shortened to tom

TOM PEPPER = Liar. A naval expression (Nelsonic period) and renowned liar of a character from the books of Mark Twain.

TROMBONE = (Tele)Phone.

'VILLE = Shortened informal name for Pentonville Prison. 'Done three months up The 'Ville'.

WALLAH = A servant, low skilled worker.

THE MUMPER

The Mumper is a book from the pens of Mark Baxter and Paolo Hewitt

"An Ealing comedy for the 21st Century". Actor Martin Freeman

It's 1985 -

Thatcher in power, Sade on the radio, print

workers on strike. But nothing in the world is going to stop Bax from meeting his friends every Sunday at their favourite south London boozer for a day of banter, extracting the urine and generally putting the world to rights.

Not even when a skinny, round shouldered fella nobody knows walks up to them one day and asks the question that became pub legend.
'Hello chaps…ever thought of owning a racehorse?'

From that simple but surreal question unfolds the story of
The Mumper, the tale of seven firm friends who embark on a
unique journey.

They would like to invite you along for the ride as well.
So saddle up and climb aboard……The Mumper is here to
take you away.

The Mumper by Mark Baxter and Paolo Hewitt
Phoenix Fiction
ISBN 978-1-7802-2044-4